I0682435

In Touch

Play On Book 1

By Cd Brennan

www.cdbrennan.com

In Touch

NOTE FROM THE AUTHOR:
This book is a work of fiction. The names, characters, places, and incidents are products of the writer's imagination or have been used fictitiously and are not to be construed as real. Any resemblance to persons, living or dead, actual events, locale or organizations is entirely coincidental. The author does not have any control over and does not assume any responsibility for third-party websites or their content.

First electronic publication: September 2015
ASIN- B0130KVNCU

First print publication: September 2015
ISBN-13: 978-0989083218 (CMD Writing LLC)
ISBN-10: 0989083217

Published in the United States of America

Sexy. Passionate. Fierce.

Irish rugby star, Padraig O'Neale, has fecked up his life and is one angry man. When caught using a banned substance for his back pain, Padraig is excused from both his provincial club and the Irish International team. Right before World Cup selection. Out of choices, his agent convinces Padraig to play for a small American club in Michigan. Just until things settle down. But when Coach asks the team physical therapist, Gillian Sommersby, to help the newest Blues player with his *issues*, Padraig finds himself trying every wacky treatment out there from stinky salves to music to yoga. Like her therapies, the therapist herself is a bit…odd. The cute college grad in Converse and glasses doesn't seem all that impressed with Padraig's celebrity status, nor gives a shite about his excuses. As it turns out, she might be exactly what he needs…

Visit me at http://www.cdbrennan.com

Books by Cd Brennan

Play On

In Touch

Love Where You Roam

Watershed (Book 1)

A World Apart (Book 2)

To the Traverse Bay Blues Rugby Club.
And, as always, to my sons, Finn and Keelan, ruggers in
the making.

Acknowledgements

First and foremost to everyone involved in the Traverse Bay Blues RFC who invited me into their world and with kindness and patience answered my ten million questions about US rugby. Huge kudos to my editor, Paige Christian, whose talent and support make this book what it is today. Thanks also to my copy editor, Georgia Macey, my critique partner, Ashlyn Brady, my friend in all things helpful, Heidi Senesac, and a super thanks to the cover designer, Tera Shanley, for her fabulous cover art.

A special mention to my alpha readers Junette Stronge for the Irish elements, and Tania Santos with Active Physical Therapy who volunteers for the Blues as their PT—both whose suggestions made this book a better read. Can never thank you enough. And to my beta reader, Coach Matt (Scotland) Szatkiewicz, the legend that he is. Any remaining inaccuracies are my own.

Anthony Dell'Acqua, President of the Blues, gave me hours of his time to speak passionately about the future of rugby in America. My husband, Dick Brennan and Dave (D-day) Wenkel offered their knowledge to help me stay as true to the club and sport as possible. A special hug for my hubby for being such a good guy about being the bad guy.

And finally, I'd like to acknowledge the National Irish Rugby team 2000-2007 who impassioned me with the sport, where I gained my love of rugby, where I watched every match with heart in throat.

Author's Foreward

The Traverse Bay Blues Rugby Club is not a Division 1 team. I used creative license for the story. As a Division 3 team, they don't have a locker room, trophy room, reception area, nor spectator stands. But they have hope and they have drive, and I believe they will achieve their dream of such soon. Rugby is a tremendous sport—the raw energy, athleticism, strength, and pride that goes into each and every game is beyond compare. Especially for your local teams in the US. The sport is on the rise, but all players are volunteers and clubs run on donations and sponsors, so I urge you to seek out your local club and support where you can. But particularly, my favorite team, the Blues, any donation will be received with heartfelt thanks. www.tcrugby.com

Chapter 1

The wind pressed against the small window, and the pane of glass moaned in return.

Gillian pulled a spare pillow over her head and squeezed. Just as she was almost asleep, another groan sounded through the room like a foghorn. A strong westerly.

Gah! She was so tired. She'd loved storms when she was younger—the thunder and lightning...the wind—all mixing to create a passionate display over Traverse Bay. And before, the ionization of the air, the excitement as the energy shifted, growing intense and bold.

Now, storms at night were just another something that kept her awake. And then the incessant worrying would start, and she couldn't turn it off. If she still dozed between wake and sleep, sometimes she'd be able to talk herself down, dream herself back into slumber with any sweet thought she could grasp onto. But once fully conscious, that was it.

The worrying began and the anxiety latched onto her like Velcro. God, it sucked. Caught between the living and the dead. Not enough energy to be active, but too aware to stop the jumble of images and scenarios that would bombard her head until daylight.

At this point, it was useless to try to sleep. All it would produce was a grumpy-as-hell Gillian the next day. With a growl, she threw back the covers and swung her feet to the floor. Bending automatically for the incline of the ceiling, she felt her way in the dark to the door.

Might as well start with the upstairs bathroom.

The door creaked. Nothing to do about that. The house was old with two of the bedrooms upstairs in an attic conversion. Each room had slanted outer walls and what she and her brother had always referred to as hobbit doors. Not full size and not fully centered, the doors didn't close on their wonky, warped hinges. When she and Andrew were teenagers, her brother had resorted to duct tape to try to retain some privacy.

Gillian grabbed the plastic grocery bag used as a liner in the trash bin in the bathroom. Only a few Q-tips and used Kleenex. It would suffice. She began her systematic search of the cupboards and the overhead medicine cabinet. Nothing. But she didn't expect much. Her parents rarely came upstairs anymore.

Her mom still kept a night-light in the upstairs hall even though Gillian was now twenty-four. The soft glow had come in handy since she'd been staying at her parents'. She didn't have to turn on the overheads during her midnight trawling.

Maneuvering the stairs, Gillian made it down to the lounge with only two squeaks. Pretty damn good for a rotting, old house. She traversed the hall and shut the downstairs bathroom door quietly before she fumbled for the switch.

Even behind the loaded drawers full of old make-up, tiny bottles of hotel shampoos and conditioners, headbands, and jars of anti-aging cream, she found nothing. Nor in the bottom cupboard that held the spare toilet paper and hand towels. Her parents were getting smarter, but she had all night. She'd find their stash. But she needed a flashlight.

She went to the utility closet first and snagged the large, yellow Eveready. A bit big, but it would do. As she turned away, she stopped, her hand still on the doorknob. She'd never checked in here. Hmmm…

How much shit could her dad cram into one small closet? Everything from baseball gloves with a ball still bedded inside to cans of WD40 and bottles of half-empty cleaning spray. She shifted the cans to the side, but when she reached around to the back, the largest fell onto the wooden shelf with a *clunk*. Shit again. She paused, listening for her parents. But nothing. She tossed the can onto a pile of rags on the shelf below and continued her search. Aiming the flashlight at the back, she was rewarded with white caps and brown bottles. Nice.

She pulled out two at a time. A bottle of expired amoxicillin tablets. What the hell? Into the bag. Her mother's Xanax. Only five milligram tablets, but that went into the bag, as well. Some generic pink stomach medicine, cough drops, a box of anti-gas tablets, extra-strength ibuprofen. Gone. She left the Tylenol. The Chinese had been using acetaminophen for over three thousand years. The safest of all pharmaceuticals on the market.

Gillian clicked off the flashlight and placed it on the shelf. She tiptoed past her parents' room to the kitchen and snagged a yogurt drink out of the fridge.

Not bad for a night's work. After gulping it down, she placed the empty container into the plastic bag and tied the top. The door to the garage creaked, so she quickly stepped through and closed the door behind, leaving it slightly ajar. Flicking on the lights, she squinted at the harsh glare of the overhead halogens. She grabbed the keys from where they hung by the switch and worked her way around her mom's old Mercury to the covered car along the far wall.

She stopped mid-step. Pain and sadness lodged in her throat. It was the same reaction every time she looked at the old car shrouded in its own misery underneath a ratty cover. The beautiful beast couldn't sit here forever.

She pulled away the tan canvas over the trunk. The body was a dark green. Painting the car was the first thing Andrew had done. He had told her if she looked good, she'd feel good. He'd spoken of the classic car like a man in love with a woman. Gillian ran her hand along the surface, leaving a finger-stripe trail through the dust. It was a pity they hadn't finished bringing her back to life.

It was time. She damn well would get the ol' girl running.

Gillian popped the trunk with the key and stashed the plastic bag inside. There were a half dozen other bags already there, mostly plastic, but one night she had resorted to an old pillowcase.

After replacing the tarp, she eyed the result. If someone looked close enough, they could easily identify fingerprints in the dust on the lip of the cover. Gillian blew out raspberries. Not much for covering her tracks, but she doubted her parents looked too closely. Of course, they could have changed their ways. She batted the air, negating the possibility they would find out, and made her way across the garage that smelled of oil and stale rubber. She flicked off the light before she opened the door to the house.

As she turned, her father grunted out, "Gillian."

She screamed, flattening herself against the door, and then covered her mouth fast, as if she could hold back the shriek that was already out.

Her dad switched on the light over the sink. He wore his holey pajama bottoms, the once red-checkered pattern now faded to pink, and an old Niagara Falls T-shirt from a long-ago family vacation. He ruffled his already disheveled bed hair. "Well, I was hoping not to wake your mother."

"If that was the case, you shouldn't have been lurking around in the dark."

He motioned toward the door with the glass in his hand. "Well, I didn't know my daughter was lurking out in the garage. I woke up and was thirsty."

Gillian was slowly inching her way through the kitchen, her small steps fueled by guilt.

"What were you doing out there?"

"Not much."

He rubbed his eyes with the palms of his hands. "You weren't out there hiding anything, were you?"

"Like what?"

"Like all the medicine you've been taking from your mom and me."

Damn.

"What? You think we are too old to notice?"

"Yeah, ancient, Dad. Ready for the old folk's home."

"We're not going anywhere just yet."

"You don't need that crap, anyway."

Her dad turned around to the sink and placed his glass on the counter. "Yeah, we do."

"No, you don't." Gillian motioned to a basket in the middle of the counter. "You have all the teas and herbs I've left for you. Even some of my new salve rubs for your arthritis. And neither of you have touched any of it."

Her dad let out a long sigh. "Gill, as much as we believe in you and appreciate the thought, we still want to do it our way." Before Gillian could interrupt, he continued. "We'll use your stuff, too, but you know your mom needs her Xanax to fly. It's not like she uses it every day. And no matter how much of your tea I drink, it still doesn't help the aches after I get home from work. Like you said, I'm ancient. And your poor Dad can't move around like he used to."

"That's the thing. You have to use the teas all the time, and the rub, too. It's preventative, not reactive care."

He dumped the remaining water into the sink and placed the glass on the counter. "Gill, we've heard this all before."

She could tell he was starting to boil, but she kept pushing. "Then why don't you try?"

"Because we want to live the way we want to live. That's not up to you."

"You don't need that shit, Dad!"

He slapped his hand onto the counter so hard it made her jump. "That's not for you to decide!" His shoulders slumped and he spoke softly. "Now, I want you to return

14

everything you've taken over the last week since you've been staying with us." He held up a hand to stop her from speaking. "If it's not already in a landfill."

"But—"

"For over six years, you've been taking our stuff every time you come home to visit. It's expensive. We have to replace it."

Gillian drew in air through her teeth. "First, I'm now out of college and a grown woman, so I don't think you can order me around." His dramatic grunt only raised her ire until she yelled out, "I'm only trying to help!" That had been her second point, but the words were lost to the emotion.

After a brief stare-down she wouldn't win, she turned and left. She was at the bottom step to the stairs when his words stopped her. "You've changed, Gill. Lighten up."

Screw this. She pivoted on her toe and took the stairs two at a time.

Chapter 2

For fuck's sake. This place was ridiculous. Fucking piece of shit hellhole.

Padraig rattled the pill container in his left pocket, reassuring himself it was still there. He stood in the locker room off to the side, gear bag in hand, as the other lads walked in and out of the shower. Confident and secure in their nudity, they laughed and joked with each other. Some shouted across the room. Lockers clanged open and shut. The acrid smell of a man's deodorant or aftershave smothered the body odor but choked the air in its extremity.

No one seemed to notice him standing there even though the facility wasn't very large, as if he blended in with the framed prints of the Traverse City Blues RFC that flanked the walls, annual portraits in a line, starting from years ago to the most recent team.

The locker room was like others he had used. When he was in *school*. Padraig swallowed the F-word that again wanted to breach his lips.

A far reach from professional facilities. Wood benches ran the locker rows with a shower room off to one side. But in the familiarity, it was all wrong. It wasn't Ireland and the Munster squad. It was a bunch of Yankees and a half-arse chance of furthering his rugby career. Feck it. This was stupid. Why had he agreed to this? How could this club be his savior?

A young, cocky face appeared in front of him. Wiry and shorter, the lad was probably part of the backs. "Hey dude, are you lookin' for someone?"

Padraig barely glanced at him, then nodded. "Where's Coach?"

"Ah, you must be that new Irish guy that Scotch told us about. Said you'd be startin' next week. A bit early, ain't ya?"

Padraig ignored his question and asked one himself. Avoidance tactics, he was good at. "Who's Scotch?"

"Scotch is our nickname for Coach McKenzie. He's from Scotland."

"You don't call a Scotsman 'Scotch,' you daft cunt."

"We know that *now*." The boy's lip curled at Padraig before he sauntered off to a locker where he gave him one last dirty look, then slammed it shut and walked out of view.

Stupid bloody Americans. Didn't know their arse from their elbow. He hadn't been in the States for a day, and he was ready to go back home to Ireland on the next flight out. This was the wrong decision, and he could kick himself for letting his agent convince him otherwise.

He was about to bugger off and find his own way to his arranged accommodation when he saw a big man with a shaggy gray beard round the corner and head his way.

"Padraig O'Neale?"

The Scotsman's large paw was outstretched before he reached him. Padraig dropped his bag and gripped the man's hand. It was larger than his own. He had seen pictures of Coach, but none of them did any justice. A bear of a man still at his age, which Padraig guessed to be in his fifties, he must have been a force in the forward pack of his team.

"Mitch told me you were here. Didn't expect you today, but you're more than welcome. Thought your agent said you wouldn't be in until Monday."

"Change of plans."

Coach lifted his chin in a contemplating manner, but then nodded. "Come with me to the office, and we'll sort you out."

He led Padraig to the back of the room. As he passed, some of the lads turned to stare, a few nodded. Padraig didn't care. With any luck, he wouldn't be at the Blues long enough to make friends. He was here to do his time, keep his body in shape and his head in the game until his agent could work his magic and get him to Argentina.

"Take a seat," Coach said, directing Padraig to a pair of chairs set in front of a large desk. Coach lowered his large frame into the swivel chair on the other side and swung around to face Padraig, who had flopped into the one on the right, dropping his duffel bag into the other. The pill bottle pinched when he sat, so he had to squirm to adjust it out of the way.

Coach folded his hands in front of him. "How was your flight?"

"Just in now, came straight from the airport." Padraig worked his way around a straight answer to keep his distance. Next thing, Coach would be asking about his personal life, and that Padraig wouldn't have. None of it.

"Your agent sent through all your paperwork, so you're good to start on Monday. Lucky you have a US passport or it would have been a heap more trouble to get you to start for this season."

Padraig grunted. "Yeah, lucky me."

Other than a subtle pinch of his eyebrows, Coach's professionalism remained staunch, even at Padraig's flippant answer. His eyes remained on Padraig as he ran his hand down his beard, pulling from his chin to the ends. Padraig couldn't hold the eye contact and looked over Coach's head out the window. Tall at six-foot-four, he could do that. "One of the best second rows to play for Ireland," *The Irish Times* newspaper had quoted. In the same article, they had also crucified him for offending the sport of rugby.

"Practices are on Tuesday and Thursdays. Conditioning training on Mondays, and we expect you to train at the gym on the off days at the minimum. The other foreign players are going once a day." Coach opened a drawer and pulled out a large, sealed manila folder. He undid the clasp and turned it upside down. A set of keys fell onto his desk. He picked them up and handed them to Padraig. "You're sharing with a couple of other lads for the moment. If you stay on past this season, it'll be up to you to find a place to live."

Not likely, but Padraig only nodded, his gaze out the window, half listening to the drone of Coach's voice.

"...most of the lads are happy to move on from sharing, anyway. As for transportation—you can get a lift with the guys you'll be staying with. Del has a car and Rory does, too. I'm sure you'll…"

The view from the window was a small stretch of the rugby grounds, some of the stands visible across the pitch. Tiny in comparison to the new Aviva Stadium in Dublin where fifty thousand fans had cheered him during the international rugby matches. Didn't even hold up to his Munster club stadium that was four times the size of the Blues' sports complex. If he hadn't been so mad, his heart would ache from the disaster his life had turned into.

"You still on the oxycodone?"

At mention of the drug, Padraig snapped his attention back to Coach who fiddled with a pile of paperwork on the cheap desk, the decorative vinyl trim peeling away from the edge. "Only when I need it," he lied.

"How often is that?"

Padraig shrugged. "Not very. Maybe after a big game, or if I get some big hits."

Coach unwrapped a piece of gum, then offered one to Padraig who shook his head. "Never chewed gum until I moved to the States, and now I can't seem to quit." He raised his gaze to lock with Padraig's again.

Was he hinting at something? "Yeah, anytime you watch any of the American sports, they're all chewing and spitting. I don't get it."

"Especially baseball." Coach chuckled. "It helps them to stay focused. All part of working both sides of the brain, they say." He changed tack abruptly, back to the subject Padraig had wanted to avoid. "You're lucky they don't test at Division 1 in America, but that might change soon."

That's why I'm here.

"Your agent said your narcotic usage was more a misunderstanding with your prescribing physician, but IRB sanctioned hard against you to show zero tolerance going forward. Something to do with"—Coach used his finger to find the note on his paper—"a Keep Rugby Clean campaign."

"Something like that." Most of it was true, but his agent had instructed him to keep the details to a minimum, to reveal as little information about the situation as possible.

"You know an Eagles player got pulled for oxycodone during the 2011 World Cup."

"Heard about that."

Coach waited, a blank stare at Padraig, as if looking for further explanation, for Padraig to connect the dots.

Padraig picked up a small framed photo sitting at an angle on the desk. "Is this your family?"

"Aye, my wife and two daughters." Still an unreadable, drawn face.

"Nice picture." Good-looking girls, but he was smart enough not to vocalize that opinion. And women were the last thing on his mind at the moment.

Coach reached across the desk and plucked the picture from Padraig's hand. "We've got some other options for pain regulation at this club you can take a look at. Got some newfangled therapist starting next week, in fact."

"It's not a problem," Padraig said.

Shoving the chair back, Coach rose and started for the door. "Well, let me know how it goes. Keep open communication with me at all times. You got it?"

Padraig understood the signal and gathered his bag and jacket. "Will do."

"Now, let's see if we can catch Del before he leaves. Then the club won't need to pay for a taxi to your place."

Coach let Padraig pass before he closed the office door behind him. The locker room had quieted, only muffled voices coming from the far side of the room. Coach walked ahead of him and shouted down the last row of lockers, "You seen Del anywhere?"

One of the men answered, "Think he already headed to the bar, Coach. It's Thursday, after all."

"That it is." Coach hitched up his pants and turned back to Padraig. "A New Zealander, who has graced us with his presence, is captain of the Blues this year. What you can do is make your way back to the office and ask the receptionist to call you a cab.

"Take it easy over the weekend and get over your jet lag so you're ready bright and early Monday." He turned to leave, but then swiveled back on his foot. "Don't let Del talk you into the pub yet. Alcohol is the worst thing you can do for jet lag."

Padraig was already in motion to get out of there, his hand on the door handle, his shoulder to the glass, when Coach spoke again. "Oh, and O'Neale? Might be a good idea to make friends on the squad, not enemies. I'm sure you've heard it before, but it's all a part of the performance of the team."

"No worries, Coach, just a bit grumpy from traveling."

The older man ran his hand over his beard again, then gave a slight nod. "I'm sure it is."

Coach had barely made it a few feet before another player had stopped him to talk. It was a good time to make his exit. Padraig retraced his steps back through the trophy room to the reception area that sat adjacent to the entrance. That was a great feckin' start. He must have pissed off the young fella, Mitch, and he had told Coach.

A blonde was on the phone when he approached, so he set his bag down quietly and waited. She caught his eye and stuck up a finger to gesture she'd be a minute. A fine, young wan but Padraig didn't even bother to acknowledge her.

More team photos and awards mounted the walls, club banners and an advertisement for the Rugby World Cup. He clenched his jaw at the sight. *He* should have been playing that tournament. Playing for the Irish team.

"Excuse me, can I help you?"

Padraig turned away from the Cup poster. "I just need a taxi, if you could call one for me."

"Of course, under what name?"

"O'Neale."

The girl was younger than Padraig and a good bit of skirt, like sex on a stick. Big, violet eyes and platinum blond hair in ringlets, not natural but still a hard-on for most lads. But it seemed nothing could turn him on these days. Even when she stepped up to him in her knee-high fuck-me boots, her perky chest straining at a button down shirt, his dick didn't stir an inch. Nothing.

"Oh yes, heard you were coming. Love your accent. Couldn't wait to see you just so I could hear you talk."

What a flirt.

"How do you pronounce your first name? Pad...rake?"

She crucified his name as he thought she would. "Depends on where you are from in Ireland. North of Galway, it's paw-rig, but in the south, it's pawd-rik." He sounded it out for her. "Like the golfer, Padraig Harrington?"

"Oh, gosh, I'm not much of a golf fan. What part of Ireland are you from again?"

The Americans always loved the accent, and his home region had one of the strongest. "Cork."

"Never been to Ireland but have always wanted to go. Heard it's beautiful and the people so friendly."

"Mostly."

She smiled at him and either ignored his grunts or didn't notice his bad manners. "Why don't you take a seat while I call?" She picked up the phone and dialed, her long, painted nails clicking on the keys. Padraig turned away but ignored her request for him to sit. She asked for a taxi from the rugby club, then louder to him, "Pad-rake, what is the address you are going to?"

She had covered the bottom of the phone in a polite manner, as she had to raise her voice to Padraig who had moved across the room.

He didn't know the address and should have dug it out of his backpack. "Sorry, have it right here…" He wrenched out a bunch of folders. He had organized everything before he came, but now flustered, couldn't remember which folder the address was in, nor could he find it as he scanned quickly through the papers.

"I thought it was—"

"Aren't you living with Del?"

He nodded as he struggled to jam the papers back into his pack.

"Don't worry. I know his address by heart." She gave him a wink. "That boy partakes in a few drinks after the matches and is always catching a taxi home."

She recited an address into the phone, thanked them, and hung up.

She walked over to him. "Is that all the luggage you got?"

"Yup, that's it."

"For the entire season?"

"Don't need much."

She raised her eyebrows and shrugged, rows of bracelets rattling when she raised her hands with the gesture. "Okay then, I suppose men don't pack as much as women do. If I was living abroad for almost a year, I'd have half my wardrobe in five suitcases." She eyed him from top to toe. "Probably don't need my help getting your bags to the curb…"

"I'll be grand." Padraig motioned out to the street. "Will he be picking me up in the front, like?"

She pointed. "Yep, right out there."

Padraig had grabbed up his bags and had turned to leave when a soft hand clasped his arm. "We've sure been looking forward to all you new guys playing for us this year. First time we've had foreign players on our pitch." Tugging at him, she was able to draw his gaze to hers. "We have high hopes. I'm sure you'll do this club proud."

His jaw tightened, and he didn't know what to say. He couldn't rightly tell her he wasn't planning on sticking around. Or this small club was a joke compared to the major provincial club he'd played for in Ireland. Nothing better than the roar of "Fields of Athenry" or the chant of "Mun-ster, Mun-ster, Mun-ster" as the crowd rallied the team when they were down, or when they were pushing ahead with a great run toward the goal, yards dropping behind them. Blood lust and a drive to get over the line.

The adrenaline rush. The noise—it made him stronger, and he didn't feel the pain. How was he going to play here?

He gave her a pinched smile. "I hope so. Heard the other boys are already here. Sorry I missed last week's training." Because his agent had still tried to the last minute to get a contract with a European club, but with no luck. Word had spread fast, the news reaching even the smallest clubs on the continent.

"I'm sure you'll fit right in and have no troubles."

All Padraig wanted to do was get away from her prying eyes. "Sure, I'll be going then."

"I'll get the door for you."

Padraig nodded. "Cheers."

He passed, and when he turned back, the receptionist fluttered her fingers at him. "See you Monday."

Out of the corner of his eye, a shape loomed up the sidewalk, drawing nearer. "Unfortunately," Padraig whispered under his breath.

He swung around, his large duffel bag shoving the person off the pavement and into the grass. She sidestepped quickly. "Whoa, there."

"Pardon me."

Jean shorts on long legs. That's what he saw first. Then a baggy black T-shirt and a long necklace with some hand pendant at the end. He took a second look. She had big, curly hair and old-style tortoise-rimmed glasses on her face. Fuzzy ringlets escaped around her freckled face. Her legs were mighty fine, but unglamorously ended in high-top black Converse.

She smiled. "No problem."

And with that smile, his stomach clenched, tightening into a lead ball at the center of his abdomen. Her grin was pure magic. Not a buzz from a woman in almost a year, and she was the one to get him going. What the fuck? It must be the jet lag.

She was still standing in the grass so he shifted his bag to the other hand. "Sorry 'bout that."

She moved back onto the pavement. "Like I said, it's no worries."

They both stood there, looking at each other. She finally broke the awkward silence with "Well, see you around."

He drew his gaze along the length of her again.

She noticed his blatant appraisal, rolled her eyes, and walked away.

Nice ass, but not his type. But thank feck his dick still worked.

Chapter 3

The smell hit her first. A combination of strong aftershave, Lynx or some crap like that, and overused Bengay. Why anyone still used the stuff, Gillian couldn't understand. It didn't really help, and there was nothing better than good ol' natural heat to loosen muscles. She made a mental note to remember her rice bags next time.

Enlightenment for the boys was the first step. Then she'd introduce her other therapies. That was going to be her strategy to get the job. Not that she needed to *get* the job. She was volunteering. Coach said the meeting was only a formality. Dress casual. Nae bother, he had said. But perhaps casual didn't mean the T-shirt and shorts she wore. Shoot, she should have made more of an effort.

Too late now. Time only to forge ahead.

She was confident all of two minutes before one of the boys on the team passed in front of her in his briefs. She gave him a pinched smile and turned the other direction. Maybe this wasn't such a great idea, immersing herself in testosterone and arrogance.

A few lingering players passed between the lockers, most of them dressed, thank God. All she had to do was walk down the main aisle between the locker rows to get to his office, the Barbie receptionist, Jenn with two *N*s, had told her. That girl was never going to leave. She'd been around sniffing at the players when Andrew had played for the Blues. She probably forgot to mention the half-naked men wandering around just to get her giggles.

Well, it wasn't going to bother her. Chin up and a straight shot down the aisle. Yep, that's where she had to go. As many times as she had watched the Blues when she was younger, she'd never made it into the locker room. That was for Andrew, early on declared a sister-free zone. And there were few places, he had reminded her, where she didn't try to follow.

Gillian launched herself forward, hoping she appeared confident in where she was going. She zeroed in on a poster advertising *Advanced Foot & Ankle Center* on the far wall. Male shapes loomed out of the corners of her eyes, but she kept going. At the end and to the right would be Coach McKenzie's office.

Just as she was about to reach the wall, a figure jumped out in front of her. Her momentum brought her smash into his chest.

"Sorry, excuse me," she said, dancing around the body.

"It was my pleasure." His purr was a cross between satisfied kitty and porn star. What a dick. Buzzed hair, over six foot, puffed out chest. Acne all over his face. Steroids probably. Stubble on his pectorals showed that he shaved. Vain, obviously. Exactly the kind of man she had avoided in the past, but who was going to be a big part of her future. At least, for now.

She smiled, trying for sincerity, but the way her cheeks ached, knew the grin must have come across more like the Joker from Batman. "Looking for Coach. Is he in his office?"

He ignored her and stuck out his hand. "Dick."

"Excuse me?"

"My name's Dick, and yours is?"

Of course it was. Absolutely perfect. When she was about to answer, a friendly face came out of the door adjacent to the last row of lockers. Shane yelled out, "Gillian, hey there!"

She abruptly walked away from Dick, who yelled at her back, "Nice to meet you, too." Grumbling followed, most likely containing the words *bitch* or *cow*. She'd heard it before. Didn't care.

Ignoring the Dick-man, she met Shane in a big hug. "You're still here."

The short, thick hooker disengaged from her arms and stepped back. "And you're all grown up."

She shrugged. "Well, it has been over five years."

Shane shifted his gym bag from one shoulder to the next. "That long? The last time I saw you was—" He broke-off mid-sentence, like everyone did when they talked about Andrew. He cleared his throat and tried again. "A while ago, you're right."

She wanted to save him from his discomfort. "Any of the other old boys around?"

"Nah, most of them have moved on. I was the oldest one here until the Blues brought in some foreign players this year."

30

That was interesting. "Really?"

"Yep, a New Zealander. He's the oldest and our new captain. And an Irish fella started today. They must be on the downward slope"—he whistled and slid his hand down an imaginary hill—"if they are playing for the Blues. Not sure, but not about to ask them."

"Huh. Coach hadn't mentioned."

"Yep, it's neither here nor there." Coach's voice boomed from the entrance to his office.

Shane punched Gillian softly in the arm. "Nice to see you again, kid." He walked backward away from her.

Kid? She was twenty-four with a university degree and a license to practice under her belt. Six years of study. Plus, all the extra classes for acupuncture, herbal remedies, and yoga instruction. Not *that* much younger than Shane.

"Come on into the office, Gillian." Coach waved her in as he moved toward the door.

After he shut it behind her, she took a seat in the first chair.

Coach plopped down across from her. "How've you been?"

"Ah yah, fine." She swallowed, then wet her lips.

"Was surprised to hear from you honestly. Didn't think you'd want anything to do with the Blues."

She'd been looping one of her curls in a finger and stopped. "I have nothing against the Blues."

Coach gave her a sad look. She hated them the worst.

"You know what I mean."

"I want to work here. I want to try my new therapies. And hey, you've got to use your connections when starting out, right?"

"Have you tried anywhere else? Not that I don't want you here." He backpedaled. "We'd be glad for a physical therapist."

Compared to last year when they didn't have anyone. Gillian knew. Her parents had kept her in the loop. Even though her dad never went to the games anymore, they had kept in touch with Coach. Then what was the problem? She pressed on. "Are you happy for me to try out some different ideas?"

Coach yanked on his beard something fierce, telling Gillian he wasn't as sure about her gig here as she was.

She plastered on a smile. "And I'm volunteering my time for experience, Coach. An offer doesn't get much better than that."

Defeat sounded in his heavy sigh. "You're right. I'm just not sure how the lads will react to some of the practices you have in mind."

Ah-ha. So was Coach just doing this for Andrew or her parents? Alternative medicine and holistic practices were all the rage in other parts of the world, but obviously hadn't quite made their way to northern Michigan.

"Gillian?"

"Oh, sorry, was just thinking of how to approach the boys with it." She reached over and grabbed Coach's hand on the desk. "Let me try, okay?"

He remained silent for a minute, then asked, "You think you can handle them? They'll let you wrap their ankles and massage their muscles, but are you willing to take on twenty men and yoga?"

Grr...it wasn't just yoga. It was the whole approach to pain management. Did she have to convince Coach, too?

As if waving her thought away, Coach answered his own question. "Ach, you'll do fine."

"I know I will. But also, the Blues will be more successful for it."

Coach nodded slowly, his gaze averted. "I'd like you to try and help our newest player, just came in from Ireland. He's taking oxycodone at the moment."

"Whoa." So addictive.

"Aye."

"Why?"

"Supposedly for pain. But it's a long story. He's come to us from a professional European club. Just see if you can do anything for the lad. You might have seen him as you came in. He's tall with dark hair. Our new number five."

He must mean Mr. Roaming Eyes. Total jock head. But Irish? That was different. She'd always wanted to go to Ireland. "What did his agent say?"

"Not much."

"Why is he here?"

Coach tapped a pen on the large calendar planner on his desk. "Don't really know honestly, but if he comes around, he could be good for the club."

"And you think I can help him?"

"We can only hope."

Chapter 4

It was time to get up. Morning sun slanted through the vertical blinds, illuminating dust particles in the air. The small, foreign room offered no comfort. His heart ached, his body heavy with dread for the day. He had no desire to play rugby. Not here.

Some days, like yesterday, his anger blinded him so entirely he couldn't even dredge up enough passion to want to play rugby at all.

He had slept away most of the weekend, barely interacting with the other boys, only once taking a cab to and from the shops to buy groceries. Hell, Del had been out drinking most of the weekend. And Ruaridh Cameron, Rory as Del called him, hadn't been around at all, but Padraig hadn't bothered to ask where. A twenty-two-year-old young buck Scotsman? Probably out with a girl.

When Padraig tried to roll over to his side, his lower back muscles seized, shooting darts of pain down his left leg. He wrapped half of the pillow around his face and bit down to muffle his groan. Most mornings he woke to an unbearable throbbing in his back, the pain increasing with movement, and no matter how gently he tried to maneuver out of bed, it always ended in a battle of wills. The last couple of months, Padraig rarely won.

At twenty-six, almost twenty-seven, he was an old man.

At each big breath out, he moved limbs, trying to ease himself from the mattress.

He stilled to take a break from the pain. Sweat trickling down his forehead to his temples, Padraig lay twisted in the sheets, staring at the ceiling. He let the ache subside and shifted until he was perpendicular to the single bed, then draped his legs over the side.

Most nights he relived the horror of getting busted by the WADA official, the entire episode playing in vivid detail. The Doping Control Officer approaching him in the locker room in front of the other lads after their victory against Leinster. The room going silent. Peeing in a cup. The man watching…everything. Padraig's utter and absolute mortification. If he was lucky, only some of the memory invaded his sleep other nights, segments flashing uncontrollably in an abstract chronology.

A tear dripped down the side of his face into his ear. Annoying, but it was nothing to the memory that awakened pain so severe, his throat swelled. He gasped, wetting his mouth with his tongue—once, twice. His nostrils flared like they did right before he lost it.

Not today.

With a growl, he wrenched himself into a seated position, letting the waves of pain subside before he stood. He rubbed his face abrasively to wake and then started his stretches, the same routine he'd been doing since before the sanction. Without accessibility to Munster's team physician or team therapist, Padraig was unsure if he needed to change the exercises, but he kept at it.

The sound of chatter and the clunk of a bowl onto a wooden table hit him before he made the stairs. The house they shared was old and small, but it didn't bother him. He had grown up in a large family in the middle of Cork City centre with less space than the three boys had. In Ireland, their terrace house was old and thick, breezeblock built, but still hadn't muffled the sounds of six kids in the family. Good Catholic breeding he was from, three boys and three girls, him the second eldest but oldest male.

He played with the bottle in his loose pocket, the tiny clicks of the pills against the plastic music to his ears. Assurance.

A younger fella was blending some sort of breakfast muck in the food processor when Padraig stepped into the kitchen. Must be Rory. He turned at Padraig's entrance. "Mornin'."

Del only raised his coffee mug in salute, then went back to the laptop that rested on the table in front of him. A bowl of Weetabix sat at his elbow getting mushy.

"How's the form?" Padraig asked as he pulled a glass from the cupboard and filled it with water from the tap. He opened the fridge, pretending to browse for food. With his back toward the lads, he quickly unscrewed the cap to the bottle and rushed a pill into his big palm. In one fluid motion, he popped the pill into his mouth as he raised his arms above his head in a yawn and stretch.

Neither seemed to notice.

"Forgot to mention my one rule in the house, bro."

Feck. Maybe Del had. Padraig swallowed the pill dry. His heart raced as he turned toward the sink to disguise his anxiety.

"No sex the night before a match."

Padraig snorted out his nose. Was he kidding? "And who made you boss of the house?"

"I did."

Unbelievable. Padraig took a deep breath. Outside the kitchen window, an older gentleman in his robe led a small yappy dog around on a leash in his front yard, plastic bag at the ready for him to do his business. This whole situation was getting worse by the minute.

"Be ready in ten, Paddy," Del said to Padraig's back, "or I'm leavin' without you."

Padraig whirled on him and grabbed the back of the wooden chair so it clunked loudly on the ceramic floor. "*Don't* call me Paddy." No one had that right except for his teammates back home.

The whir of Rory's blender stopped, filling the room with silence as Del and Padraig stared each other down. The nickname was non-negotiable, and Del must have sensed the same.

Del's face remained expressionless except one raised eyebrow, his fingers hovering like claws over his keyboard. "No worries, mate, what you want us to call you then?"

"How about my name?"

"Nah, everyone on the team gets a nickname. Plus, your name is too hard. Like Rory's, except his nickname sounds like his real name."

Padraig pinched his brows together, lifting his hands in wonderment. "For who?"

37

Del had started typing again. "For everyone."

Padraig pushed off the back of the chair and turned. He pulled a bowl from the cupboard, ripped open the paper packet of instant oatmeal, and poured it into the bowl. "Whatever."

There was a pause, and out of the corner of his eye as he topped the dry cereal with water at the sink, he could see Rory trying to smother a laugh at whatever Del did behind his back.

Del's deep voice continued in his slow fashion. "I think something simple. Like…Irish."

"To Irish." Rory raised his breakfast shake and drank.

When Padraig popped his oats into the microwave, Del's chair scraped loudly along the floor. "Ten minutes, mate, and we're leaving."

"Not a problem, *mate*."

Rory raised his glass to Padraig. "You wanna try?"

"No, thanks, that looks like shite. I'll stick with my porridge."

"It's good for yees—it's got yogurt, spinach, eggs, and blueberries."

Ugh, fuck that shit. Padraig ignored him and sat at the table, shoveling big scoops of steaming cereal into his mouth. "Ye have a good weekend, then?"

"Aye, good enough, spent most of my time training."

"On the weekend?" Padraig looked at him skeptically.

"I go over there to do sprint exercises and practice my kicking." Rory gulped his green shake in one go, plugging his nose to get it down. Was this kid for real?

"What position are you playing?" Padraig asked him.

"Full-back right now, but hope to move up to center."

No chance in hell. Good height but the kid was a stick.

"Let's go!" Del yelled from the front door.

Padraig and Rory clambered from the kitchen, and the men and three large gear bags crammed into Del's two-door banger with rust around the wheel arches. How the mighty had fallen. Some of the Irish players that had sponsorship, like Keating and Mahony, were driving around sports cars. Here, because he was the new bloke, he had to move the front seat forward to squeeze his large frame into the rear. When Del pushed the driver's seat back, Padraig's legs cramped up around his ears. He buckled himself in and turned his body so that he could stretch the length of the backseat.

The Kiwi couldn't have been driving on the right side of the road for very long, and sure enough, he peeled in reverse out the driveway, the tires squealing as the car looped around to face the wrong side of the road.

Rory laughed, but Padraig bit his tongue, shaking his head in silence.

Once they had come to an abrupt stop, Del drove slowly, to Padraig's relief, passing rows of boxy houses, most with front porches like their own and manicured lawns with the same bushes and flower baskets along the fronts.

They turned onto a main road that led to a T-junction and the main artery that ran along the waterfront and through the city. Hooking a left, they passed the same way the cab had brought him in on Thursday.

Traverse City hadn't looked like much from the airport until they'd hit the shoreline. The area catered to tourists, classy downtown and a nice waterfront, but too many resort hotels blocked the view. Lake Michigan sparkled from between the buildings. Padraig was riveted to the glimpses of blue that passed in short bursts, a staccato performance of man against nature. Sad, but the buildings won by a long shot.

It was Padraig's first time in the States, unless he counted when he was a baby, which he didn't. Nothing like Cork, a beautiful city with lots of character. The rest of the world was so busy looking at Dublin they rarely saw what a great city Cork was. The coast was even better. In the summers, his ma and da had driven the family out of town past Ringaskiddy, a patchwork of light and dark green fields flowing into the Atlantic ocean, to the colorful town of Kinsale where his ma's sister lived, the buildings painted in bright oranges, blues, greens, and yellows. Trawlers and sailboats filled the large harbor, sometimes tied two or three thick to the docks.

Padraig missed home already.

When they finally arrived at the sports complex, Padraig's back was aching. He wished he could pop another pill real quick, but there was too much activity around as the lads fed into a stream of players heading into the main entrance of the clubhouse.

Bodies jostled and teammates called out to each other, the room reeking of male testosterone. Since Padraig still hadn't been assigned a locker, he stood off to the side and watched, dumping his bag by a wall. There were some big fellas on the team, larger than he'd expected. But he hadn't expected much.

Coach weaved around the men down the center of the locker room to the far end, passing right under Padraig's nose without even an acknowledgement. The boys naturally followed and gathered around Coach, some sitting on plastic stackable chairs, others leaning against the lockers and walls.

Padraig trailed behind the rest, then sat on the end next to Rory.

When the room quieted, Coach spoke, his back to a white board. "A few things I want to talk about before we get started on the pitch. First, I want to introduce you to the newest member of the team"—he waved at Padraig to his left—"Padraig O'Neale. Straight in from Ireland."

All eyes on him. There was some applause, but nothing hearty in it. He held his hand up in a half-wave to acknowledge them, though none was needed. He was the only new guy in the room. One of the lads with thighs wrapped for lifting, black electrical tape and tubing, nudged the guy next to him. No contest. Padraig had inches on him.

"Padraig will be starting lock forward, our number five. He comes to us with more experience than the team put together with the exception of Del."

The Kiwi snorted, jerked back his head like a disgruntled horse, and crossed his beefy arms in front of his chest. "You got that right."

Coach ignored him. "He has over one hundred caps for his previous provincial club, Munster, and thirty caps for the Ireland International team." He referred to his notes. "He was with Munster when they won a Heineken Cup and the Irish team when they won a 6 Nations Championship."

No response from the lads, as if Coach was speaking Chinese. "Give O'Neale some respect," Coach said.

At the cue, the players shifted noisily out of their seats and stood. With a single loud clap from Del, they started a rhythmic clap and stomp routine. It lasted only a minute, but Padraig couldn't hide the smirk. What the hell were they doing? Must be some ritual they performed when someone did well in a game or maybe even at practice. What were they, in kindergarten? Rewarded for good behavior? The haka he could understand. The Kiwis and other islanders had been doing a war dance before matches to intimidate their competitors for years. And it worked. It was daunting. He had stood in front of the almighty All Black team before, and there had been some serious passion, energy, and power radiating off them.

But this?

Every passing minute in this club seemed a bigger, fatter joke.

The team looked to him for some sort of reaction. What did he do in return? High-five them all? Pat their bums, which American sportsmen seemed so fond of? He only nodded. "Thanks, lads."

He felt Coach's stare on him and turned. Hard to read, Coach—the shaggy beard hiding his expression. He spoke to the team. "Thanks, boys." They resettled into their seats, some throwing glances at Padraig, and none in a friendly manner. "Next business…" Coach began. "As you are all aware, the World Cup is next year." Murmurs started between pairs of mates that Coach subdued with a raise of his hand. "We've been waiting to hear when the scouts are coming around to view the team in action, and we got a confirmation letter today." He glanced down at the sheet. "Looks like they won't give us a definite date, just that it will be one of our home matches at the end of this year."

There were loud groans, and then one of the players piped up. "At least it's a home game. We'll have some advantage."

"Not much," scoffed Del.

"Settle down," Coach said as the banter reached a feverish pitch. The noise continued, so Coach backed up and pounded on the white board.

As it quieted, Rory leaned into Padraig and whispered, "It's not like any of us have a chance. Don't know what they're getting so excited about." Padraig couldn't agree more. Who in this motley crew would be called to represent their international team? Not one of them.

"The only players not eligible for selection are Del and Rory. Mr. O'Neale is lucky enough to carry an American passport."

All eyes turned to Padraig again. Feck. The possibility hadn't even occurred to him. No way could he play for any team but Ireland, even if that wasn't going to happen. And then play against his old teammates? What honor was in that? He bowed his head with the thought and had nothing to say.

Coach saved him by continuing, "So let's drive it hard the next couple of weeks, get us up to where we want to be. Anything that we had put on the backburner to address later, we're gonna work on now. I'll break you into special units to work on strengths and weaknesses."

"Excuse me, Scotch?" A lad with coifed hair raised his hand as if he was in school. "I don't think I can make it to most games in November 'cause I gotta pull extra shifts at my job to save more money for Christmas."

Coach held up two hands in front of him. "We'll talk about that later, Austin, see what we can do to help. Any other questions?"

Silence prevailed. A few stared out into space, as if lost in the dream. Only Padraig, and he was sure Rory and Del, were itching to get onto the pitch. Get out of that room and do something. Get moving. It was the longest Padraig had gone without training in years, and it looked like he was going to have to do most of it himself.

"So that leads me to the last bit of business. She should be here any minute." Coach glanced up at the clock. "Since we are trying to give this club and you lads the best chance of success, management have decided to introduce a specialist for the team." He cleared his throat and rushed, "And she's volunteered her time."

Just then a soft knock occurred on the back door that led to the pitch. Without waiting for an answer, the brunette from Thursday walked in. Today, she wore black leggings with a funky pattern at the bottom, an oversize white collared shirt, and a fedora.

"This is Gillian Sommersby, and now the Blues physical therapist."

She passed a quick look over the men, resting at last on Padraig at the end of the row. A moment of recognition tweaked in her smile.

"She's all right," whispered Rory when she stepped in front of the semicircle.

What the hell was *he* looking at? Fair enough, she was cute, and again today, his belly had roiled at the sight of her, but her getup was...odd. This whole circus was strange and made Padraig mighty uncomfortable.

She clasped her hands in front of her. "The Traverse City Blues has asked me to come on board to help you with injury rehabilitation and pain regulation."

Padraig's heart skipped a beat. Did this have anything to do with him? Couldn't be. They wouldn't get a specialist just because he needed pain meds to play rugby. Lots of the lads were on them. They just didn't get caught like Padraig had.

"You can regulate me any day," Dick joked, which received a few laughs.

That didn't make Coach happy, anger furrowing his brow. He hitched up his pants over his belly, then pointed at Dick. "You're a starting member of this team, Dick. Act like it."

Coach motioned toward her. "Sorry about that, Gillian, please continue."

"Like sports medicine?" The short hooker with the beard piped up. She gave him a grateful smile.

Gillian walked over to the table at the wall and set down a worn brown satchel with musical notes patched on the front. "Yes, similar, but not only in the traditional sense. Meaning, I incorporate traditional physical therapy with alternative methods to get the best response from your body."

Snickers and laughs, and one guy even let out a whoop.

"So give the lads an idea of what you mean," Coach prompted from behind her. Having surrendered the floor to Gillian, he was now leaning against the row of lockers at the back.

45

"Well, not only do I work with muscle and joint mobilization, but I also incorporate acupuncture, acupressure, massage, yoga, and herbal supplements. Whatever is needed. It is a holistic approach to injury and body management." She cringed. "Have I lost anyone yet?"

She waited, and then continued when only feet scuffles replied to her query. "Coach, can I borrow your white board?"

"Aye, sure, Gillian. Just let me wipe the plays off first—"

"No problem, I can do it," she said as she grabbed the eraser from Coach and stepped to the board.

She bent over to retrieve the marker cap she dropped. Now, that view wasn't so bad.

She took her time drawing a rough sketch of the human body. She made short strikes in a star around the left knee. "Let's say you have a knee injury, and after a hard hit, you suffer from pain for the rest of the game." She took the marker and highlighted around the kneecap. "You can mobilize muscles and joints through therapy, and the pain seemingly goes away, but really you are only covering up the injury. Because when the body is in pain, it will try to assist, and often overuses other parts to compensate." She then drew long circles around the outside form of the upper leg. "The knee injury could lead to a thigh muscle injury, as is seen in most cases, because the body will try and balance for the lack of strength in and around the knee by putting more strain on certain leg muscles." She seemed to pause for effect. "And the next thing you know your groin is out."

Half of the lads groaned, some of them cupping their dicks.

"Yep, works every time." She laughed, but there was an evil tinge to the chuckle. Padraig would bet money she was getting a kick out of their discomfort.

Coach walked over and stood next to her. "I'm going to put a timesheet here," he said, motioning to the table with Gillian's bag. "Each one of you will sign up for a twenty minute slot with Gillian." A couple of the lads hooted, but Coach silenced them with a finger. "Over the next week, she'll go through any past or present injuries you have or had, any current pain when you're playing on or off the pitch, and any other health issues you feel you need addressed to perform at a peak level."

Before Coach had stepped away, several boys jumped up and swarmed the sign-up sheet. Coach had to yell to be heard over the noise in the room. "As soon as you're on the sheet, get out on the pitch for warm-up."

Padraig stayed well back from the pack but watched as a couple of the lads engaged Gillian in conversation. She was animated in her discussion, as if she was excited about what they had asked.

When he finished taping up his thighs with the electrical tape and tubing for the lifts, the room was empty and the signup sheet had been knocked to the floor. Grabbing it up, he perused the options. But there were none. Every single slot was filled. Fuck it. He tossed it onto the table and throttled through the door to the pitch. He didn't need any hocus-pocus new age bullshit to help him with his pain. That was what the pills were for. And he had his exercises. He'd get by. He had for the seven years he'd played professionally. It wasn't like there were going to be big hits on this field.

He had to do his time until the drama blew over and he'd be back with Munster, the returned hero, better than before he left. Reformed. Who didn't love a fallen hero to rise up once again better than the Irish? He'd get there.

By the time Padraig placed his first foot on the Blues rugby pitch, the rest of them had finished warm-up, high-knees, shadow runs, and butt-kicks, and Coach was trying to organize them into specialty groups. Padraig headed for Del because he was the captain of the team and Padraig wanted some answers.

An insane noise blared from the loudspeakers when he was a few strides from reaching Del. Moaning whales and whimsical harps? Combined, they created a vomitous sound that retched out of the stadium speakers. As one, the team turned heads toward Coach. Padraig felt bad for him. Even at the distance between them, Coach appeared flustered, an awkward walk-run on his way into the building. Gillian ran out the door to meet him halfway at the try line, and an animated discussion ensued.

Most of the team had gathered around Del and Padraig. "Hope Coach doesn't let her sound this shit off while we practice," one of lads said.

"Why couldn't she play some hip-hop or something?" Mitch asked no one in particular. Padraig was thinking the same. If you wanted to pump a bunch of athletes up, this new age elevator music wasn't the way to go.

"Coach is coming back," one of them said.

Del introduced Padraig to the two players beside him. "Padraig, mate, this is Dick and Damian, they're the

Blues' wings, also known collectively as Dick-n-Mouth." Both shook Padraig's extended hand halfheartedly, too focused on the happenings at the other end of the pitch.

"Hoo-wee, and she's coming, too," Dick said. "Right this way, boys." He puffed out his chest and began to do some warm-up exercises, whirly gigs with his legs, like you did when you were cold going onto the pitch. What a feckin' eejit—Dick was acting the peacock.

Gillian approached them at a fast pace, the piece of paper in her hand clipped and bent with the breeze she created. She stopped directly in front of Padraig, out of breath, her chest heaving. Padraig didn't want to stare so looked down at her shoes instead. The same black Converse she had worn last week.

"Mr. O'Neale?" she asked.

"Yep, that's me."

"You didn't sign up for your initial consultation." Her hat was gone, and as her breathing settled, she pulled strands of loose curls away from her face and tucked them behind her ears.

Out of the corner of his eye, he could sense the other boys moving away. At least that Dick fella had stopped his ridiculous warm-up routine. What a muppet.

"There weren't any spots left, but I don't mind. I don't need an appointment." He teased the last word as if it was a joke, but Gillian didn't appreciate it. Not one bit.

"I'm already late getting started or I'd offer to add you to the end of the list, but there won't be time today."

"No problem. Whenever."

"You don't seem too enthused with my services."

Padraig glanced away briefly, then turned back to her. "I don't need your *services*."

49

"That's not your choice. Coach McKenzie is your boss. You are employed with the Traverse City Blues Rugby Club, and this is part of your tenure."

"Listening to this?" Padraig's temper was rising. He could feel it in his jaw, and his back pain was making him a cranky prick. "What the feck is this shite?"

"Music therapy."

"For what? The dead?"

She bit her lower lip, and he could tell she held back the thousands of oaths she would have spewed forth if she wasn't in a professional environment. At a pub, he probably would've deserved a slap.

"I apologize," Padraig grunted out.

"As you should." At that moment, the music changed to a twinkling of piano keys, a soft melody almost like a lullaby. A small but sure breeze lifted strands of her hair outward like static electricity from a balloon. Her gaze locked with Padraig's, and for a moment his life softened, the edges not so cruel and bitter. It was as if she had radiated a calming spell onto him. With all the funky clothes she wore, maybe she was a witch. His ma believed in the banshee, so he supposed anything was possible.

When one of the lads shifted into his peripheral vision, breaking the spell, Padraig cleared his throat and looked away.

"I'm working group sessions all day Thursday, but you can stay late after practice, and we can do your interview then," Gillian instructed.

Payback obviously. She was standing her ground, letting him know she wouldn't be walked on. Even though he understood, and would have done the same himself, that agreement didn't relieve his irritation. Not a request. A

50

command. Either he could follow through and put himself right in her and the club's eyes, or he could flack it. Not go. But for now, she was waiting for an answer. "Sure 'nough, I'll wait around."

A slight nod of her head in recognition. "I'm sure you will."

Whether it was sarcasm or not, Padraig couldn't tell. He didn't know her from Adam.

"Well, I'm late starting this morning, so I'll talk to you then." Without acknowledging the other fellas, she turned on her heel and headed back to the complex.

The entire squad watched her walk the pitch until the door closed behind her. A strange one, she was.

Chapter 5

Gillian's best friend, Junette, drove up as she was opening the garage door. Music blared from Junette's open window. Gillian called out, "Come here and help a sister out."

Junette climbed out of her compact car, dragging an oversize handbag with her. "I'm coming. Hold your horses."

"Can you hop into the driver's seat? I'm going to push the beast out of the garage, and when it's halfway down the driveway, you step on the brake."

Junette dropped her bag on the grass. "You're all gung ho, aren't ya? Haven't been here two minutes and you're on me like a fly to shit."

Gillian laughed. "I'm feeling good about this whole thing, so yeah, let's go!"

After Junette hopped in, Gillian went around to the back to push the car out nose first. "Ready?"

"Don't you need the ignition on for the car brakes to work?"

"The car won't start, ya dork. Why do you think I'm pushing it out of the garage? For exercise?"

Junette stuck out her tongue before shutting her door and rolling down the window. "So I'm not mechanical. Sue me." With a wave at Gillian to go ahead, she said, "Go on, then, Fix-it Felix."

With a laugh, Gillian pushed hard against the trunk. Her feet slipped as she found traction, but the beast finally started to inch forward. When it picked up momentum on the decline, she let go. "Brake!"

The car came to a jerky stop with a short squeak of the brakes. Junette shifted it into park and hopped out. "Shoot, that was tough going. I've worked myself up a thirst."

Gillian pointed to a green reusable grocery bag on the lawn. She ducked her head under the hood, but could hear her friend rifling through sack. A bottle of beer appeared in Gillian's line of sight.

"No thanks, no beer, but can you open my wine?" Gillian swiped a dirty finger down both sides of her face like war paint. "My hands are greasy."

"Still off the beer?"

"Yup."

"Like the feather, by the way."

Gillian tapped her head until she found what Junette referred to. "Oh, yeah, found this gull feather on the lawn this morning. Thought it added to my warrior look."

"Truly hard core." More rustling, and Junette said, "I found the six-pack, but no bottle of wine."

Gillian balanced the troubleshooting manual on the engine block, wedging it between some clear tubing and what she had identified as the radiator. She weighted the first pages down with a wrench so the book would stay open. "It's there at the bottom."

Junette snorted. "You mean this airplane-sized bottle of Cab Sav?"

"One glass of red wine a day is beneficial. Finally recognized by the US health system, known for centuries by the Europeans."

Gillian turned in time to catch Junette making crazy eyes at her. "What?"

"Nothing. I guess that means I get to finish this six-pack off myself. I'm good with that."

"All yours."

"So how was your first day with the Blues?"

Gillian shrugged, then took a sip of the wine and set it on the ground. "All right." She unscrewed the cap on the air filter and lifted it off.

"You don't sound too enthused. Not like when you talked about it this past spring." Junette pulled a portable camp chair from the lawn to the car and took a seat. "Maybe it's not such a good idea. You can't change people if they don't want to be changed."

Gillian couldn't look at her best friend so busied herself inspecting the guts of the car, not really seeing anything. She'd started out in college as a music major, but changed her second year to physical therapy. So much happened that year, and she had been determined then, as much as she was now, to have a career that might help others. If she only impacted one person, that was enough. But to her surprise, she found she was good at it, too. In her own non-traditional ways. "No, but I have to try."

"That's honorable, Gill, but why don't you just get a job as a PT in an established practice like everyone else out of college? That would be better for you."

"Because I'm not everyone else."

Junette snorted. "Ain't that the truth."

Gillian eyed the air filter, blew into the creases, and then placed it back into the circular receptacle.

"Gillian, did you hear what I said?"

"Sorry, no, what?" Gillian walked around the side of the car to give it an appraising look. All the work. Years of fixing the rusted frame, replacing piece after piece from entire doors to floor pedals, updating the engine, everything. Andrew was the talented one as machines went. She had mostly handed him wrenches and contributed her pennies. She should have watched more closely, should have listened when he spouted off his mechanical wisdom.

"I said would you turn this shit off? Every time I come here, you're playing the same crap." She swirled her beer in the air. "Like hello, we left the eighties over thirty years ago."

Simple Minds was singing "Don't You Forget About Me" and hell if she was going to turn it down or off. It was one of her favorites. "Eighties music is the best. So much passion and ingenuity. Folk will catch on and my music will come back full force. I'm just way ahead of the rest of you."

Junette blew a raspberry. "Whatevah."

"Plus, it's a beautiful night for it." Gillian opened her arms and did a slow twirl. "A warm summer evening in Michigan. Lawn mowers buzzing, sprinklers sprinkling. The kind of balmy night you want to sit out and turn up the music until the mosquitoes drive you nuts and you head inside. The kind of summer night you'd love to be in love." Gillian let her arms flop to her sides and turned back toward the car. "I was born in the wrong era."

"Old news. Let's move on."

"No, I'm serious. I don't get it these days. It all seems so complicated. All this technology and pace. I can barely breathe trying to keep up."

"It's not complicated. You just have to embrace it."

"Embrace what?"

"Life."

Gillian gathered the socket wrenches from the tool box and haphazardly laid them in the engine block, as if she knew where they were meant to be used. Heavy clanks of metal on metal kept Junette from going on about Gillian's life, or lack thereof. She'd heard it before.

"Maybe you'll meet a nice fella this year. Are there any hotties playing for the Blues?"

Gillian chose to avoid answering Junette outright. She wasn't into jocks and their small minds. She was there to help, and that's all. Although, the Irish fella with his dark hair and bright eyes… He'd probably turn out like the rest of the meatheads. Rude. Full of himself. More muscle than brain cells. Hell, he was already popping the pills. That was like a gigantic red X over the top of him. With a buzzer.

But sexy as hell if you were into that type of guy. Coach wanted her to help him, and she would because he'd asked. And that was the only reason.

"I'm still holding out for Lloyd Dobler."

Junette growled. "Gill, he's a fictional character. He doesn't exist."

"In my heart, he does." With a dramatic sigh, she rested her hip against the car door. "He's absolutely perfect. Sensitive, caring, responsive, intuitive, intelligent—"

"Geek."

"Yes, but that's a good thing. He doesn't feel the need to prove himself like other men. That's the point. He's different. Do you not remember that scene in the movie when he is kickboxing?"

"I try not to."

"Well, he's totally cut. Great body. But you never know because he hides it under that big trench coat."

Junette shook her head slowly from side to side. "Oh, Gill, you are lost to me."

"Better to be a dreamer than dead in the water. You married the guy you dated in high school. *And* you've got a kid. You're not even twenty-five."

Even though Gillian regretted the words as soon as they left her mouth, Junette didn't seem bothered at all. "That's why I'm here on a Monday evening drinking light beer and watching you struggle over your fucking car. It's actually fun and interesting compared to Mickey Mouse Clubhouse and poopy diapers."

Junette had been Gillian's best friend for as long as she could remember. For as opposite as they were and their very different paths in life, there was no one she felt more comfortable around. While Junette shifted in her chair and crossed her legs, Gillian took a moment to soak in the wonderful woman next to her. "You still look fabulous, Junipers. You know that, don't you?

"Aw, you're full of lovelies this evening. Still look fabulous, even though…" She motioned for Gillian to continue.

Gillian shrugged. "Nothing."

"That's bullshit. You were going to say, even though I've had a baby."

"Maybe, but it's still a compliment. Why do you hide your fab figure behind those blousy shirts?"

"Um, because I've still got a baby belly, and although some people think it's okay to flash their muffins, I do not. And you're the same. Look at you and those baggy T-shirts and ugly shoes. And why do you wear glasses now? What happened to your contacts? What the hell? I've seen you naked. You have an awesome body."

"I like my style. It's shabby chic with an emphasis on shabby." Gillian laughed at her own joke, but Junette didn't follow suit. "Nothing like the local Goodwill store to help with all this greatness." She motioned down her body, and then Junette did laugh.

"There's more to life than how you look. I've got more important things to do than worry about clothes and shopping. It's not like I was ever really into it before, so what's the go now?"

"All I know is if I could turn back time—"

Gillian started humming a few bars of the tune by Cher.

"No, please don't start singing. What I'm trying to say is that I'd love to be all sexy and young and single again some days. Not that I don't love my boys, but these are *your* days, Gillian. Have fun. Live a little. Shake a tail feather. All that stuff."

"Who says I'm not?"

"I do."

Her dad's work van pulled up to the curb, which saved Gillian from having to bolster her defenses. He poked his head out of the window. "Almost done, Gill? I'd like to get into my driveway at some point tonight."

"Yep, sorry, Dad. Will be done soon. If you leave your keys in your truck, I'll park it after I move the beast out of the way."

"Hi, Mr. Sommersby," Junette piped in.

"Heya, Junipers," Gillian's dad said as he exited the van. He pulled an old battered lunch box and Thermos along with him. "How's that little boy of yours?"

"Awesome. He's already started having tantrums."

"At fifteen months old?"

Junette exaggerated a smile for Gillian's dad. "Just lucky I guess."

He turned back toward Gillian. They'd been walking on eggshells around each other since the other night. "You staying here or your new place tonight?"

"I might as well take the leap."

"Okay, hon, pop in before you take off."

"Will do."

"Nice to see you again, Junipers."

"You, too. Tell Mrs. Sommersby I said hi."

"I will. Goodnight, ladies."

Neither said anything until Gillian's dad disappeared into the front door. Then Junette asked, "How are they taking it?"

"Being on their own?"

"Yeah, you having your own place now."

"Fine, I think. I couldn't stay here much longer whether they wanted me to or not. Too many memories."

"I'll pop over next week and see how you've decked it out. Hopefully you've given up on posters and bean bags for interior decoration. We *are* mature women now, you know."

Right, she'd do something about that this weekend. Gillian laughed, then danced her eyebrows comically at Junette. "You'll have to wait and see. Maybe I did. Maybe I didn't."

"Oh God, please say you did."

"What do you think of lava lamps for ambience?"

"Just say no, Gill. Just say no."

Chapter 6

"So what do you think of our new therapy sessions?" Del asked as he turned into traffic.

Padraig was in the front seat this time, thank feck, since Rory had stayed behind again to work on his kicking. He admired the young player his commitment and passion, but wasn't about to go overboard for a club he might only be with for a couple months. He knew he'd get his groove back. Right team and right tournament, he was sure to be back full strength.

"How is that supposed to help our game?" Padraig asked sardonically.

"Don't diss it altogether, bro. Music is a huge part of my culture. You know, I'm half Maori, and music and ceremony is important to my people."

Del's Maori side showed. He stood just over six-foot, built like a house, and moved fast as a leopard on the pitch. He had a massive black tribal tattoo that sleeved his right arm from shoulder to below his elbow, and a dragon tail wrapped the bicep of the other, disappearing under the sleeve of his shirt.

The All Blacks Padraig had played against had been covered with ink. Some of the Irish squad had a few less visible designs, most from their cultural heritage, like Padraig's Celtic band circling his left forearm. He had always wanted another one, something bigger and bolder, but could never decide what he wanted on his body for the rest of his life that held enough significance. And the pain to get it done. Sure, didn't he have enough of that in his life already? Perhaps one day.

"Okay, so tell me, do you feel any better after listening to that at training?"

"Nah mate, but maybe it takes time to get into our system or something."

Padraig looked out the window at the passing streets. "I doubt it."

"Hey, you want to stop for a quick pint before we head home?"

Padraig scoffed. "Hell, yeah."

"Mate, you need one after that tough session."

Tough workout? Not so much. Harder than he'd expected, though. And more organized, more professional that he had imagined. Except for the bloody music piped out the speakers. Coach had let it play throughout the training session again.

Del pulled his old junker into the Sail Inn off the main road. The large sign at the front read "Karaoke Mon Thurs nights."

"Can I give you a little bit of advice?" Del asked over the hood as they exited the car.

"As my captain?"

"As another foreigner playing for this club."

They walked into the windowless building, scattered with only a few patrons since it was a Tuesday evening. There was an L-shaped bar directly to their left as they entered. Padraig approved. The place reminded him of some of the pubs back in Cork except for the large moose head behind the bar and mounted fish along the walls. The smell of stale beer and smoke permeated the air, but the place looked clean enough.

"What's that got to do with anything?" asked Padraig as they approached the bar.

Del ignored him, ordering the beer an obvious priority. "What'll ya have, bro?"

"Guinness if they have it."

Del asked the bartender, a bit 'o skirt with a ponytail and a tight T-shirt over skinny jeans, who looked bemused at the request before she plastered on a smile again. Her cheerful façade was all fake as she whined out, "No, sorry."

"Not in luck today, Irish. How about a Blue Ribbon for the Blues?"

Any numbing agent would do at this point.

As she poured, Del continued where he'd left off. "It's probably a good idea if you try to be mates with the other guys. Easier on you"—he set one pint in front of Padraig—"in the long run."

"I'm not worried about the long run."

Del glanced sideways at him briefly, but then nodded to the girl when she set the other pint in front of him. "How much, hon?"

"It's happy hour still, so five bucks altogether."

Del pulled out a tenner and set it on the bar. "Keep the change."

She smiled, leaning onto the bar so her breasts squeezed together, showing a long vertical crease in the V of her cleavage. "You guys aren't from here, are you?"

How original. And not a movement in his nether region. But Del was saddling up for a bit of a flirt, crossing his arms on the countertop, his foot up on the barstool rung. "Nope, how can you tell?"

"Big guys like you." She winked. "Where you from?"

Padraig had enough and grabbed Del's arm, tugging him away from the bar. "Not here," he answered for them over his shoulder. The beer sloshed from his pint glass as he turned them abruptly to a high-top table on the far wall. When he looked back to make sure Del had followed, he noticed the same had happened to him. Del flicked the beer off his hand, then wiped it on his jeans. "Mate, that wasn't cool. Plus, she was hot."

"And probably underage."

"Nope, already checked up on that. They have to be eighteen to serve alcohol in this state. So they're all legal."

When Padraig sat at the table, Del remained standing. He crooked his head to the side, motioning in the other direction. "Let's go outside."

Scraping his chair back, Padraig rose and followed Del out the double glass doors where a wooden sign over the entrance read Portside Patio.

Del gave a wide-ass cheeky grin to an older waitress clearing empties from a table. Fuck, what was he like?

As he sat, he finished half his beer in one long drink. "It'd be better if you were on good terms with the other lads, mate."

"It's not my job here to get along with the other lads."

"Well, see, that's the thing. You, me, and Rory are the only paid players on the squad. And I don't think Rory gets paid much, but he's here for the experience."

That was news. There wasn't a player for any of the Irish provincial clubs that didn't get something. "So they are all volunteers?"

"Yep, all of them hold regular jobs, mate." Austin's comment in the locker room made sense to Padraig now. He couldn't imagine not being able to play because of work or family commitments. Playing rugby was his job. He had no other and hadn't for years. Not that it wasn't hard work. It was, and it came with a whole heap of shite he reckoned other jobs didn't have. But he loved what he did, so he was luckier than most.

Del continued, "Think of it this way. Not one American rugby player in US Union is paid. Not one. So all those lads that compete in the World Cup are up against professional year-round players. For the most part. Some of the Americans play for overseas clubs, but most don't. That has to say something for their dedication."

He had a point.

"So all we have to do," Del said, waving a hand between himself and Padraig, "is worry about training and playing rugby. All the rest of the boys have full-time jobs they have to maneuver around. Some have family and kids. But they make the sacrifice because they love the game."

"So I should feel bad for them? Is that what you're saying?"

"Not at all, mate. That's the last thing they'd want. But they can help you do *your* job better. All I'm saying is think on it."

"I'm not sure I need their help."

"Oh, you will, cuz. That's what a team is." Del chugged the rest of his beer and thunked the glass on the table. "Goin' to the loo." He scooted out of his chair. "Be right back."

Finally a minute to himself. He wrestled the pills from his pocket onto his lap and shook one into his palm. He glanced around to see if anyone noticed, but the few punters on the patio were busy smoking or talking away to each other.

Discretion. Always important, but he felt like a junkie in Cork City centre. Feckin' hated that he felt this way.

As he washed down the pill with a drink of beer, he noticed at the doors a young woman with a kerchief tied around her head and a stack of glasses up her arm staring straight at him. He wanted to tell her to feck off, but he had manners. Or at least he used to. Everything these days made him angry. But who could blame him?

His mum would be mortified if she knew how Padraig had treated his old teammates, coach even, and at times his agent. *That's not how you were raised, Padraig O'Neale*, she'd say, waving her wooden spoon at him. That spoon was both threat and punishment, having been whacked on the back of his calves more than a few times in his youth.

But for the most part Padraig had been on the straight and narrow. A bit of bushin' when he was younger, drinking on the streets with the boys, but until recently everyone considered him lighthearted and ready for a laugh. That was the Padraig of the past. Now? That man was too far gone to be able to conjure up again.

He rolled his shoulders, then cracked his neck to each side. Where the hell was Del? The girl was still staring at their table. She didn't move an inch until Del approached the doors, and then shifted away to allow him through. She watched him saunter toward Padraig in his easy lope. Strangely, she was the first woman Del didn't notice.

Del set two new pints on the table, pushing one toward the other pint of Padraig's, only half empty.

"Thanks, I could have gotten this round."

"No worries, mate, it's all good."

"So, why are you with the Blues?" Padraig asked.

"Why not?"

Padraig smirked. "I can think of a hundred reasons." Avoiding Del's stare, he finished the last of his first drink, the foam settling and dripping down the side.

"It's not that bad if you give it a go."

Padraig swirled the dregs around the bottom of the glass. "I watched you on the pitch. You're more than good. Seems to me you could be playing a bigger club in New Zealand, even the All Blacks team."

"Nah, mate, I tried out for the Maori All Blacks, you know the team only the indigenous fellas can play for, and got in, but I woulda been sittin' the bench most of the time."

"So big fish in a small pond kind of thing, eh?" Padraig asked.

Del turned back to Padraig. "Something like that. And I wanted to travel, get away from home for a bit."

"Why not Europe or South America? That's where I wanted to go. Or Biarritz or Lyon. Even Parma in Italy for you."

"So why aren't ya then?"

Lifting his shoulders in an exaggerated shrug, he answered, "Didn't get in."

As if he understood there wouldn't be any further discussion, Del picked up where he left off. "America's a good place to be right now in rugby. Most guys don't get that, so I'm ahead of the rest of you. They are doing some innovative stuff here, mate. They weren't rugby powerhouses in the past, but they're getting there and will be a force to be reckoned with one day. And I want to be a part of that. So if that is a big fish in a little pond, I'd rather that than a small kakapo in a big forest. At least I get to be a part of making plays, leading the boys, offering ideas and solutions. Over there, mate, I'd be some stuffed dummy the boys used for scrum practice."

Padraig knew what he was talking about. Sure, everyone had to work on the way to the top. Padraig had tried out for the Irish National team three times before he got a spot, so there was no guarantee. Ever. And when you got older, you lost your jersey to the younger kids and your name no longer appeared on the team sheet—the starting players for the next match.

"What's your real name? I mean, how did you get the nickname Del?"

"Now, I'm gonna tell you, Irish, because I think we are on the same level. No one else knows, so if I hear you told anyone my real name, your ass will be mine on that pitch. You got it?"

He seemed serious enough, so Padraig acquiesced. "No problem. My lips are sealed."

"My first name is Rydell after my mum's dad. The rest of my name is tribal, but mum is a white girl so she wanted Rydell. I came with my own nickname, and the boys were good with that. I mean, who's going to mess with me? I got their respect. It's important you let them call you by your nickname, Irish. It's all a part of the"—he waved his hand in the air like an eggbeater—"feng shui of a team."

"Hey, boys."

Padraig and Del jerked up in the seats to the sound of Gillian's voice behind them. Her hair was pulled back today showing off a slender neck, strong lines that slid into pronounced collarbones. She had her satchel draped over her shoulder. Padraig's stomach dipped again. This time, he acknowledged the sensation, rubbing his hand back and forth over his belly.

Del turned on the charm. "*Kia ora*, Gillian, you come to meet us boys for a drink?"

She dropped her bag down beside the table, still holding the strap loosely in her hand. "You're unlucky tonight. I'm here to meet a friend of mine."

"Too bad, we'd love the company of a fine woman like yourself."

She smirked. "Aw shucks, Del, you sure do know how to make a lady feel special."

They shared a laugh while Padraig remained silent, spinning his glass around on the table.

"Hi, Padraig." Gillian nodded to him. Full lips, he noticed. And she'd pronounced his name correctly. "How are you settling in?"

Padraig pinched a smile in return, making a concerted effort to look her in the eye. She hadn't been too pleased with his perusal last week. Gillian had changed to a gray skirt with the periodic table printed on the front, and even though she wore another T-shirt that had "Nerd" written across the chest, he could still tell there were some nice breasts underneath. "Grand," he answered. "Couldn't be better. Nice shirt."

She squinted her eyes at him, slow to respond. "Thanks."

"Well, I'll leave you boys to it." She hitched her satchel back onto her shoulder. "I'll see you on Thursday. I have a surprise for group session."

"Can't wait," Padraig said dryly. He took a large sip of his beer, showing off his nonchalance to Miss Sommersby. "Perhaps some more music therapy we can look forward to?"

"Perhaps." Gillian leaned down between them, an arm on the back of each chair, her chest directly at Padraig's eye level. She smelled of lavender. "Think doggie style."

She briefly smiled at Del, then turned to Padraig. He could have sworn she pinned her gaze on him a nanosecond longer than she had Del. Was it a challenge? What did she see?

"That'll be a beaut, Miss G! Padraig and I are already lookin' forward to it. Aren't we, Irish?" Del asked, slapping him on the back.

Padraig didn't respond, but instead caught Gillian's gaze to make sure she knew he was up for the contest. Whatever that might be.

"Okay, see you then." She pinched a smile at them and left, making her way, with a nice swish of the hips, to a table at the far side of the beer garden. She sat across from an older man with long gray hair, wearing crazy-striped hippy pants and rows of leather and silver bracelets up his arms.

"Mate, there is something very sexy brewing under that there Miss Gillian," Del said when she was out of earshot.

"You think every woman is sexy, *mate*. Why would we want to get involved with American girls when we're going home?"

"At some point, yes," Del agreed, "but not right now." He rose from his chair and Padraig followed suit. "Right now, anything can happen."

Chapter 7

The first thing Gillian saw when she walked in the door was Padraig. With Jenn, the receptionist, picking lint off his shirt. She had him up against the desk, her legs alternating with his. She stopped her grooming of the Irishman and worked her phone in front of her, punching buttons. Today, she wore a short summer skirt, tank top, and fashionable heels that looked like ankle boots, but were sandals. A bit much for the club, in Gillian's humble opinion.

Padraig was sitting, his hands to each side, grasping the edges of the desk. And unlike most men pinned in that position, he wasn't staring at her chest, but rather out into space, his gaze unfocused and sad.

Whenever she saw Jenn, Gillian always felt an immediate pang of envy, but it was quickly squashed by her logic. She didn't want to be that type of girl, never had, never would. Sure, Jenn looked fantastic, gorgeous even, but gah—there was something so chintzy about her. Overdone, over-the-top fakeness that most men just didn't seem to get. Did they actually believe her act was for real?

That she wanted only him? That all the batting of her eyelashes and syrup-sweet smiles were genuine? God, she could gag.

Supposing with men's egos, they would. Her brother was the same, always gawking over scantily clad women that whispered "no class" to Gillian, but obviously were yelling something else in his ears.

Conscious of her own sloppy cut-off shorts and baggy hoodie, she cleared her throat to interrupt the intimacy before she made a total fool of herself. The last thing she wanted was for one of them to look up and see her staring.

Jenn turned and sat next to Padraig. Practically on his lap. "Oh hi, Gillian. Didn't see you there."

Of course not.

Jenn ran her fingers back through her hair so that her chest rose. "Didn't think you were coming in today."

"Special favor for *Coach*," Gillian said, emphasizing the last word, as if she could conjure him to appear and save her from this awkward situation. Invading the space of the vomitous love birds. She'd give Jenn that. She moved quick. And now that Gillian thought of it, what the heck was Jenn doing here on a Wednesday? Obviously trawling for meat. The foreign boys were here for some extra practice and Barbie must have gotten wind of it somehow. What a leech. She needed to get a life outside of men.

When Gillian met Padraig's gaze, he returned it steady, no flinch or show of emotion. But he'd been like that since he'd arrived. Flat. Zombie-like. Half-dead.

"I just need to borrow Padraig a minute."

Jenn crossed her arms over her chest. "What for?"

Was it any of her business? It was as if she'd already staked her claim on Padraig and was his keeper in all things receptiony. "Because I told Coach I'd work on his back." And why the heck were they talking about him like he wasn't there? She walked up to Padraig. "Do you have a minute?"

He eyed the door. "I'm sure the lads are about ready to go, and they're my ride home."

"It'll only take a minute."

"If he doesn't want to, he doesn't have to, Gill—"

Okay, that was about enough. "Jenn, I'm sure he appreciates your loving care, but this is about the club, so if you wouldn't mind butting out a minute. Hell, we could have been done by now if we'd just gotten on with it." She waved her hand out toward the physio room. "Mr. O'Neale, if you would please? I've already worked all day but made a special trip out here to help." She had, and she *was* tired. She'd volunteered her Tuesday and Thursday evenings for the club, and now she was here on a Wednesday. Seeing him with Barbie didn't bother her. Not one bit. Her grumpiness wasn't about that—at all. But she had used a special olive oil treatment in her hair this morning. Not for him, of course.

He shrugged before he rose from the desk. He grabbed his bag and hoisted it to his shoulder. "After you, Miss Sommersby."

"I can give you a ride home if you need one, Irish," Jenn purred.

Padraig held up a hand in a wave. "That's all right. You go ahead. If I miss the boys, I'll get a cab."

As soon as Gillian closed the door, she launched into him. "It's none of my business, but you should be careful with Jenn. She works her way through all the boys."

He dropped his bag, a half-smirk on his face. "You're right on the first account. It isn't any of your business. I'm a big boy. I can take care of myself."

"I'm not worried about you. I know that Coach doesn't like it when the boys get together with Jenn." Even when Andrew had played with the Blues, Jenn had been a tease, having started her flirtations young at the ripe old age of sixteen. She had some sort of connection with the club, an ex-player's niece or granddaughter or something. More than one player had been off their game after fooling around with her. She played the lads against each other, and it was rotten.

Padraig had stepped around the physio table and into her space. God, he was big. She stood her ground. No alpha gorilla behavior would intimidate her. "Just giving you fair warning, is all."

"I'm good, thanks. Now, we done here?"

What? They hadn't even started. "No. This isn't about Jenn. Coach really did ask me to help with your back pain." Gillian unzipped her bag where she'd placed it on the table and grabbed a small jar of ointment. "I'll use one of my special treatments on—"

"I'm not interested." Padraig took a step back.

"I can show you some exercises specifically for the lower back, and if you apply this cream twice a day, you'll notice a change within a week."

His fist clenched at his side. "I told you I'm not interested in your help. I have a routine that my physio back home gave me. That's working."

"You're not in pain?"

He crossed his arms over his chest. "Nope."

But she could tell he was lying by the way his eyes had darted to the corner of the room and back before he'd answered. The way they shone, all glassy. The way he walked with stiffness in his step. She wouldn't take no for an answer. Not anymore.

"Take your shirt off, please, and lie on the table with your head at the far side. I'm sure you are familiar with massage. Head goes down in the center."

She pulled her hoodie over her head and hung it on the hook on the back of the door. She bent at the waist and shook her hair down, bunched it up, and pulled it through the ponytail holder that resided permanently on her wrist. When she stood up, Padraig was staring at her as if she'd grown two heads. Maybe she had a ketchup stain on her tank top. She held the shirt out but saw nothing. Huh.

At his almost imperceptible nod, her courage grew. Just like any client. "Lie here on your stomach."

He did as instructed and settled his head onto his overlapped hands, elbows jutting out like chicken wings. In gentle, fluid movements, she un-tucked each hand and arm and let them trail down the sides of his body. She lifted his hips to lower his track pants so they rode low on his bum. Sweet mercy. His ass was divine. Rounder and juicier than a summer cantaloupe.

But she was a professional, and he, a client. And a jock. A deep breath in and out. Gillian uncapped the jar and rubbed her palms with the ointment.

"What the hell is that smell?"

"None of your worry. It works really well. Hasn't anyone told you the smellier the concoction, the better the results?"

"Just like Rory. You are all mad," came muffled through the table.

"Crazy knows crazy. Now shush."

She started at his lower lumbar and moved her hands in sweeping motions up his back, around his side, under his armpits, and finally over his shoulders. She began again at his lower back and kneaded and rolled along his spine, then outward, circling her palms over knotted muscles. Hitching his pants lower, she delved under his boxer band, massaging the top of his bum, smoothing the muscle out and away from his spine.

As normally happened once she was in rhythm, the time ticked by. After a few repetitions along his torso, she stopped to check on him.

He appeared to be asleep. The endorphins released by the massage weighted him to the table, as happened with most of her clients when they fell into a peaceful lethargy. So quiet, she couldn't hear him breathe. Wide back, broad shoulders, dark, tousled hair. A man any woman would want. Except for Gillian. He was no Lloyd Dobler.

So not to startle him, Gillian withdrew her hands from his back with a soft swish of her fingers. With a deep breath, she took a step back and waited. But he didn't move.

She should really be getting him up and out the door so he could catch his lift from Del, but she couldn't get herself to do it. Instead of waking him, she decided to let him rest. So she took a seat on one of the chairs along the wall. Leaning her elbow on her knee and resting her jaw in her hand, she watched him sleep. A dark, manly brow that had finally relaxed. Black, thick lashes. Strong nose and a top lip that came to a defined point.

He was gorgeous, really.

She was so mesmerized that when his eyes blinked open, she screamed. Just like in a horror movie when the corpse comes to life. She had scrambled halfway up her chair when he let out a laugh.

Her hand over her racing heart, she didn't see the humor, but then, he'd only opened his eyes, which didn't normally elicit such a dramatic response. She was still shaky as she gathered her gear together. Out of the corner of her eye, she saw him move, first to sitting where he waited a few beats, then onto his feet.

As he was pulling his shirt over his head, Del barged through the door. "Everything all right here?"

Both she and Padraig responded in unison. "Fine."

Del raised a brow. "Uh-huh."

Rory crowded in the door behind him and said to Padraig, "You ready to go?"

"Yeah, all set." He stopped at the door and turned back to Gillian. "Thanks."

And then he was gone, and Gillian was still breathless.

Chapter 8

When Padraig stepped into the locker room on Thursday, there was a buzz of activity around the bulletin board, the boys pushing and shoving to get a look at the one piece of paper tacked under an announcement for the season's fundraiser.

He ignored the commotion and turned toward his locker. In passing, Rory stopped him with a comment. "She's having us do yoga today in groups. You're in the first one."

What the fuck? Padraig knew the *she* to whom Rory referred. Who else would have them take precious time out of training for something so incredibly stupid? Magic hands she might have, but he hadn't signed up for this. Hell, he didn't really want to be here in the first place, and this was only making it worse. Plus, he had his bloody interview with the woman after training so couldn't even escape home.

"Brilliant," Padraig grunted as he passed Rory straight to the toilets. There had been no opportunity to take his pill this afternoon. Del had them out the door as soon as Padraig, who had been running late from the gym, stepped into the kitchen. What he needed to do was keep a glass of water in his bedroom, but he'd forgotten that, too.

He threw his gear bag at the wall of the bathroom and shut a cubicle door firmly behind him, turning the privacy lock. His anger and pain shook his hands so that he struggled with the cap. He had to squeeze both sides while turning, the childproof mechanism catching every time he almost had it opened.

"Fuck!" Padraig stopped and drew a deep breath, then let it out slow. Tried again with the cap, and he got it on the first go. He rattled a pill out of the bottle and swallowed it dry. He flushed the toilet even though he hadn't taken a piss. After grabbing his water bottle out of his gear bag, he drank deep, then headed for the lockers.

Most of the lads were outside already so the locker room was quiet, only the soft mumble of a few in the area by the white board. He took his time stripping off his tracksuit bottoms and hoodie before donning his rugby shorts and jersey. He pulled his change of clothes from his bag and neatly refolded them on the top shelf, then placed the pill bottle in the front left pocket of his jeans for later.

"You comin', Padraig?" He heard over the tops of the lockers.

"Sure, be right there."

When he rounded into sight of the others, his throat seized, and his body tightened in response to the view of Gillian's backside. Here he'd been stripping down to his underwear only a few rows over. Bending at the waist, she fiddled with a portable CD player. She was dressed in tight leggings to her knees and a tank top that finally revealed her perky breasts. Even with the top sporting an owl. The way the boys stood, hands over crotch, they were having the same reaction as Padraig. No glasses, and she had braided her hair to the side, again showing off her fair neck. Underneath all her crazy, she was most certainly edible.

In front of Gillian was a single yoga mat, and then five other mats in a row facing hers. There were four others, including the left wing, Dick, all of them huddled together laughing too loudly at a joke he had told. Some slow willowy music started, and she turned toward the group of lads.

The boys shifted about, trying to jostle their bits imperceptibly. Gillian didn't seem to notice as she stepped to the front of her mat. "Ok boys, today we are going to start one of the oldest practices in both body and mind management." She paused. "Yoga. If you didn't get it by now."

The hooker with a beard said, "My wife goes to yoga on Wednesday nights. She loves it." He stepped forward onto a mat and mirrored Gillian's stance. The other three reluctantly followed, Dick and another young one elbowing each other as they waited. Juvenile. He wasn't sure about this new-age shite either, but at least they could act like they were out of school.

"Most people do when they get into it," Gillian said, then motioned to Padraig. "Mr. O'Neale, are you going to join us?"

There was the one mat left on the far right side, and without a word, he casually stepped to the top.

"Thank you," she said quietly, then repositioned her feet. "Yoga originally was a discipline to attain a permanent state of peace. Now, in Western culture, we use it mostly for the physical rewards—body toning, breathing exercises, control, flexibility, strength, and endurance. I'd like you to notice that all of these benefits are what you also need as professional athletes."

The lad right next to Padraig, whose name he had yet to learn, mumbled under his breath, "Professional, my ass."

Gillian ignored it, but Padraig felt the pressure of four sets of eyes on him as they recognized the paid athlete in their midst. He kept his gaze straight ahead, standing solid, his feet slightly apart.

"So yoga will now be introduced into your training once a week in group sessions such as this." The music strained higher until it peaked at a crying violin, then retreated into a more subdued refrain.

"Let's get started. I'll talk you through the positions and your breathing. Stand with feet slightly apart, comfortable." She pointed to the hooker. "A bit farther apart, Shane." When he shifted, she continued, "That's perfect. Now raise your arms up and let them fall back to your sides. Each move is partnered with a breath—in for one movement, out for the next. Now, swoop down until your fingertips touch your toes. If you can't touch now, don't worry, we'll work on getting you a little bit closer each time."

Gillian took one step back, then another, her bum up in the air in an inverted V. He tried to follow along with her but was mesmerized by the movement of her body. So beautiful and graceful. And he looked as much an idiot as the boys next to him.

"This pose is called the downward dog. Get used to it. We use it a lot."

Snickers came from across the room, but they continued the routine. Gillian led them through a sequence of movements that she called the sun salutation, and a basic starter, she explained, for novice yoga practitioners. Which they all very much were. When they were in their second downward dog, Padraig shifted his gaze over to the lads next to him to see how they were faring. Was he the only one embarrassed as fuck about this?

All their beefy hands were spread at the top of the mats, the downward pressure causing white knuckles and fingers. At least he wasn't the only one with crooked legs. None of the boys' legs were straight, all bent with their bums sticking up at awkward angles, like sprinters at the blocks.

During the third round of the sun salutation, Gillian said, "Okay, I'm going to go around to each one of you to help with your positions. I'm happy to see you can all do the plank well, not a far stretch from a push-up, but correcting the others will do wonders for your flexibility. Also, try not to jerk from position to position. Smooth. Go from plank to cobra in a smooth motion."

She started at the far end with Shane, but Padraig could see no more for the large bodies between. When he pressed up into downward dog, he noted her at Dick's shoulder. "Press back into the balls of your feet so there is a nice line from your hands on the floor along your back. That's better."

They had to hold the placement for five breathing repetitions. His bad knee was fine but his back ached. Padraig wanted badly to shake out his hands, just for a moment to relieve some of the pressure. But there wasn't a chance in hell he was going to be the first one.

She stepped out of the corner of his vision. As per the sequence, he took one step, then another forward until his feet were between his hands. As he lifted his head to stretch his back, he felt her hands along his spine. He shivered with a small jerk, which he hoped she hadn't noticed. If the boys felt what he did, none of them wanted to rise out of the current position to stand in front of her. Every one of them would have a hard-on, not easily disguised when you were stretching your hands in the air, lengthening your body upward. And there, a big boner standing to attention. Why did Coach let her continue with this alternative therapy? Didn't he realize how embarrassing it was for the boys? Did it even help? Padraig had his reservations, and in the midst of "breath in...breathe out..." he determined he was going to have a word with Coach. Fuck this.

"When you stretch out with your palms on the ground—or in your case, your fingertips, but don't worry, the more yoga the do, the more flexible you will become—make sure to keep your back straight." When he curved in his head to bring it to his knees, she gently applied pressure to his shoulders so that his knuckles rested on the ground. "See? Every time you stretch, take it a bit farther. Without hurting yourself, of course."

Of course, thought Padraig. What would she know of pain? But then...there had hardly been any pain today. Whatever she had done with her magical hands yesterday was just short of a miracle.

"That's the last of sun salutation. I'm going to walk you through a few yoga floor stretches now to cool down, a brief meditation, and that will be it."

Thankful to be able to move, to adjust his shorts around his front, Padraig flopped to the ground. The other boys did, too, joking about the downward dog in the only way a man could, references to sex rampant. Dick was mid-joke when his voice broke. All eyes were on Gillian as she kneeled on all fours on her mat, arching her back up like a cat, then a few breaths later, lowering it until her belly curved downward, her back bowed, her head and chin lifted to the ceiling.

That had to be one of the most erotic things Padraig had ever seen. And unfortunately, he had to share it with four of his teammates, two of them immature little pricks. Padraig couldn't move. He was frozen, sitting on his mat, mesmerized by the movement of her body. The motion and the curves—so beautiful. Her braid dangled over one shoulder; her toes pointed like a ballerina.

"C'mon boys, you have to do it, too." Her voice broke the spell, and all five of them scrambled to do the same. As majestic as it looked on Gillian, it was mortifying for Padraig. God, he hoped she didn't walk around helping the lads with the floor exercises. They all looked fucking ridiculous.

But she didn't. After the cat pose, she took them through some leg stretches with their backs on the floor. One of the lads farted loudly when they had to tuck both of their knees into their chest, rolling on their lower backs.

When the others started laughing, Padraig couldn't hold back and chuckled, too. Then Dick farted louder, as if he had forced it out, and that led to more laughter. The pain in his lower back eased as he gently rotated it back and forth along the floor. It felt good. To laugh. To let it out. Because he had been serious for too long.

She must have known she wouldn't be able to keep their attention after the farting so asked them all to take ten minutes for personal meditation, lying supine on their backs, arms and legs relaxed. Padraig released his knees so they bent naturally, feet on the floor, his hands behind his head. He lay there, staring up at the light fixture. It was a typical locker room light, long and rectangular, black bug spots piled up at the corners. How did the flies get in there?

Gillian's face, thrust in front of his own, broke apart his reverie, shattering it into pieces like a ball through a window. Strands of her hair fell down to him like threads. "You're pretty flexible for such a big guy."

"Thanks. I've worked with some of the best physios in the world."

"I've heard. But that doesn't mean I can't help you." She had squatted behind his head, but he couldn't read her expression as gravity had puffed out her face.

"What are you going on about? I'm doing what you ask me to."

"But you don't believe in it."

"Oh really? How can you tell?"

"Your attitude."

"And all the other lads are lovin' it, I guess."

She tilted her head as if she was pondering that one. "I can't say they are all on board with everything—"

"Really? You think—"

She hovered a finger over his lips, and Padraig waited for it to drop so he could get a small taste, his eyes fixated on the tip. "Ah-ah, don't interrupt me. You didn't let me finish. I was about to say, the others are at least

86

approaching it with more of an open mind. It's like you don't give a shit about what we are trying to do here."

She rose without another word and walked toward the table where her bag sat. As she passed Dick, he flicked out his wrist and pinched her ass. If Padraig hadn't been watching her bum himself, he would have missed the slight movement.

He roared to his feet, and in two steps, pushed Dick at the shoulder. "What was that, ya cunt?"

Ugliness painted Dick's face as he snarled at Padraig. "What are you talking about? I didn't do anything. And watch who you're calling a cunt, or I'll kick your ass."

Padraig glanced to Gillian who hadn't moved a muscle since she'd swung around in search of the culprit. Her mouth was slightly open, but she said nothing.

"Apologize," Padraig directed at Dick.

"For fucking what?"

Again, Padraig tried to engage Gillian, but she had turned back to the table where she donned her glasses once again. Ignoring the boys, she slipped on her oversized hoodie and walked out the door that led to the pitch.

Had he imagined it? No. Not with Gillian's reaction. He pointed a finger at Dick. "You better apologize."

"Whatever, ya *paddy.*"

Padraig could have torn his throat out, but instead he punched an end locker on the way to his own. So much for not getting involved.

Chapter 9

Padraig left the pitch a bit early to make his appointment with Gillian and headed to the showers. He'd been surprised on many levels today. First, his body felt as limber as it had in a long while, and second, the boys had played hard today. Their scrum was tight, their wings fast, their centers navigated the pitch, and their scrumhalf was a creative wee devil. All in all, not a bad bunch.

But then there were moments he was back in junior club rugby. Their technique was lacking and even with Del's leadership, there were plays where it was mere organized chaos. But they had potential, something that Padraig hadn't seen on Tuesday.

He grabbed his towel off the rack, and then walked dripping over to his locker, scrubbing his face and hair. After a quick wipe-down, he wrapped the towel around his waist and jerked open his locker. None of the cubbyholes had a combination or padlock. Coach said they didn't play that way. Fair enough. It didn't really promote goodwill in a team if everything was on lock down. They had to trust one another, but it still made Padraig nervous.

Before he deodorized, he patted the pocket of his folded jeans on the top shelf, checking for the pill container. His throat tightened when the hard cylinder shape wasn't there. He pushed the panic back and retraced his steps in his mind. He was almost sure he had secured the bottle in his jeans before training. He had been running late, but always took a minute to place it somewhere safe.

He yanked out his jeans, then his shirt, socks, and shoes, patting down every piece of clothing—but nothing. Adrenaline raised the bar, and his world focused, every nerve ending poised for fight or flight as panic set in. Flight wasn't an option—he hadn't had a chance to get a refill on the pills, no backup, not even fucking Motrin here or at the house.

He dove through his training shorts and shirts, then his cleats. Unlikely places, but when desperate… He went through every inch of his locker and bag again, zipping and re-zipping, his rage bubbling like a teakettle. And he had the feckin' appointment in ten minutes. He couldn't even get to a pharmacy by then. Where was a fucking pharmacy? Not anywhere near the club, he knew that much. But he had no control, relying on Del for lifts everywhere.

By his third search, panic and anger overwhelmed him, and he kicked hard the bottom of an adjacent locker. The boys had started to filter in from the pitch, chatting and laughing, splitting up to their different locker rows. Head down, seeing red, Padraig started to shove his dirty gear back into his bag.

A shape loomed up to his right. "You looking for this?"

The sound of rattling pills snapped his attention to Dick, who shook the container like a maraca.

Padraig raised himself up to his full height, expanding his chest, dominating the space. He was only four inches taller than Dick, but he outweighed him by a couple stone, twenty-five pounds, at the least. "They're mine," Padraig said, wanting badly to say "ya prick" but Dick held the pill case, not Padraig.

Dick threw the bottle at him, but it was only a gesture, and he laughed when Padraig reacted, jerking his hands out to catch. "What is this"—the ignorant tosser squinted at the bottle—"Oxy…co-tin you are on? Some good stuff, O'Neale? Must be, the way you were looking for it just now."

A few of the other lads with lockers near him had gathered around to see the fuss. Padraig was barely holding his rage in check, but didn't want to make a scene. The towel still wrapped around his waist, and he had to get dressed to meet Gillian in Coach's office in less than five minutes.

At least he was calmer than before. Dick wasn't helping, the cunt, but the pills were in sight. Not lost or gone, so there was still hope. He tried to play it cool. "Thanks, I thought I had lost them."

"So the all-powerful Padraig is on drugs."

Padraig shook his head, rolling his eyes. "They're just pain meds for my back. Not much stronger than anything you can get over the counter here in the States."

Dick hesitated, and Padraig could tell he was considering whether it was the truth or not. He tossed the container up in the air and caught it, then repeated the action faster, over and over. All the while Padraig watched the bottle up and down, up and down.

"Well, if it's no big deal, maybe I'll keep them for myself. I did find them after all."

In a second, Padraig had slammed Dick up against the locker, his forearm pressed into Dick's neck. "Did you fucking take them out of my locker?"

The commotion brought the team running. For good measure, Padraig lifted him and threw him back into the metal, an almighty clang echoing through the room. "Did you?"

Dick's eyes showed no fear. With all his teammates around him, he knew he was safe and Padraig was making a show of himself. To make Padraig look even worse, he gasped out, "I found them on the floor this morning. Just under there." He freed his one arm to point under a bench across from Padraig's locker. The hand he pointed with also held the bottle.

"Hand it over." Padraig motioned with his free hand.

Dick slammed the plastic container into Padraig's outstretched palm. "You're an asshole, you know that?"

"Let him go, O'Neale." It was the Kiwi, behind him with the rest of the team.

Dick's face had turned red, his eyes bulging from lack of oxygen. With one last stare-down, Padraig released him, and Dick's body relaxed off the lockers.

"Pretty big words for such a small prick," Padraig sneered and turned his back on him.

Wrong move. Dick shoved him hard from behind into his open locker with a mighty *crack*. Having lost his towel, too, Padraig swiveled around to face him again, all naked fury. Dick stood his ground, his hands fisted in a boxing stance. "C'mon, ya Irish junkie, have a go, then."

"Stop! Don't act like stupid knuckle-grazers."

All heads turned to see Gillian standing with her hands in her hoodie pocket. And there Padraig stood in all his glory. Bad enough all the team sided with Dick. Now he looked ridiculous standing there butt-feckin-naked in front of the team physio.

"You're late for our meeting," she said. Her eyes lowered to the pill bottle in his hand. At least, that's what he hoped she was looking at.

He scooped his towel off the floor and haphazardly wrapped it around his waist and held the two sides together. "Give me a minute."

"Okay, lads." Del clapped his hands loudly together once, a big whack. "Who wants to go to the pub?"

Some murmurs, and the boys began to disperse. He waited for Dick to move on. His locker was in another row. No reason for him to have been here in the first place. With his chest puffed out, his shoulders back, Dick pointed two fingers at his eyes and then at Padraig. He mouthed, "I'm watching you."

Padraig didn't bother responding. Dick finally pranced away on the balls of his feet. Within minutes, the rest of the boys in his row had left, as if their proximity made them guilty by association. Guilty of fealty to the new guy, guilty of taking meds themselves, guilty of...what? What exactly was Padraig accountable for? Thousands of athletes took medication to help with injuries. But, going natural was all the rage these days, and medicating was voodoo.

He stood there, staring into the darkened space of his locker. He re-tucked his towel. His breathing under control, he untwisted the cap, shook the pills until one spilled onto his palm. It went down with a quick sip from his water bottle.

He probably could have done without one, the pain bearable today, but he was seething with rage. He quickly dressed in jeans and a short-sleeved Irish rugby jersey, tucking the pills into his pocket. Outside, it was still warm so he slipped on his flip-flops and headed to Coach's office.

The door was open. Typing away, she had her laptop in the center of the desk. He knocked on the opened door and remained standing in the entrance. She looked up, then glanced at her watch. "Glad you could make it. Please take a seat."

Padraig took the same chair he had the first day he'd arrived, laying his arms along the wooden rests. Since the age of nineteen, he had been his current height, the last eight years filling out the pounds and muscle. Rarely did he fit into normal chairs comfortably, and this was no exception. He was wedged into the chair, his knees bending well over the edge.

She shifted her laptop to the side so there was a direct view between them. The obscene overhead office light reflected off her glasses, but the boys were right. There was something about her. A bit of something. Especially in her yoga gear.

"So what happened out there?" she asked, jerking her head toward the locker room.

"Nothing important, and you're not Coach, so none of your business."

She seemed to expect his smart-arse reply. She ran her top teeth over her bottom lip, sucking it gently before letting it be. More titillating than Padraig wanted to admit.

"It is if one of you guys get hurt."

"Well no one did, but doesn't mean no one *will*, if they don't stay out of my business."

She nodded. "Is that the business of your oxycodone?"

He was taken aback for a moment until he realized Coach must have told her. "It's a prescription…and legal," he added when she didn't respond.

"It is, but may not be for long. What is your dosage?"

Fine. If she had to have the information, he'd give it to her. He dug the bottle out of his pocket and tossed it to her without warning. She was quick and snatched it from the air. She turned the bottle around, read the label, then set it down on the desk. She didn't push it back toward him or offer to return it.

When Padraig leaned forward to retrieve the bottle, she wrapped her hand around it, making a small fist.

Padraig took a deep breath through his nose. If she wanted to play games, then fine. He sat back and tried on his best nonchalant pose.

"When were you issued the oxycodone?"

"By the team doctor after my back surgery. It's called OxyContin in Ireland."

She shrugged. "You're not in Ireland now." She waited for a response that he never gave, then continued. "Pain relief is often prescribed post-operative, but from Scotch's notes, it says your surgery was over six months ago."

"Yeah, well, it obviously didn't work."

"Oxycodone is a highly addictive pharmaceutical. Have you been taking it since"—she ran her finger down some notes on a legal pad—"last December?"

He mirrored her and shrugged. "Doc gave me a prescription for it, and it helps, so I take it."

"Just five milligrams once a day in the morning?"

"And at night." And in between.

"You know that oxycodone is a banned performance-enhancing substance by WADA."

Only too well. Funny she called a game a performance. Maybe in the US it *was*. For him, rugby was life, and it didn't end when he walked off the pitch.

She looked once again at the label and read, "Prescriber—Doherty. Is that your family physician?

"That's none of your business, either."

To Padraig's surprise, she twisted off the cap and peeked inside. She shook the bottle up and down in quick motions. What her intentions were, he had no clue. She finally tightened the cap, set it back on the table, and pushed it toward Padraig. "Are you done after this?"

His stomach twisted at the thought, but he'd been planning since he came here to get the new team doctor to refill the prescription. Little had he known, there wasn't one. "Sure," he lied, nodding in affirmation.

She cocked her head to the side and pursed her lips. "Great, because there really are so many other options."

"What? Music and yoga? I don't think that shite can really help on a professional level."

"It can, and it will." She typed fast, her fingers flying over the keys. "First, I'm going to do some acupuncture on your back. Anywhere else you have injuries that still cause you pain?"

"My left knee."

"Okay and your knee. We'll concentrate on that for now. I'd also like you to try an herbal remedy for chronic pain. It takes a while to take effect, so I want you to start it immediately. It's a salve and you need to rub it into the areas three times a day." She cleared her throat and looked away. "It's the same stuff I used on you yesterday."

That smelly shite? No way in hell. "Great, are we done here?"

She tilted her head in a thoughtful expression. "Yeah, I think so." There was a long pause, and as Padraig was rising to leave, she spoke again. "Thanks for saying something to Dick today."

He hesitated. "No bother."

"Do you want to go get something to eat?"

Whoa. That was unexpected. He sat back down on the edge of his seat, holding the arm of the chair in a death grip.

"Do you mean on a date, like?"

"Uh-uh. No." She lifted both hands in defense. "No, no, not a date. It was nice of you to defend me earlier...and I thought I could pay you back."

She was flustered, Padraig could tell, curling a strand of hair around a finger, and looking at anything but him.

"We're both hungry, right?" she directed at the wall. "And I can give you a ride home."

"Sure... Let me tell Rory. He was going to give me lift."

"Okay."

"Right."

But he didn't move, nor did she. They both looked at each other, waiting to see what the other would do. He wanted to go. If nothing else, get out and do something in this godforsaken town. But he didn't get it. He'd only been rude to her so far. He'd heard the old saying, "treat 'em mean, keep 'em keen," but he had never put much stake into it. Probably because he was brought up better than that.

So why would she ask then? He hadn't done anything that any other decent guy wouldn't have done. He slapped his knee, reminding him that it was only business. She probably wanted to pick his brains about the oxycodone and convince him of her *alternative* methods. Bunch of shite, really.

He rose and grabbed his bag where he had discarded it by the door. "I'll go see if I can find Rory, then."

She had already started packing up the laptop into her satchel. She raised her gaze to him. "Okay, see you in five."

Casual. Easy. Her body language whispered to him that the invite was nothing. He was new to the club and to the country, and she was being polite. Gillian wasn't his type. She was…different. Sexy and different, but more than a little eccentric. She was the type of girl you had no idea what was coming.

Chapter 10

Gillian drove a cream-colored station wagon with wood paneling. From the rearview mirror dangled a Blues pendant on a black leather strap. At one point, Padraig had stilled the pendulum locket with his hand, but she said nothing.

Peppy, synthesized music played in the background as they'd made their way from the sports complex. Del had told him she was straight out of college, another notch against her, but he could tell by her car that she struggled. Most Americans wouldn't be caught dead in the piece of shit, but unlike most, she didn't seem embarrassed.

They'd spoken little, but he'd taken the chance to steal glimpses when she was busy with traffic. She still wore her hoodie but had changed into a black skirt and a pair of black and white striped leg warmers, along with flat shoes. At least she wasn't wearing those shite high-tops that she always did. In all his days, he had never associated with anyone like Gillian. She didn't seem to fit with the athlete crowd. Like a sea crab that had chosen the wrong shell.

She parked her car in front of the Sail Inn, the same place he and Dell had visited a couple of days ago. He held the door for her when they entered and was rewarded with a smile. Her small dangling earrings swished back and forth. Like a fish to a lure, Padraig followed.

Gillian led them to the same high-top Padraig had chosen the other day with Del, and whatever they had agreed on before in Coach's office, to Padraig, this was a date. The same middle-aged waitress offered them a menu each, then left them promptly after the usual niceties that Padraig ignored, anyway.

He pretended to examine a classic touch to pub dining in the make of a cardboard six-pack for beer that held the tomato sauce, mustard, salt, pepper, and other condiments, but snuck in glimpses of Gillian across the table. When she caught him staring, he cleared his throat and busied himself with the menu. There wasn't much. The usual pub grub, but they had fish and chips. That would do.

The waitress stopped back at their table while Gillian was still studying the menu. "Are you ready to order?"

Padraig waited for Gillian to answer first. "I'll have the cheese and veg quesadillas."

"Anything to drink?"

Working her mouth back and forth, Gillian contemplated for what seemed longer than necessary to Padraig. She briefly met Padraig's gaze before looking away. It was as if she was making a life-or-death decision.

"I'll have a glass of red wine," she said on a whoosh of breath.

"What kind? We have Cab Sav, Merlot…"

"Either of those is fine."

The waitress raised an eyebrow. "Okay, and what about you, big guy?"

"Fish and chips, and I'll have a pint of Blue Ribbon."

When the waitress had gone, Padraig stretched his legs out to the side of the table. Gillian sat with hers clasped in front of her, only moving when the waitress set her drink down. They both reached for their glasses.

"Do you miss—"

"What made you—"

They had spoken at the same time so Padraig apologized. "Sorry, you go first."

She asked about Ireland and seemed interested in his Irish childhood, how the culture and food differed, his private Catholic school, his sisters and brothers. Gillian kept asking questions about everything from their school uniforms to the strict Catholic instructors to the discos they went to when they were teenagers.

After their food arrived, she motioned at his hands. "See that? How come Americans don't eat that way? You never set your fork and knife down."

"You mean, why doesn't the rest of the world swap utensils to cut their food?" Padraig smirked but Gillian wasn't offended.

Instead, she shifted her fork to the left and picked up her knife in her right hand, like Padraig. "I'll give it a go, but it might take me a bit. It's very efficient."

"Exactly. We can shovel it in better this way." He made Gillian laugh, and he decided he preferred that over making her angry. Her smile transformed her face. She didn't do it enough, Padraig reckoned. But the same had been said about him in the last year. Maybe she, too, struggled with some unknown.

Padraig began to relax. Perhaps she wasn't going to interrogate him after all. Only once did their conversation lead to Padraig's Irish rugby experience, but more about the rugby fanaticism in Cork County. The Munster fans sang the famous song "Fields of Athenry" at their rugby matches, which had been adapted and now sung at the international matches, too. He had mentioned how powerful the song was during a match, how the Irish voices could rally the team. Patriotism, like in the US, was massive in Ireland, and there wasn't a prouder moment than when Padraig took the pitch for his country, the green, white, and orange flag proudly flying.

Every time he asked about her childhood, she waved it off and told him it was boring comparatively, just a normal American middle-class youth, and would redirect the conversation back to him.

"What I don't understand is why some of the Irish names dropped the O. Like yours, O'Neale still has it, but lots of Americans have lost theirs over the years."

"Not sure why the Irish dropped it when they moved here, but I can tell you a story from back home. The Irish are very proud of the O still on their name. Did you ever learn of the potato famine in Ireland?"

Gillian winced. She tucked the loose hairs behind her ears, nudging her earrings so they swung like a magician's pendulum. Padraig was hypnotized. She seemed embarrassed when she replied, "A little? Unfortunately, we didn't get a huge amount of world history in high school, but I've read *Angela's Ashes* by Frank McCourt."

They both laughed.

"Fair enough," Padraig said. "Anyway, so you know that Ireland suffered during the Great Famine from 1845 to

1852." To not embarrass Gillian, nor make him sound like he was spouting off, he added, "And the only reason I remember the years is because the nuns beat them into me."

"Seriously?"

"Nah." Well, not entirely. Padraig was no stranger to the crop, but she didn't need to know that.

"Many argue this to be an overgeneralization, but there is a story told that during the famine in the mid-nineteenth century, some Protestant organizations offered soup to starving people on the condition they received Protestant-based religious instruction and dropped the O, Mc or Mac from their name. People who took the soup, and changed their religion in exchange for the food, were known as 'soupers' or 'jumpers.'"

"God, I'd have taken the soup if it saved my family."

"I'm sure many did just for that reason, but my family is still proud of the fact that we have our O"—he chuckled—"especially since parts of Cork were particularly affected in the famine."

"Obviously that shows the strength and pride in your heritage."

Padraig squirmed under her admiration, shifting in his seat.

"Do you still speak Gaelic?"

Padraig smiled at her effort. Not Gaelic. Their language was referred to as Irish or *Gaeilge*, but now wasn't the time to correct her. "I don't personally, but there are some places that speak it as their first language instead of English, like in Connemara in County Galway. And of course, we have telly that is in the Irish language."

With her look of disappointment, Padraig added, "But we all have to learn it in school from day one."

Her face brightened. "Oh yeah? Say something for me."

Aw fuck, he should have known that was coming. He took a long drink of beer as he wracked his brain for a suitable phrase. Not something corny or crass. But that's all he seemed to be able to remember at the moment, phrases that the boys would throw out at each other while they were drinking at the tournaments overseas.

Then it hit him. He looked her directly in the eye. "*A chuisle mo chroí.*"

"Hold on... How do you say it again?"

Padraig sounded it out for her. "Ah khush-le mo chree."

She repeated it. "That's beautiful. What does it mean?"

Literally *pulse of my heart*, but Padraig asked instead, "Have you ever seen the movie *Million Dollar Baby*?"

"The boxing movie?"

"Yeah, that's the one. They spelled it wrong in the film, but anyhow, if you ever get a chance to watch it, you'll find your answer there."

"I heard it was a tear-jerker."

Padraig paused, his heart caught in his throat at the amazing woman in front of him. "Yeah, I might have spilled one or two." He smiled to make her comfortable.

Gillian punched him playfully on the arm. "Aw, go on, ya big softie."

They laughed.

Somehow, Gillian had drawn him in, in all her peculiarities. He wasn't sure if it was the setting or that they'd removed themselves from their environment, but here, her brilliance was true. Kind and smiling, she had grace and style. And when he took the time to look, she was beautiful. And after the yoga today, he knew she had an amazing figure along with the package. Why she chose to hide it, he couldn't imagine, but her indifference was refreshing. Titillating. Sexy in its own way.

After his second pint, a full belly, and great conversation, Padraig was buzzing. Maybe Gillian would like to go out again. She was a slow eater, daintily picking at her food. Using her utensils the Irish way had prolonged the meal, but Padraig didn't mind. While she refolded her napkin and placed it on her plate, Padraig struggled to decide if he should ask her out again. Get the awkward moment out of the way before they got to the car.

But then the waitress returned to collect their plates, and the chance was gone. Gillian asked for the check and folded her hands on the table in front of her. Then she shoved them into her lap, only to raise one again to twirl a curl of hair around a finger.

He was about to save her by offering up more conversation, but she began, "I was wondering about the oxycodone you're taking…"

Oh fuck, here it comes.

"Did you start on a larger dose and reduce down to what you are on now?"

Fuck! She'd roped him in and soothed him like a babe in a cradle. Softened him with her smile and laugh. Subdued him with her wit and charm. He should have known. He *had* known. But then they'd been getting along so well. He'd really enjoyed himself. "Is that really why you asked me out for dinner?"

She had twisted her finger tight around the curl and was now yanking on the strand. "No! I mean, maybe a little, but mostly—"

The waitress cut her off when she laid the bill down in the middle of the table. Padraig was so mad he didn't even offer. Feck it. She'd said she wanted to pay him back. Well, they were square now.

"I don't want to talk about it."

"I just thought that maybe if you haven't started to reduce the dosage—"

"Just stop," Padraig interrupted, but she kept talking in her same calm tone as if they were continuing their lovely conversation from before.

"That you should. Your body will develop a tolerance, and you'll actually need more."

Padraig shoved the chair back and stood to leave. "This is none of your business. Why do you keep prying?"

"You'll get headaches, dizziness, and most likely liver damage."

"I'm outta here." He had walked two paces when she finally raised her voice.

"Especially combined with alcohol."

Some punters at the bar had swiveled in their stools to watch the commotion. Padraig pivoted and walked back to her chair where he bent and stuck his face in hers. He was so close he could count the freckles on her nose. "Why do you give a shit?"

God help her, she didn't even blanch. Didn't slink or move away, but held his gaze. "Coach asked me to—"

"Yeah, I got that before, but why do you give a shit about me and what I do?"

She said nothing. And right now, as he held her gaze, he was more disappointed than anything else. Why life had to be so complicated was beyond his comprehension. Why a meal with an interesting girl couldn't be just that.

He turned and left. He'd walk home.

Chapter 11

Gillian looked at her watch again. Padraig was ten minutes late. She wouldn't be surprised if he didn't show at all. They hadn't spoken since Thursday night. She still had his gear bag in her car, and he'd made no attempt to get it back, through Del or Coach or anyone else.

It was a beautiful Sunday, though. Low eighties and a slight onshore wind from the lake. She'd still go for a swim one way or the other, but she really hoped he listened to Coach's request. Not for his sake or the Blues, but for her. She'd mucked things up horribly and wanted to make it right again with him. She had gone about helping him the wrong way. She was the Blues PT, not their psychotherapist.

Another glance at her watch. Fifteen minutes late. She was certain she'd given Coach this exact location but hadn't considered how Padraig would get here, or if he even knew how. She'd give him another ten, and then she was in the water.

The car metal was hot where she was leaning, so she grabbed her bag and headed for a picnic table just past the parking lot. The beach was busy, lots of families and tourists out for the day. She should have picked a more secluded spot, but that would mean a bit of a drive out of town and she hadn't wanted to give him any excuse not to come.

Her bathing suit was crawling up her ass, so she tugged through her beach wrap and released the fabric.

"Brilliant."

Gillian spun to see Padraig standing there with a towel in his hand. Behind him, perpendicular to the parked cars, Del waited in his banger. Her face flushed with heat.

Del waved. "G'day, Gill."

"Hi, Del. Thanks for giving Irish a ride."

"You okay to give him a lift home?"

"Sure, no problem."

When he drove off with a wave, Gillian turned to Padraig. "Thanks for coming. For a minute there, I didn't think you would."

He walked past her. "I needed my gear bag."

She followed. "I have it in the car."

He pulled his flip-flops off and stepped onto the sand.

Gillian did the same and slipped hers into her bag. The apology that had been nagging her for days bubbled out. "I shouldn't have brought your meds up. I shouldn't have ruined the evening." They started walking, seagulls dipping and circling above them. He remained silent so she continued, "It was nice. I had a good time."

When he looked her way, she met his gaze and smiled. This was going much better than she'd imagined. And she had thought of little else since that night.

She led him to the far side of the beach where fewer sunbathers had laid claim to spots in the sand. "We can leave our stuff here." She dropped her bag.

He pulled off his jersey and threw it and his flip-flops on the ground. "Me, too."

"Yeah, leave your stuff here."

"No, I meant I had a good time, too."

"Oh, well, that's great." That's great? A four-year-old could think of a more charming and witty comeback.

He was obviously confident of his physique as he stood waiting for her to undress. The bravado she'd summoned earlier to wear her two-piece was gone in the light of day and a public beach. She was supposed to be working, and a bikini wasn't really professional attire. And unlike the rest of her wardrobe that consisted of blacks, grays, and browns, her bikini was a bright Kelly green, the same one she'd worn in high school. She should have worn her Speedo one-piece. Unless she worked in her hoodie and beach wrap, which would be stupid.

She undid her sarong and laid both that and her prescription sunglasses on top of her bag. Taking her hoodie off would reveal all, and so she stalled. "Have you had hydrotherapy before?"

He lifted his arm around to his back and stretched, his bicep muscle defining and shifting with the movement. Sweet divine. "Nope," he said, popping the *p* sound at the end.

"Right, okay, well usually you do it in a heated pool, but the only public pool in Traverse City isn't open on Sundays. But you can make your own arrangements during the week. One of these days, I'll have a therapy pool at my practice... Did you want me to talk you through it?"

He smirked, almost as if he understood her procrastination, and jerked his head toward the shore. "In the water."

"Righto, then." She turned her back on him and sucked in a deep breath through pinched lips. Here went nothing. In one quick motion, she flung off her hoodie, grabbed her white plastic cutting board, and stalked toward the water's edge.

A seagull flew over, calling out as it went. Two kids splashed and laughed as they pushed each other off an inner tube float. The breeze picked up the farther out she went. Or maybe that was the wind velocity from her speedy exit. She didn't turn to see if he followed and didn't stop until she was in the water up to her chest.

Normally, she would have eased herself into the cold Michigan lake. Storming the deep water as fast as a Napoleonic soldier hadn't allowed for acclimation, and her nipples puckered just below the surface. Right. A bit deeper then. No giving him an eyeful of that.

She placed the cutting board in front of her chest, turned, and let out a squeal more girly than a tweener at a Bieber concert. He had followed close and was practically on top of her.

God, she needed to get herself together. Professional. Cool.

When he grabbed at the cutting board, she pulled it back to her chest.

"Planning on some cooking instructions along with your water therapy?"

"Ha ha. I'm going to use this for one of your exercises. Normally, the board would have slots in it to increase or reduce the amount of tension, but this will have to do for now." When he didn't speak, she rambled on. "I still have to buy a bunch of equipment so I'm improvising. Nothing's perfect at the start…"

Anyone looking at them from afar would think they were intimate, he stood so close. She took a step back. "Okay, so first thing, just walk through the water slowly." She pointed to an orange and white swim buoy. "To there and back."

"Just walk?"

"Yep, but slowly. Go back and forth twice, and then twice again, but faster."

He took off without another word. He was being really good about this whole thing, which was a bit of a worry. She should feel relieved, but there must be a catch.

On his way back, she realized she'd been staring when his gaze flicked up to hers. Caught by those blues again. But there was nowhere else to look. Nothing else to preoccupy herself, and when he turned to go back the other direction, she breathed a sigh of relief. Everything was so intense with him. Or maybe it just felt that way since years had passed since she'd been attracted to someone. Head down, study hard, work hard, make a difference. And of all people, a Blues jock just like her brother had been. Life was twisted.

On his last lap back to her, he seemed fixated on her person, but she couldn't tell without her glasses until he got closer that he was staring at her. She squinted. He was staring at her chest! There were her boobies bobbing in the water in all their Kelly green splendor. When she relaxed, she had forgotten about the board in front of her and let it float to the side.

Before he reached her, she was babbling, with said board again in place in front of her. "So the basics. The buoyancy of the water"—*oh, ugh*—"supports your body weight and reduces the pressure through your spine and joints. Improving the malleability in your back will reduce stiffness and increase spinal movement. By easing the pain and making exercise easier, hydrotherapy can help you recover faster."

"How long did you practice that for?"

"What?"

"Never mind. What else ya got?"

She was loath to give up her board, but she had to show him. And to do that, they'd have to go into shallower water. She led him in a few feet and demonstrated how to lean into one bended knee and use the board to push and pull water to and from his chest. She repeated the motion and then reluctantly handed over her only defense.

Gillian pretended it didn't mean a thing and placed her hands on her hips, hoping the bravado rang true. "Go on, then. Give it a try."

Without a retort or any snide remark, he did as he was told. When he was finished, she had him swap legs and showed him another direction to use with the board. He was doing it all wrong, so she dunked under the water and felt along his leg, repositioning as she went. When she popped back up, wiping water from her face, he laughed. "You could have just asked. Not that I didn't like you copping a feel."

Her face burned so she ducked under the water again in the guise of clearing her hair from her face. When she came up, she said, "Irish, I'm your physical therapist and here to help. That's all."

His brows pinched together. "Right." But from him, it sounded more like "Royt." He handed the board back to her. "I was just joking, like."

He, like everyone else, thought she was uptight, that she needed to loosen up. All right. She could do this. Be professional *and* have fun. "Are you a floater or a sinker?"

Now his hands were on his hips. "What the fuck?"

"Can you float on your back or do you sink?"

"I can swim."

"That's not what I asked."

"Fine. I'm a floater."

She'd hoped for a laugh from him, but got irritable Padraig back instead. Hell, he was so up and down, she barely knew what to do. "Okay, well then lie on your back. This is another alternative to allowing your back muscles to relax and stretch before you start the other water exercises."

He fell back into the water with his arms out like a cross. While sculling water with his hands, he struggled to keep his body lithe along the water surface. When the two kids in the inner tube ran into him, he swore and jerked to standing.

The boys moved away from him but not before one shouted, "You shouldn't say that word!"

Gillian laughed through a pinched mouth, the reined chuckle tightening her gut and chest. "Well, I guess they told you."

When he grabbed his head with both hands and looked as if he was about to explode, Gillian calmed him. "Move down here away from them a bit and try again. I'll help you."

113

He followed and then sank into the water up to his neck. He tried again, but his butt dipped and his head came up.

"The key to lying supine in the water, totally relaxed, is to keep your head back. Try again." When he did, she pushed up his butt with her hand. He floundered, lashing his arms around, but then stilled. She laid the board on his chest to free up her other hand. Keeping upward pressure on his bum, she tilted his forehead back and then raised his chin. As he relaxed, she ran her hands underneath him, adjusting and lifting arms and legs, then settled again at his lower back. With his crotch right at eye level. A glance at his face confirmed he was looking up at the sky and not at her. Phew. "I think you got it."

To be certain, she left her hands on his back, his skin smooth in the water. His chest hair had curled with the damp and his nipples had puckered with the cold. She stared at his ribs, mesmerized by the body in front of her. What would it feel like to kiss the hard planes of skin? Move her hands over his muscles like a car on a rollercoaster?

"I'm good." He interrupted her musings, and she dropped back into PT gear.

"Yeah, just keep your head back. You might get some floats to help you at the pool."

"What?"

She raised her voice since his ears were submerged. "Never mind."

His body stilled until even a finger didn't twitch. With quiet movements, she moved away from him and stood. His eyes were closed. Her throat tightened at the image—his long, strong body floating toward the shallows, the waves urging his body forward. His arms spread wide like a crucifix, his dark hair floating like seaweed around his head. And a white plastic cutting board on his chest. Ha. She smiled.

And it was then, in that moment, Gillian realized her path with Padraig was irreversibly set. There was no going back, only forward, as if the space behind her had closed over with vines and branches, messy, an entanglement too fierce to try to attempt, while the path forward was clear.

For now.

Chapter 12

Padraig followed Gillian around to the driver's side and grasped the door handle to open it for her. A gentleman to boot. He had proven her wrong in many ways over the last couple of hours, but she was still uncertain what to do about it. He was a Blues player, everything she didn't want, but when she'd seen him standing nude in the locker room the other day, her thighs had gone up in flames. And she'd *never* experienced that before.

He swung the door open for her, and instead of ducking right into the car, Gillian turned to face him. She tried for nonchalance and rested one arm on the top of the door, the other on the roof of the car. Not exactly screaming seductress with the wet spots on her boobs and crotch where the damp from her bathing suit had leaked through, but she didn't want the day to end. Something had to happen now, either one way or the other.

Padraig paused, half turned to walk away, probably contemplating what the hell she was doing. What the hell *was* she doing? Her mouth went dry, and the streetscape around her went fuzzy.

Padraig stretched, his jersey rising up his belly. "You ready, then?" He tapped on the car roof with his knuckles, but he didn't move away.

Gillian ran her finger along the top of the door on the rubber seal, which was dry and cracked, some chunks completely missing. "Are you?" With that witty response, she'd give Shelby Fero a run for her money. Sweet Jesus, she was out of practice. If she had ever been *in* practice.

Padraig stood motionless for a beat too long, in Gillian's opinion, but then stepped forward and withdrew her sunglasses slowly from her face. He folded the ears and passed them back to her. She pocketed them in her hoodie and left her hands there.

His hands replaced where hers had rested on the roof and door, joining them in a strange metallic connection.

Her heart raced, and a buzzing started in her ears, but she held his gaze, although his features were unfocused to the point his face had become abstract. No longer Padraig, but just a man. Water ran down the back of her neck from where she'd tied her hair on the top of her head. But if she moved, then she'd break the potential that harbored quietly in the moment.

He stood there looking at her, as if still contemplating the pros and cons of a simple kiss. If that was what this was.

Someone had to do something, so she did. Her mouth was so dry she licked her lips, then stepped into his space and kissed him, a quick peck on the lips. When she withdrew, he followed, stooped, and brushed his lips softly against hers again.

Gillian had learned in a physiology class how the human lips were the most exposed erogenous zone of the body, and even a light touch sent thousands of bits of information to the brain to decide whether a person wanted to continue or not. Was that going to be it? Was that his testing?

Her heart raced, very aware of his one hand that had moved to her waist, the other still resting on the top of the car. Gillian had decided what she wanted, but was still convincing herself she wouldn't care if he wanted the same or not when he swooped to her mouth again. At first, the kiss was awkward as they both found their rhythm, lips open then shut, tongues dancing in and out. He drew her out and pinned her against the fake wood siding on the car.

In a fog, she could still hear the sounds of traffic, voices on the beach as they rose and fell in play. But she didn't care a wink like she normally did. Absolutely no one would have caught her sucking face in public before. But his lips were thick and juicy, so much to suck on. He was patient with his tongue, waiting for her own movements before adding his own.

He pressed his hips into hers, grinding back and forth until she groaned. The ache swelled intense, strong…beautiful. As he began to move away, she grabbed his waist and pulled him back in. Padraig grunted when she slipped her hands over his ass and squeezed him closer. Their hips rocked together, the pressure building with each fusion of their bodies.

Right in the middle of the parking lot. But she was too far gone to care. This had never happened before. Her head had always been in control, and her body never a part of the equation.

He moved his hands under her hoodie, up her sides where his thumbs grazed the outside of her breasts before he slipped them down to her hips again. He caressed the skirt fabric up and down over her thighs, catching on the bikini strap underneath.

She bunched her fingers into his hair at the back, tugging hard, groaning into his mouth when he moved his right hand down, his fingertips grazing her center, then back up again to her hip.

Holy hell.

Pulling away from his lips, she stayed near to him, her cheek resting on his, and whispered into his ear. "Come with me." Very bold, but this must be what other woman had talked about. The urban legend. The myth of fantastical proportions. The urgency and desire to get screwed as soon as possible. Not after she'd drunk five beers and felt horny. But an all-out cry from her body to consummate. That very minute.

Without waiting for an answer, she popped into the car and slammed the door. She squeezed the steering wheel as she waited to see what he would do. Maybe he'd knock on her window and motion for her to roll it down, to tell her it wasn't a good idea, he'd get a cab. And she'd accept that. Her body, however, would not.

Instead, Padraig sprinted around the front of the car, banging his hip on the right bumper. She laughed when he swore and hopped the rest of the way, favoring his right leg. She hadn't meant to. It wasn't funny ha-ha. The laughter was a release of nerves.

She couldn't define her excitement, not having felt it before. It was a bubbling effervescence of giddiness.

Maybe it was like a drug high. She didn't know, but she'd heard stories.

"In Your Eyes" by Peter Gabriel was playing when she started the car. How ironic. Padraig was so far removed from her usual type, and not for the first time, she wondered if she was doing the right thing.

She turned up the music. She didn't want to talk to him. She couldn't. It would have changed everything. And luckily, he didn't speak either, only tapping his finger along with the music on the armrest of the door.

Gillian turned into the drive to the small nondescript brick building that hosted her start-up practice and living area in back. With the ticking of the cooling engine, embarrassment set in. Because really, she was trying to establish herself as a professional and taking home one of the players within a week seemed juvenile. Like the car engine, some of the heat from earlier had worn off, and doubt crept in like a spider up her leg.

"Well, come on, then." She plastered on a smile and a look of confidence, she hoped, and took the lead to retrieve her beach bag from the backseat.

His presence behind her threw off her equilibrium when they approached the door. She fumbled the mail she drew from the box, leaflets and advertisements floating to the ground.

"See you like your number fives," Padraig said as he stooped to collect the paper.

What did he mean by that? When he handed her the mail, she must have looked confused because he continued, "You know, I play number five and your address is number five…"

"Oh." Her voice came out a breathy chuckle. "Right."

She swung the door wide and stepped back to let him through, as much to see the look on his face as for courtesy. Did he still want this? Or did he want to run? Supposedly, he was a celebrity in Ireland, and her place was humble, to say the least.

Too late now. With a deep breath, she flicked on the lights, the strong halogens above causing her to squint. With a sweep of her hand, she introduced him to her small client space. "This is where all the magic happens." She tried to joke, but he said nothing. The magic of a small desk and chairs, therapy table, and second-hand treadmill must not have been magic enough. "Through the back door is my place."

After unlocking and leading him through to the apartment, she said, "Make yourself at home."

He kicked off his flip-flops at the door. She had left the lights off so most of the kitchen and living room was in shadow. She wouldn't make the mistake of turning them on. She was botching the romantic interlude badly enough as it was.

Gillian dropped her bag on one of the stools at the island that divided the kitchen and living room. She stood waiting as he scanned her personal space. The living area was divided by a couch and end tables. On the other side, she had converted a small dining area into an exercise room, small free weights were lined in order on the floor, her yoga mat rolled in the corner, her trumpet case off to the side. Thank God, she hadn't left it out. Nothing like a brass instrument to scare Sex Jock away.

He nodded in clipped shakes of his head at her music posters on the walls, as though he was about ready to go nuts. Uh-oh. Time for intervention. She bit her lower lip. "Yeah, I meant to take those down last week. All except the one in the middle. She can stay. In fact, I might take them down now…"

As she was scooting by him, he reached out his arm to stop her. "Don't."

"All right, yep. You're right." His lingering hand on her arm drew her gaze to his. Her knees went weak with the intensity. "Probably not the time for it…"

"It's a nice place, Gillian." He picked up her Rubik's cube. Andrew and she had fought over that damn thing for years. It had originally been her dad's, but at some point when they were young, they both wanted it, and it had become a type of game. One would take the cube from the other and hide it like treasure. The other would find it and do the same. Back and forth until one day, Andrew no longer cared and it stayed in her possession, hidden in a drawer of feminine hygiene, her best hiding place yet. Gillian could have played the game forever. She had imagined them taking it into their adult years when they had kids of their own, searching each other's homes when they visited for barbecues and birthdays. But that was never going to happen.

Padraig set the toy back down again. "Lots of throw pillows and candles, which I hear from my sisters is the epitome of comfort for a woman."

Phew. "I'll just light a few for us then." She slipped from their slight connection to the kitchen where she rummaged in her top spare-everything drawer. No matches. As much as she had envisioned herself floating about like an ethereal spirit to light the candles, she only had a very unromantic child-proof plastic lighter thingy. It would have to do.

Barely. With each candle, she had to use one hand to press down the child safety mechanism, the other to click the lighter. Click-click-click. If he hadn't lost his hard-on by the posters, Gillian was sure he was now as flaccid as a monk.

When she'd finished, Padraig was standing in front of the print of *Music, Pink and Blue No 2*, one of the few she'd had professionally mounted, and a stark contrast to the U2 and Duran Duran posters flanking each side. His hands in his pockets, he seemed to be studying the framed picture.

"Who painted this?" he asked finally.

"Georgia O'Keeffe." She stepped up behind him. "She's an artist that believed music could be translated into something for the eye." Looking at the print over Padraig's shoulder, Gillian noted how much the picture looked like a vagina. The folds pink and purple, but yep, very much a woman's coochie. She'd never had a man in her apartment, so how could she have known how cringe-worthy it all was until now? She should have listened to Junette. He was going to think her a fruitcake. Which she was...

Taking a deep breath, she wrapped her arms around his waist, resting her chin on the middle of his back. She squeezed her eyes shut, waiting for an answer.

When none came, not even the removal of his hands from his pockets, she tugged gently on the bottom of his shirt. She'd come this far, and even if he was uncertain, even if she was confused, she would see it through. To do any less would have been worse. Would have been ridiculous. When she lifted his shirt over his abdomen, it got stuck at his shoulders, but he helped by pulling the jersey over his head. He turned, his shirt in hand, which she then took and let drop to the floor.

She traced her fingertips along his belly up to his chest and then over his shoulders to his arms. But she couldn't look at him, concentrating instead on the movements her hands made along his skin.

When she finally worked up the nerve to meet his gaze, his face was serene, the flickering of the candles shifting dark spots to light and back again. A small faded scar ran the length of his chin.

Gillian trailed down his arm to his hand, tugged gently, and led him over to the large, patterned rug. She shifted the wood coffee table aside, then knelt and patted the floor. Now what? He'd barely said a handful of words since they'd arrived, and she was flying blind. All the heat and passion at the car was long gone, and she questioned again what the hell she was doing. If only he'd make a move or give a sign if he didn't want to.

He grabbed a pillow off the couch, threw it on the floor, and lay down, the pillow scrunched under his head, his legs crossed at the ankle. He folded his arms behind him and closed his eyes as if tired.

She rose and removed her hoodie and beach wrap, then stood there, unsure what to do next. He lay motionless on the floor. Music to entice him? All she had available was the *80s Greatest Hits* or her meditation music that he hated. He was sure to run for the hills.

Right. It was time to spice things up a bit. Gillian wanted desperately to get back to the intensity at the car.

The craving. Her body demanded it. Beyond that, she didn't want to think. How often did a girl have an Irish hunk in her living room? Jock or not.

She dropped down and crept up on her hands and knees. She kissed him along his chest to his waistband then tugged his swim trunks down his legs. He stirred, and she was glad to see she'd affected him, that he still desired her.

As she crawled back to Padraig, she locked gazes with him until he dropped his to her breasts. She hovered above him, her hair falling to both sides of his face so a tunnel formed, each at an end. For a moment, he didn't move. So she didn't either.

When he finally returned his gaze to hers, she wet her lips, inviting him to make a move, do something. How much more did a girl have to do?

It must have been enough. He grabbed both of her breasts, rubbing his thumbs over her nipples. At her gasp, he tugged down the bikini to expose them. Lifting his head, he took one nipple into his mouth and sucked. When he circled his tongue and nipped, she bit her lip to hold in a groan. He moved to her other breast, doing the same, biting gently on the nipple, then blowing air.

Her throat tightened from the emotion. So long. It had been so long since she'd allowed someone into her physical space. She swallowed the tears that brewed behind her eyes.

She kissed him, soft at first, then stronger, her tongue digging in and out. She sat up, straddled his erection, and removed her top. His hardness was overwhelming. She'd needed this. To feel so strongly again. For anything.

He moved his hands to her butt where he began to rock her gently over his length. Candlelight flickered over his face. He was beautiful. Such dark eyelashes around bright blue eyes. With each pressure against his erection, Gillian felt herself slipping further into that surreal world of pleasure—comfortably numb, the sharp edges of life blurred to soft borders like smudged charcoal.

Her mouth dry, she went to suck his ear to create moisture, her dangly earring feathering over his face. She sucked his lobe and wet her tongue in his ear. If they didn't break soon, she would come from humping his cock through her suit bottoms. And that wasn't enough. She wanted it all. For the last five years, her sole purpose had been to ease the pain of others. Now, she would take from him.

Padraig grunted. She could tell he was close, too. In a flurry of movement, he pulled her down and grabbed her bikini strings. He yanked them off in the midst of a tangle of legs.

Completely bared, she sat upon his thighs and took his dick into her hand.

The pillow had shifted away, and his head thumped back onto the floor as he groaned.

Loathe to break the connection, she had to ask. She hadn't been down the condom aisle for so long. "Do you…have anything?"

"My wallet," he grunted.

She squeezed his length once more, then lunged for his jeans where she found a brown wallet. In a hurry, she flailed with the tiny pockets, then commanded herself to slow down. When she found it, she ripped the foil open with her teeth and rolled the rubber over his dick slowly.

When she lowered herself onto him, the room fell away, phosphenes dancing behind her closed eyes. So good to be whole again. When the lights fizzled, she opened her eyes to see Padraig staring at her. His hands grasped her hips, then led her up and down. She rolled her own nipples, wanting that, too. He joined her with one hand, squeezing one breast, then the other as they moved together, first slowly, then building faster until he pounded out his release. And when she licked two fingers and rubbed her clit, she came full and fast, the image of his ecstasy pushing her over the edge.

Chapter 13

Gillian had dropped him off at the end of the block, and he had walked the rest of the way to the house. Both wanted to avoid the other boys and their questions. And although neither had said much on the ride over, didn't even broach the subject of what was next, Gillian had kissed him goodbye, a long and lingering taste of her lips.

Two mornings later, and he still woke up to that kiss. Sometimes, when he was in the heat of a moment, right in the midst of amazing, he didn't understand the impact until the whirlwind had passed. That's where he was now.

She was an enigma. Underneath her façade, there was an ocean of perplexity. But also beauty, grace, intelligence.

He scratched his scalp furiously. Fuck, he shouldn't be getting involved. If he'd wanted a shag, he should have just gone out with Del to the bar and found a one-nighter. But it was like he couldn't resist. Now, what the feck was he going to do?

Most incredibly, he had forgotten to take his pill last night.

He opened the bottle and shook the pills out into his hand, then counted. Twenty-four. And since he hadn't taken one last night, then all of them were there. If he could cut it down to only two pills a day, he'd be able to last two more weeks. Almost. By next Friday morning, he'd have to organize a doctor's visit. Maybe he could borrow Del's junker to get there.

There was no pain in his back this morning, but he popped one anyway. In the morning before training and one at the end of the day, he promised himself. That was it. That was all he would take.

Only Rory had been up when Padraig had returned, watching late-night television, some comic talk show host, Tosh-O, a sarcastic and edgy fecker. Rory hadn't said a word even though he must have heard him come in. But the Scot was good like that, kept to himself, didn't get involved.

Unfortunately Del wasn't going to be so easy. When Padraig made his way into the kitchen, he immediately asked, "Where were you Sunday night?"

"Here."

"You didn't show up at the pub, and you weren't here when I went to bed."

"What? Are you my captain and mother now?"

Del's chair scraped back, and he rose to his full height and girth. At first Padraig thought Del was going to have a go at him, but instead he picked up his bowl and placed it into the sink, turning on the tap to rinse. He leaned against the counter and crossed his arms over his chest. "Just making sure you're all right, bro."

"I'm grand." Padraig moved to the cupboard to grab out a bowl for breakfast.

"So where did you go after your therapy with Gill? I thought you were going to meet up with a few of us at the yacht club." What the boys affectionately called the Sail Inn.

Padraig wanted to tell him to shove it up his arse and it wasn't any of his business, especially where Gillian was concerned, but he liked Del for the most part, as much as he knew of him. "I went for something to eat, then walked home."

Which wasn't an out and out lie. He did get something to eat in the way of Gillian, and he did walk home, from the corner at least. He couldn't pull off a full fib if he tried, as he wasn't practiced in the art. Had rarely been dishonest in his life. That's partly what had gotten him into this mess. When he was younger, his mum wouldn't smack him with the spoon when she caught him out, but the look of disappointment she'd give him was far worse that the sting of the wood on the back of his leg.

"Yeah, I s'pose after what happened Thursday in the locker room, you weren't too keen on having a drink with the rest of us."

Padraig sat at the table and grabbed the box of Weetabix. "I'm not too bothered."

"You should be."

"Why's that?"

"What I said before. We are visitors to this country and paid employees of the club. At least show some respect, mate." He paused until Padraig met his eye. "Or I'll personally ask that your arse, as you put it, is booted back to Ireland."

That wouldn't do. Not until he had secured another place to play. And Gillian complicated things. He didn't want to get her involved with his mess. He conceded. "All right, I'll make amends."

"Awesome." Del stepped away from the sink and clapped Padraig on the back. "There's the proud Irish I've heard about. Now, check this out." He turned his laptop on the table so Padraig could see the page. There were pictures of three men with their biographies to their right.

"Yeah, so?"

"Those are three of the scouts who travel for the Eagles looking for players for the Cup."

"How the hell did you find that?"

Del winked. This morning he was chewing a piece of gum, so his face seemed to spasm with delight in himself. "I'm a master when it comes to finding information."

"Have you shown anyone else?"

"Nope, maybe Coach knows, but he hasn't said. Probably doesn't want the lads to know what they look like. Might make them nervous if they saw one of them watching a game. You know what I mean?"

Padraig nodded, then shoveled in the rest of his cereal.

"Not interested?"

Padraig shrugged. "Not really."

Del rolled his eyes to the ceiling, thumping his hand hard on the table. "You can't even see what you got right in front of you. An American passport, man, and a chance to make the Eagles."

"You're a New Zealander. Would you play against your country?"

"Irrelevant, I don't have a US passport, so it's not even a question."

"But if you did, would you?"

"I don't know." Del pushed away from the table and chucked his gum in the rubbish bin. "Maybe."

"I doubt it."

"Fuck, mate, I'm starting to like it here. Maybe I'll find a nice American woman to settle down with and stay."

Padraig jerked out of his chair and threw his bowl and spoon into the sink. "I'm out of here."

When he entered the club that afternoon, Gillian had Dick's leg up in her lap as she taped his ankle. Feck. Anyone but him. Padraig glared at them both until Dick noticed him there and flipped him off.

He turned away toward his locker, trying to ignore the envy that burned in his chest. He never wanted to be, but jealousy ran strong in his blood. Before, he had controlled his urges by joking around. But the drama over the last year had stiffened everything that Padraig was about. Loose had become rigid and light-hearted had become stone.

It wasn't like she was his type. It wasn't like they were dating. It wasn't like he planned to stay.

A minute later he smelled her soft lavender scent and knew she leaned against the lockers on the other side of the door. He closed it gently, then stretched an arm over the top of her. "Do you have to do that? Dick's such a dick. And Del wants me to patch things up with the wanker."

She laughed, a chuckle and a smile that made her eyes go squinty. "It's my job, Irish."

He nodded. Fair enough. "So..." He couldn't help himself and tugged on a braid she wore over her right shoulder. "You want to do something again tonight?"

She tilted her head. "I'm sorry, but I have other stuff to do tonight."

"What other *stuff* that's so important?"

Pinching her eyebrows together, she made a small movement away from him. Not noticeable to the human eye, but discernible to a sensitive heart.

"Well first, I have plenty of other important *stuffs* in my life, O'Neale." Ouch, on last name basis again.

She softened and laid a hand on his forearm, but then removed it quickly, darting a look around for any notice of her gesture. "Second, I have physio appointments tonight."

"At night?"

"Any time I can fit them around the Blues schedule."

"Wow, one of those overachiever types, eh?"

"No, just realistic. I have bills to pay, including my student loan for my degree and rent for my office and apartment."

Padraig reckoned she should add a new car to that list. "So why bother volunteering for the Blues?"

She rolled her eyes, then puffed out a sigh. "For so many reasons. But mostly"—she held up her finger, then pressed it down on her opposite hand so that it created a cross—"they let me practice and get experience with alternative physical therapies, and"—she pressed down a second finger—"I can help."

"I admire your philanthropy, but is it worth it?"

She cocked her head in consideration, but dipped her head when she spoke. "So far, I think it is."

He didn't want her to leave. "So, any suggestions on how to clear the air with Dick?"

She gave him a look like he was daft. "Umm…maybe apologize?"

"Not for him pinching your ass!"

Gillian grabbed his pinkie finger and tugged, a subtle gesture that no one would see. "No, definitely not that, but maybe going a bit overboard when he found your pills."

"Found them, my arse. He took them."

"Okay, well then for practically strangling him to death."

"He started it."

Gillian choked on a laugh. "Perhaps, but you sound like a kid now."

Padraig rolled his eyes to the ceiling. "Fine. I'll buy him a drink at some point."

"It's good for team bonding, no?" She nodded in a sarcastic way, her eyebrows raised.

Padraig laughed. He tapped the locker lightly with his knuckles. "But ya see, I'm not sure I want to be *in*." He raised his fingers in double quotes at the last word.

"Why not?" she asked.

He shrugged, then picked up his tape roll, tossing it into the top of his locker. He hesitated, choosing his words carefully. "I'm not sure this club is the right fit for me." There. He'd said it. But it didn't feel as good as he'd thought it would to be more open about his intentions. The dynamic had changed, and that was because of the woman standing in front of him.

"I know you have your hesitations, but it could be great for you. I also know it's not on the level you were playing previously. I could tell that straight away from your resume. But it's all what you make it. Maybe there's a reason you are here."

There was a call from Coach that echoed in the room. "All right lads, on the pitch."

A scramble of footsteps sounded as the boys made it out the door. Gillian, her ass on display today in black leggings, disappeared around the bend. "Have fun."

What was she thinking? "So tomorrow night, then?"

She popped her head back around the corner and motioned *shhh* to her lips, but smiled so Padraig grinned back.

He dreaded going onto the pitch. All he wanted was to get her alone again, stay tucked away in her apartment. For days. Weeks. Months even. But then reality hit as Rory paused at the end of the locker row. "You comin', Irish?"

As he took his first step outside the door, the music started. Today it was similar but more melodic than last week. Didn't sound so much waves and sea mammals as it did harp and Enya. Or a good Enya impersonator. Feck, if the lads wouldn't have totally taken the piss back home about this. It reminded him that he needed to call. Everyone. His mum, his agent, his old coach to let him know how he was getting on. Not that his old coach cared, although he said he did. He had promised Padraig a spot on the Munster team again if he could kick the pain meds completely and get into top physical shape.

It was furnace-hot and humid; *close* they would call it in Ireland. Padraig walked onto the pitch, but it was like stepping into a sauna. He raised his eyes to the gray mass of clouds overhead and then to the west, like at home, to see what weather was on its way. Hopefully rain would come and break the humidity. The sticky heat fouled his mood further. And today's training was about new plays. Brilliant.

Some of the boys were practicing their kicks at the far end of the pitch, but most had gathered around Del in the center. There was some commotion going on as Del's head popped up and down in the midst of the circle. What the hell was he doing? The haka? Some were warming up, but they were all engrossed, and when Padraig stepped up to peer over the tops of their heads, sure enough, Del was just finishing the last of the war dance, his tongue stuck out long down his chin, a thumb slicing across his throat. The manic look on his face would have intimidated anyone.

The boys clapped, some cheered, and then they dispersed, only a few hanging around to chat with him. Padraig approached, a crooked smile on his face. "Looked good, Del. As good as I've seen."

Del grabbed Padraig's arm and turned him away from the others, walking him to the center line. "Thanks, mate. It's the first time I've shown them. Some of 'em have seen it on telly, but none of them have witnessed the pure strength and energy live and in person."

"You plan on rallying this bunch of wallies with the haka?"

"Might do, mate." He blew a big breath out puffed cheeks. "We need something."

The whistle blew, and Coach divided the lads into two teams. Coach assigned Del captain for one side, Padraig for the other. With Dick on Padraig's team. Things had just gotten interesting.

The lads were keen. Padraig had to give them that. It was difficult for him to remember those days, it was so long ago. But he had believed in everything then—he would go all the way with rugby. And to every player, that meant the World Cup. He had been certain he would be with the Irish squad next year.

He rolled his shoulders to release the bitterness. That wasn't going to happen now.

Their fly-half, Kevin, nicknamed Keys because he was always losing them, dropped the ball and then on the upward bounce kicked as his own team surged ahead. Padraig's team ran forward toward Del's team. The game started with a high, hanging ball into the far right corner to give them time to get down the pitch and into position.

Damian caught the ball and ran forward, tossing the ball to Rory, then on to Josh, right in front of Padraig. Josh tried to fancy-foot around him and slipped, an easy tackle for Padraig. That's what youth and inexperience got you. They wanted to do it all on their own, showcase themselves, instead of looking for help, passing the ball into a better position.

When the ball was loose out of the ruck, Padraig pounced before Champ, their number eight, could pass it to Del. Padraig stripped the ball easily before his knee touched and turned it over.

Del was almost on him, so he passed the ball off to Dick who appeared out of nowhere, running up the sideline. And then Padraig got hit. Hard. By a bunch of Del's team. But the ball was already gone. As they all scrambled off the ground, Coach's whistle blew shrill. A try. Padraig heaved as he walked toward his team who all congratulated the left wing. Dick still held the ball, even though it was only a practice try, and beamed at the others as they patted him on the shoulder or bum.

He held a hand out to Dick, who looked skeptical, but then grabbed it in an awkward handshake. "You came out of nowhere. Nice speed," Padraig said to him as they walked to the posts. Dick shrugged. "Whatever." Then he jogged away when the conversion kick went wide.

Well, Del couldn't say he hadn't tried.

Coach rearranged some players, swapping the inside centre from Del's team with the number eight on Padraig's.

Padraig's team had scored, so Del's team restarted with a drop kick, Padraig's team receiving once again. Padraig noticed most of his lads had clumped together, leaving large spaces for the ball to fall into the other team's hands. He yelled to the boys to move, but they ignored him. Del's team surged forward with the kick. The falling ball bounced off Rory's chest straight into Damian's hands. When Damian found an easy hole to get through, Padraig yelled louder, "Get back there!" Even if he was only captain for training and nothing else, he'd get his fuckers in line.

Damian was halfway to the try line when Mitch finally clipped his ankle in a swiping dive. The right wing stumbled, but the break was long enough for some of the others to get in front of him. He ended up kicking the ball into touch, gaining another fifteen yards. That meant Padraig's team lineout. He was the jumper and rocked the lineouts.

The teams assembled into the parallel rows of men, the opposing teams about a yard apart and facing the sideline where they awaited the hooker's throw-in. Shane, or Shano to the other lads, the Blues hooker and one of the best players on the team, took a few extra minutes to wipe the ball. Fair enough. There was enough moisture in the air to soak their shirts through before they'd even started running. Now, their T-shirts clung to backs and chests. Padraig would have preferred the rain if he was going to be this wet.

Shano called out the play. That meant Jimmy and the loosehead prop, Dave, would lift Padraig on the count of two to catch the throw from the hooker. Dave was nicknamed Pickle because of his love for the juice, on occasion chugging it after a game. He swore by the regenerative properties and constantly quoted findings from a study a few years back. Pickles halted post-workout cramps in eighty-five seconds. It also restored electrolytes faster than Gatorade.

When the lift came, it was awkward and unbalanced, the loosehead prop boosting him higher than Jimmy, and Padraig tilted toward the other team. In slow motion, the ball came toward him and, as his fingers nicked the side of the ball, the tighthead prop shifted and the ball sailed over Padraig's head to land in grunts and a scuffle behind him.

The prick! He'd done it on purpose, leaving Padraig looking the fool. But worse, it appeared as if he hadn't done hundreds of lineouts before. The props dropped him like a hot kettle, and then bodies were everywhere on top of him, around him. When someone dug into his hand with their cleat, he considered biting down on their calf. The pitch was dry, the grass coarse like a Brillo Pad, chafing his arms like pine needles. The ball evaded hands as each player tried to control it in the ruck.

The hard weather he didn't mind. He got plenty of that back in Ireland. It was the indecency on the pitch with these thickos who didn't know what professionalism was.

As the ruck dispersed at the whistle, Padraig was slow to get up. There was a penalty for a knock-on, so the ball went to the defending team in a scrum. His back ached and his knee throbbed and this was only practice. They had a game on Saturday. Looked like he was going to have to get his meds refilled earlier than planned. His hand supporting his lower back, he limped toward the assembling teams.

Gillian stood next to Coach on the sideline. She had donned her fedora cap with the patterned band, but damp hair laid limp against her neck and where it had loosened around her face. When he caught her eye, she smiled. Then stuck out her tongue, and Padraig wondered if the lads had noticed. Playful little tease. Feck, he wished he could get a repeat on the floor tonight.

Not the best time to get a hard-on, especially when the flanker was about to wrap his arm over his back. Both teams set, and with the call from Coach, the men heaved forward with a collective grunt and collided in the middle.

Padraig's talent was in the lineout, but he enjoyed the scrum the best. The raw energy and power and strength of eight men on each side, head to head, vying for the smallest movement over the ground. In that moment, Padraig always forgot his pain. It seemed illogical. Common sense said there should be more pain, but because those minutes, sometimes mere seconds, were so intense—digging in, pushing, willing his entire body to respond—his focus was not himself, but the team.

It was pure animal strength and guts that drove the men, sometimes mere inches, to try and gain control of the ball. It was instinctual, the desire to win, to overcome your adversary, and nothing reflected that better in rugby than the microcosm of the scrum.

After all that work, it fell and crumbled. A blow of Coach's whistle saved them resetting. "All right boys, that will be enough for today. You all look like limp fish. Go on in for a shower."

A few of the boys laughed, but some had anticipated the end and had already started heading for the locker room.

Padraig scanned the area where Gillian had stood, but she was gone. Disappointment fizzed through him, but he had no time for a self-pity party since Del was at his side.

"They're not going to listen to you until they respect you, bro."

Padraig shook his head in frustration. "How's the form today, Cap?"

"I can see what's going on, and since I *am* the captain, I'm gonna try and fix it."

"Let me ask you this. Do you think they are even worth the effort?" Padraig asked.

"I do," Del said simply.

They approached the locker rooms, and Padraig held the door for both of them to enter. Some of the boys were in the shower, but most had gone, probably preferring their own hot water at home than the drizzle that these showerheads put out.

Padraig and Del stopped at the end of lockers where they would divide to go to their different rows. "Why don't you go to the team social after the match on Saturday? Have a few beers. Get to know the guys."

"I hadn't heard about it. Don't think I'm invited."

"Everyone is invited, including the Grand Rapids players, and Scotch and some of the boys are bringing

141

their wives and girlfriends. Shano is even bringing his kids."

"Like I said, no one said anything to me, not even Coach."

"Well, I'm saying something to you now, bro. And right now, even though you've got the most experience on the team, *you are* the weakest link."

Chapter 14

It had turned chilly, the wind picking up off the Great Lake. They were walking along the beach, the one the boys always passed on their way to the complex. When they first set out, Padraig thought Gillian was taking him home after dinner, but then she'd turned toward his house and pulled into the Traverse City State Park. A few trees sheltered picnic tables on a grassy area, a clean sandy beach beyond. Off to the side was a children's play area, blue and red slide and climbing bars, yellow swings.

Padraig zipped his fleece to his collar and stuffed his hands in his pockets. He had yet to touch her, but wanted to. Badly. "How is it twenty-five degrees one day here and fifteen degrees the next?"

"Well, since this is the summer, I assume you are talking Celsius."

"Why can't the States match the rest of the feckin' world?"

"Easy, grumpy, or that's what I'm going to start calling you."

Padraig smiled out at the water, unable to make eye contact. "From you, I don't mind."

She rotated them both toward the waterfront, then pulled him down into the sand. "It's funny. I get a sense that you'd be a different person in Ireland."

"I get a sense you'd be a different person in Ireland, too."

She said nothing.

They sat side by side. Even though they'd had a nice dinner, chatting as much as they did the other night, Gillian hadn't shown any outward signs to him that they were any different after their sexual relations. Most girls latched on, held your hand or arm, marked their territory by grooming you—fixing your hair, picking off fuzzies. Like Jenn had. He wouldn't have minded if he had felt the same about her, but the receptionist had tried to stake a claim without Padraig's acquiescence. That was, and would always be, a bunch of shite.

Both of their knees were bent in a relaxed, reclined position, as if they were sunning themselves. Gillian leaned her head back, and with her eyes closed, Padraig took the opportunity to move behind her. He wrapped a leg to each side, and as he'd hoped, Gillian leaned her head back on his chest so he could rest his chin on her shoulder, his cheek pressed into her own. "I'm going to use you as a wind block."

She laughed. "Wow, you are a gentleman."

They were quiet a moment as they gazed out at the bay. Two sets of white sails spotted the distance. In his peripheral vision, the waterline stretched out to the right and the left, where it started swooping southwest.

Traverse Bay was beautiful, Padraig admitted, but too populated for him. Even though he grew up in the middle of the city, if he was going to the sea, he picked one of the many secluded bays in West Cork. There was nothing quite like the Atlantic crashing on the craggy shores of Ireland.

"So...I'm curious. How did you decide to become a physical therapist?"

She didn't respond so he nudged her in the back of the head with his nose.

"Hey!"

"Is the question that hard, like?"

"No."

She faced the lakeshore so he couldn't get a read off her expression, and had decided to drop it, when she spoke up. "Do you think what a person does for a career defines who they are?"

"Definitely not. But I'm trying to get to know you as a person. How you came to be here right now with me."

"I didn't start out in physical therapy. My first year of college I was a music major. That was my first love."

Padraig chuckled. "I can totally see that."

She slapped his right shin. "What is that supposed to mean?"

Padraig dragged in a big breath and let it out, letting his focus stray to the horizon. One of the boats must have tacked in as the white sails had grown larger as it headed their way. "I don't know...you just seem more music than PT."

"By the way I dress? You mean because I don't wear Under Armour shirts and yoga pants every day?"

145

"Maybe... Or maybe it's the way you don't seem entirely comfortable working with the boys."

She stiffened. "How so?"

"It's not one thing I can put my finger on. Just an impression, I guess."

She sat up and away from Padraig. A cold wind blew between their bodies. "Wow, thanks for your honesty. So you think I'm a crap therapist?"

"I didn't mean that at all." Wow, he was fucking this up.

"Then what did you mean?"

"Ya know, I'm not sure." He just didn't want to piss her off anymore. "Maybe it's just your methods that don't fit me, but I'll try."

She looked back over her shoulder. "Thank you."

Padraig pulled her back into his embrace, to which she succumbed. He wanted badly to wipe away the conversation and start over. Luckily, Gillian did just that.

"You're one of the best rugby players that the Blues have seen on their pitch. Yet, you care less. It breaks my heart, really."

He rubbed his forehead in frustration. She hadn't mentioned his meds, but it seemed like every time they spoke of the Blues, it was there, an elephant in every word. "I've just got a bit going on at the moment, Gill, but trust me when I say that rugby is my life."

All the pain he suffered every day was a result of that passion. His love for rugby and nothing else. But how could he tell her about his past? Where he had been and how far he had fallen? He had learned that words didn't work well with him. When he tried to rectify his behavior through explanation, it turned out wrong, turned against him to play out his worst fears. The media had taken all his comments, his defense, out of context until he had sounded like the biggest langer in the world. He'd learned the hard way to keep his mouth shut.

But he could show her.

He trailed kisses down the back of her ear, along her chin, then to her neck. Her small gasp of pleasure was all he needed to suck on the pulse zone in the fleshy part between her chin and neck. He dipped his right hand down to massage her clit through her shorts, using his other to squeeze her left breast, gently applying pressure against her nipple when he circled up over her fleece.

"Oh, God," she whispered. The words carried away with the wind. He had massaged her to the point where Padraig thought she would come, then stopped. Not because he didn't want her to, but because a young family walked by at the edge of the water. Each of them had their pants rolled up to not get wet, but still could enjoy the sensation of lapping water around their feet.

She wiggled to a sitting position, her eyes still glassy from arousal. "I think I might approach Scotch about water therapy for the team."

Padraig groaned.

"I'm serious. All the big rugby teams in Australia do resistance training in the water a couple times a week."

"They have the weather for it."

"We can make arrangements with the local pool on a Monday every other week instead of conditioning training."

Even though Padraig was still unsure of her therapy methods, her passion was a turn-on. All the new-age music and yoga. All the acupuncture and salves that she applied to the boys' ankles and shoulders that stunk to high heaven. She believed in it so strongly he couldn't help wanting to believe in it, too. But wanting was the key word. He wasn't ready to give up his pain meds, no matter how sexy and wonderful the woman was.

She now sat up cross-legged in the V of Padraig's legs stretched around her. He ran his hands up the back of her sweatshirt, then circled around to grasp both breasts in his hands. He caressed them under the bulky hoodie, using slow and deliberate motions for discretion. There was something so erotic about sitting in a public place and pleasuring a woman. She hadn't put a stop to it yet, either.

He ran his fingers over each nipple, the thick buds pronounced through her thin bra. She leaned forward into his hands, small soft grunts of *ah* escaped her as she dug her fingers into the sand on either side of his legs. The world had dropped away, the traffic noise and voices a distant resonance, as if they were both submerged in water. Even the lakeshore and horizon had blurred into abstract shapes and colors as his focus turned inward.

His rubbed himself against the thickness of her short's waistband, and even though he knew they should get up and go, he couldn't get himself to stop.

With a quick movement of body and sand flying, Gillian jerked away from his hands and turned to face him on her knees. Placing her hands on each side of his face, she laid a gentle kiss on his lips. "Irish, I need you in me right now. Let's go." She yanked at his hand to rise.

He was more than willing, following Gillian to her car, the squeak of sand from their bare feet loud in his ears.

As he rounded the front of her station wagon, he asked, "Are we going to yours?"

"Nope, your place is closer. I don't think I can hang on much longer." She hopped in as Padraig did the same. When inside, she turned in her seat and locked her lips to his, forcing them into a deep kiss, tongues and lips sucked to swelling. "That should keep us till we get there."

"What about the boys? They'll see you. They'll know then."

"Screw the lads!" she said in a mock Irish accent. And this from a woman who proclaimed such integrity for their discretion, to not cause any trouble within the team and to keep a professional distance at all times.

He laughed, then louder as she peeled out backward. "Watch out, there might be kids!"

"Oh, shit. Oh, no." She peered into her rearview mirror. "Thank God, there wasn't. I'm acting like a lunatic. I get this way around you." She grabbed his hand and held on, driving the car with only her left. "I don't know what I'm doing."

He could relate, but couldn't find the words. He understood the loss of control he had when they were together. All the energy was both liberating and frightening as hell. It had been awhile since Padraig had been caught up in such a whirlwind of emotion and need. With a female at least. Rugby had always been his first love.

His house was less than a mile away, the red glow of sunset behind them as they headed east away from the lakeshore. Before they turned off the main street onto the cul-de-sac where the house was located, Padraig suggested they park around the corner and walk in, but Gillian was having none of it.

"If they are going to know, they will. I don't like to be sneaky." She turned to him in the car. "And I'm not embarrassed of you or the situation. Are you?"

A little, but he squeezed her hand for reassurance. "Nope, not at all."

Del's car was gone when they pulled up on the curb in front of the house. That was a bit of luck. Padraig still clicked his door shut quietly behind him.

As they strolled along the lawn together to the front door, Gillian hooked her arm through his. Brave. He imagined much of her lust had rescinded like his, but she was still determined. A feisty lass his ma would be proud of. Nothing but the best for her eldest son, she had always said.

He held the door for Gillian as they entered. The telly was on in the living room, an evening newscast, and he could hear commotion coming from the kitchen, a pot set hard onto the cooker, and cupboard doors clunked shut. Must be Rory and his late-night snacking. The young man was a stick yet ate non-stop.

He put his finger to his lips and motioned up the stairs. They might just get away with it. They both laughed, acting the teenagers. And when he closed his bedroom door behind him, he became shy. She had never been in his space before. Not that there was much Padraig had added.

He did a quick skim of the floor to make sure no dirty underwear was lying about and moved to the small desk where the pill bottle sat out in the open. He had taken his workout pain relief, but had left the bottle behind when they met for dinner. A big step for Padraig. He rarely separated the pills from his person. She knew he took the meds, but he didn't want to bring it to her attention. He muddled about as if he was stacking papers and clearing the area, discreetly opening the top drawer and swiping the container inside.

He jumped when she came up behind him, wrapping her arms around his waist. "Nervous, Irish? I know it's not your first time," she joked, "but I'll still be gentle with you."

Her husky voice and sexy banter brought his focus back to the room, to her head resting between his shoulder blades. He turned in her arms and kissed her gently. "The boys will recognize your one-of-a-kind car, especially since it is sitting up on our curb in front of the house."

She laughed and shrugged. "We'll have to deal with any backlash together. Not that there will be much... I don't think." She grabbed a curl and twined it around her finger, her gaze fixed to the middle of his chest, her teeth worrying her bottom lip.

"Right so, then let's get it on," he growled into her hair, pushing her back onto the bed. He ripped open a condom and placed it on the table beside his bed.

Another laugh from her notched his heart up a couple of degrees. But his giddiness and fun turned to hot fire when she grabbed his ass with both of her hands and tugged him against her crotch, his hard-on nestling between her legs. "Doesn't mean we shouldn't still try to be discreet...ya know, for respect for the team and the club..."

Silencing her with a deep kiss, he'd worry about the club later. Right now, Padraig wanted only Gillian, tasting her in different places, first her brow after he had lifted off her glasses, soft pecks that returned the wanted result when Gillian shivered beneath him. Keeping his eyes locked on hers, he slowly removed her hoodie, then singlet, kissing each mound of exposed breast on his way down to tugging off her shorts.

She laughed when they got stuck on her high-tops, which he discarded with a yank. "I hate these feckin' things." The shoes he rarely saw her without.

She laughed. "I love them."

He rolled off to the side to look at her. In her bra and knickers, she was the sexiest specimen he'd ever laid eyes on. It was funny. Gillian wore sexy underwear under a load of weirdness, as if she was in juxtaposition with herself. She had the body of an athlete, but the clothes of a nerd.

Her nails were chewed short. Her hair was long. Her toenails were painted a bright pink, but covered up by her worn high-tops.

So she had her own skeletons. Fair enough.

He ran his hand down the soft skin from her breasts to her belly, then teased over her mound and down her right leg, the one exposed and not half tucked under Padraig's weight. When he looked up, she was staring at him, the sedate expression in her eyes a strange mixture of passion and relief, as if she, too, had waited too long to find this.

He didn't want to rush, only to linger and enjoy the responses her body involuntarily gave to his touch. When he pushed her panties off and cupped her pussy, her eyes glazed over. He ran his hand back up her leg, over her thighs and then hip, to settle for a moment around the side of her belly before continuing up to release the bra straps off her shoulders. When her breasts came free from the silk, he groaned at the beautiful sight in front of him.

He plunged in, as much as he wanted it slow, but her nipples had peaked and it took all his strength to pull back from sucking until they bruised. Their sex was so hot he'd never get his fill. The more he felt, the more he wanted.

He tugged at his T-shirt, which Gillian helped to get over his head, then in one motion removed his shorts and boxers. The condom on and with a subtle nibble on her lips, he slid home, his length surrounded by warmth and sweet pressure.

There was a loud knock at the door, and Del's voice muffled through the wall. "Mate, there better not be anyone in there with you."

For feck sake. Gillian smiled at him, and he buried his head in her shoulder. "Go away, Del, I'm busy."

He began to slide in and out, slowly, covering Gillian's small gasps with his mouth to hush the sound.

Pounding again. "Mate, I'm serious, no sex the day before a match. My one team rule."

"For feck sake, Del, I'll be out in a minute."

Gillian laughed out loud with Padraig still deep inside her.

"I heard that, mate. I know she's in there," Del yelled again while thumping the door so hard, the hinges whined from the strain.

"That's your rule, not mine!" Padraig yelled over his shoulder, but Gillian gently turned his face back to her own, shushing his anger with small soft kisses around the outline of his lips.

"We can finish this later. It's important to Del, and Del is important to the club."

"Feck it," Padraig said as he withdrew. He lay still on top of her, holding her tight, trying to get his composure back together.

Del burst in the door. "I knew it! Look at your ass hanging out there, Irish. No mistaking that shit. Get your prick out of her and your ass downstairs where I can see you both."

"I'm out!" Padraig yelled.

"Hi, Del." Gillian cupped her hand in a small wave.

"You're not helping any, either, Miss Sommersby."

"I was just giving his back a massage. I get better leverage this way with him on top of me."

Del chuckled. She had handled the situation with grace, even with her legs up and wrapped around Padraig's backside.

"I'm goin'." Del paused a second. "Nice legs, Gill."

"Get outta here!" Padraig grabbed his phone off the bedside table and threw it at Del, who was already halfway out the door. It smashed into the wood and fell with a *thud* onto the floor.

Gillian tweaked his nipple. "You forgot to mention Del's rule."

Padraig rolled off to the side of her, pulling her into a cuddle. "I didn't realize he'd enforce it. Plus, having sex before a match affects players differently. I play better."

Chapter 15

But he didn't. Padraig had a horrible game. Gillian cringed when he knocked-on the ball. And when he got into a pushing match with the opposing team's center after a dirty tackle, it turned into an all-out brawl between the teams before the ref and coaches stepped in to break it up.

He kept his attention away from the sidelines. During practice, they'd catch each other's eye, and Gillian almost could believe they were in a real relationship. Relationships she'd envied in the past, watching from a distance, never engaging in herself. Relationships where they shared secrets and mundane daily activities with the same frequency and enjoyment.

By the looks the other players threw at Padraig, they thought him at fault for the fight, which rarely happened in rugby. For as much physical contact as there was, there was still a sense of decorum and respect between players that resulted in few conflicts on the pitch. There was an understanding that because the game was one of the most strenuous of all sports, full cardio for eighty minutes and plenty of opportunity for an elbow or knee to end up in the wrong place, the offended player let things slide. For the *most* part.

What triggered Padraig? It must be the drugs, the oxycodone changing the lighthearted joker into a man full of rage, like Jekyll into Hyde. Her brother had been the same, but she hadn't recognized it for what it was back then. To her, he was just being an asshole big brother, but she knew better now.

They lost the match, but all the boys were still in good spirits except Padraig with his long face, dragging his feet around. As they lined up to congratulate the other team, the Blues joked and called out to one another. While Padraig proceeded down the line, half-heartedly slapping fives to the Gazelles, Gillian decided to make an exit. She had things to do, and dealing with Padraig's alter ego wasn't one of them. He wasn't invested enough for her to take on his baggage, as much as Coach wanted her to help. As much as she desired him, she had her own demons to deal with, including a classic car that wouldn't start.

Without saying her goodbyes, she gathered her gear up quickly and made it to her wagon without being caught. She should have stayed around to help the boys with icing their muscles and made sure they took care of any injuries properly, but she was a mess. And a bit embarrassed from last night at Padraig's house with Del catching them in the act in bed.

Never had she been so brazen. Always a bit shy when it came to her sexual exploits. But there was something Padraig did to her that had unleashed years of pent-up sexual energy. And she was mad for more. What if she became one of those sex addicts? Maybe addiction ran in her family, like a genetic inclination or something. Shit.

She was confused, and not having talked to Junette about it, her bemusement replayed constantly in her head. *Have fun, then let it go* vied for *maybe there was something there*. But with a jock? She'd hated them for years. Vowed to hate them after Andrew.

Maybe she'd just use Padraig for the great sex. And company. And conversation. And that sexy-ass accent. Sure, she'd watched her brother and his friends go through the girls with no remorse. Why couldn't a woman do the same?

Time for grounding with her folks and a serious mechanical outlet to straighten things out. Then, she'd consider going to the game social or not.

When she arrived at their house, her dad was sitting outside in a lawn chair, drinking cans of beer with the neighbor. Her dad was still dressed in his work gear, Carhartt pants and a cotton shirt with his plumbing logo above one pocket, Sommersby Sewage & More. Gillian left her Plymouth on the curb and approached them with a wave. "How are you boys doing today?"

The older gentleman, Phil, from next door answered first. "It's a great day to sit out and shoot the shit."

"You here to work on the car?" her dad asked.

"Indeed, I am. I am so close to getting her running. Is Mom around today?"

"She had an early shift at the hospital. Should be around soon if you plan on staying for a bit. I think she saved some leftovers in the fridge from dinner last night if you want."

"Aw, that's nice of her, but I only planned on getting the ol' girl running and then was going to head to the cabin."

A look of disappointment crossed her dad's face, but he said nothing.

"Did you want to go with me?"

Her father shook his head, then took a long swig of beer. "No thanks."

As if Phil could sense the sadness that had settled over both of them, he changed the subject back to the beast sitting in the driveway. "She sure is a beauty. You did some good work there."

"We both did." Gillian looked pointedly at her father. "Both Andrew and I. He did way more on it than me."

Her dad grunted. "I'll be happy to get it out of my garage."

Although her love for her dad was boundless, her ire spiked from his comment. With the exception of a framed family picture Gillian's mom kept on her dresser, anything to do with Andrew had been wiped from the house. Unhealthy as all hell, but that's the way her dad wanted it. The car was the last reminder. It would have been long gone, Gillian reckoned, if not for the tarp that had disguised it all these years. And she'd fought for it.

"I used to tinker with cars when I was younger," Phil said. "What's wrong with it?"

Gillian shrugged. "That's the thing. I can't figure it out. And there's not too much to those old motors. No computers or anything to work around. I've replaced almost everything on the damn thing, and it still won't go. It'll fire up, but then it sputters out." She'd pumped any extra cash over the last two years into the car. She'd eaten crap ramen noodles at college, created "casseroles" with cream of mushroom soup and saltine crackers, just so she could save to fix this fucking car. But she loved it, and she was determined. Plus, it was the last project she and Andrew had worked on together, and he'd want to see it finished.

"Plenty of gas?"

"Quarter of a tank."

"Spark plugs?"

"New."

"Air filter?"

"Check. Also, new."

As if to engage her father again, Phil asked. "Have you taken a look at it yourself?"

"I'm a plumber, not a mechanic." Her father rose, hiking up his pants. "Now, if you'll excuse me, I have to take a leak."

When her dad was gone, Phil asked, "Still not taking it well, huh?"

Gillian kicked at the grass. "He doesn't like to hear Andrew's name spoken. Puts him in a bad mood. Seems wrong to me, but I'm just the daughter, so what do I know?"

"Men deal with things in their own way."

She rolled her eyes. "I guess." She thought of Padraig. She didn't know the full story, but he was in some sort of denial as well. The pain meds. Only when he was away from the sport's complex did he seem like another person. Almost happy. At least fun to be with and more lighthearted than when he was in rugby mode.

"Let me get under that hood and have a look."

Gillian popped the lever on the inside and walked around the car to join Phil with the hood up. He wiggled the leads on the battery then asked for a socket wrench to remove a spark plug. Eyed it, then tightened it back in. He didn't bother with the filter, but ran his hand down the hoses from the spark plug leads to the distributor, pinching along each one as he went. "Those look solid."

"And new," Gillian repeated.

He unclipped the distributor cap and removed the part, the cables still attached. "Ah, here is your problem."

Gillian's heart leaped out of her chest. "Seriously?"

"See this here." He ran his finger on the inside of the plastic cap, showing her a thin crack spreading the width. "You have a cracked distributor cap. That's going to interfere with your spark."

"No way. We replaced that new."

"Well, if it sat for a while in the elements, it could have cracked again."

Her dad had walked out to join them at the front of the car, handing Phil an old rag. Gillian was ecstatic. "Phil here has figured it out!"

"I see that." Her dad still seemed sad. The deep creases around his face, the dark circles under his eyes spoke of the pain he still held close. Only in his late forties, he had aged to a man twice that. "Why don't you let me buy you that last part that you need?"

"Really?" She swallowed the tears that wanted to surface.

"I know you are working hard to get your practice going…"

She hugged him, a big squeeze around the waist. "That would be awesome, Dad."

Chapter 16

As the team returned in pairs and groups back to the locker room, Del approached Padraig and swatted him on the back. "Not too bad of a game there, Irish."

He grunted. What a lie. He'd played better when he was in secondary school.

"So are you coming along with me and Rory to the social?"

He looked over Del's head for Gillian, but she had gone, most likely to rub down one of the lads in the locker room. The thought was enough for Padraig to bite his bottom lip, *fuck* slipping out on a forced breath.

Del turned to follow Padraig's gaze, but there was nothing to see. Only the boys and their families, huddled together to collect folding chairs and coolers full of drinks and homemade sandwiches. He grabbed Padraig's arm and started walking. "Be good for ya, mate, to get out and socialize with the team."

It was the last thing Padraig wanted to do. "Maybe. We'll see how I feel after a shower."

"Nope, no time for a shower. We're leavin' in five. You can have a swim in the river when we get there."

"Didn't bring my togs," Padraig said.

"Just wear your rugby shorts. No one's gonna give a shit."

At his hesitation, Del added, "I'm sure Gillian is going to be there. In a bikini. All the boys gettin' a good view of—"

Padraig glared him down. "All right, I'll go."

Del nodded his head in a knowing matter, a smirk on his face. "Okay, so let's go."

Instead of heading toward the big lake, they headed inland. Padraig wasn't about to ask but was glad when Rory did. "Where's this place at?"

"On the river. A bunch of the old boys bought a cabin for the club's use."

"I think they're called cottages here," Rory said from the backseat. He had unbuckled and leaned forward between the two front bucket seats.

"So if they have a second house, they call it a cottage, while the rest of the world, their cottages *are* their houses." Padraig hmphed.

"And then they travel way over to Scotland and Ireland to visit our cottages, as if it was the best shit they've ever seen." Rory laughed.

"Don't be too hard on the Yanks, they've got their hearts in the right place," Del defended as he turned left off the main road. He held up a piece of torn paper with scribble on it, and Padraig realized he was following some sort of directions. "Look for a sign that says River Pitch."

"I thought we were going to Spider Lake?" Rory asked.

"Mate, I'm just reading the directions that Shano gave me. Said it was on this road." The road was narrower but still paved with woods closing in on both sides. The smell of earth and green was fierce, the air thick with oxygen that filled Padraig's lungs as he took a deep breath.

Although not entirely sold on Traverse City, he could see the beauty in this part of Michigan. Small houses, or cottages, periodically broke out of the trees, a mailbox on a post at the end of the drive, or a cabin or house name on a painted board.

When Del slammed on the brakes, Padraig lurched forward, Rory half in his lap from the back seat. "This is it."

He took another sharp left and they trundled over a set of railroad tracks, and immediately after the bumpy dirt came to a T-junction, a house visible to the right and a longer road filled with potholes on the left. They took the one on the left, Del barely slowing to accommodate for the rough terrain. Padraig's head hit the roof of the car at each howl of delight from Rory as they dipped and jolted back up again.

No number of growls or swear words at Del could slow him down. He was on a mission for the drink.

The cabin was actually a couple buildings, a small main house and another low rectangular building off to the side. Cars were parked haphazardly in the grassy area in the middle of the circular drive. Del did the same, driving the car into a spot in the middle, barely cramming the junker in between another vehicle and a large wooden sign of some sort. The area surrounding the clearing was heavily wooded. Birch, Padraig knew, from when Gillian had pointed out some of the different trees in the area.

When Padraig opened his door, it smacked against the sign post.

"Hey, don't hurt my girl," Del snapped.

"Well, you didn't exactly leave me much room." Padraig squeezed his large frame out of the wedge the open door had created, his knee banging painfully against the metal edge as he tried to hop on one foot to maneuver the other leg out. When he closed the door, he came face to face with a memorial plaque dedicated to Blues players. He scanned it briefly, then came to an abrupt stop. *Andrew Sommersby*. Any relation to Gillian? What were the chances? Perhaps an uncle since Padraig knew her father was still alive, but she hadn't been forthcoming about much of her past now that he thought about it. Actually, they almost always talked about Padraig.

"C'mon, let's have a quick look around." Del pointed to a small narrow building on the left with a sign that read Blue's Clubhouse. "Must be the real deal."

Padraig dipped around the post to follow Del. A couple young kids came running around the corner of the main cabin, squealing at the top of their lungs. The one in front carried a rugby ball, the other chasing, a determined look on his face.

Rory waved him and Del off and continued to a covered barbecue area, a wood box beside it with flamingos painted on the front. Coach stood with tongs in hand that he waved precariously close to Josh's face as he spoke animatedly with the young flanker. Smoke billowed from the barbecue, and the pleasant smell of burning wood and cooking meat drifted over to Padraig with the shift of wind.

The property was in the bend of the waterway with the cabin facing one shore with the other beach off the parking lot, overgrown trees and shrubs along the edge that connected the two. Dick-n-Mouth were getting into oversized black tubes, like the ones for large lorries, or semis as they called them here. Damian squealed like a baby at the temperature of the water when he dropped his bum into the center of the tube and immediately shot out into the middle of the stream. He was lost from sight behind the trees. Where the property turned from mowed grass into untamed bush, there was a green road sign with one direction that read Forwards, the other Backwards. How ironic.

Del said, "You should give it a go later."

Padraig shrugged. "Maybe."

At the "clubhouse," Del opened the door to a long room dominated by a pool table. A UFC match was broadcasting on an old-style telly, bulky on a metal stand just inside the door. Framed posters and team flags covered every inch of the rest of the walls, rising with the angle of the roof. On the far side of the room was a small bar and stools where the scrum-half, Mitch, was pouring a pitcher of beer out of a refrigerator keg, the young fly-half, Kevin, on a stool at the bar, a full pint in front of him. They greeted Del as they entered, but only nodded to Padraig.

He had to admit the clubhouse was a great space for after the matches. Triangular pendants hung high on the walls, and old rugby balls were stacked over the doorway to the bar with a framed red jersey above.

Mitch poured Del a beer. "One of the lads that played for the Blues now plays for the Eagles and donated his last World Cup jersey back to the boys. Pretty awesome, eh?"

Padraig nodded and Del said, "Nice."

"Through there"—Kevin pointed out the back window beyond the bar where a small wooden shack with a door had been added to the building—"is the sauna. Va-va-voom."

Intentionally leaving his face deadpan, he responded. "Not bad." Not bad at all, actually. They should have something like this back home, a place where the team could hang out with no bother.

Del headed to the pool cue stand on the wall next to the bar stools. He pointed out the Steinlager All Blacks flag that was backdrop to the sticks, but Padraig had already noticed.

"Want to shoot a game? Just you and me. Mono-le-mono."

"I think you mean *mano a mano*."

Del waved his hand, dismissing Padraig's correction. "Whatever."

"Maybe later."

Once outside, they followed the noise around the front of the cabin via the deck. A huge fire pit was holed out of the ground, long benches on either side. Chairs and people, family and friends of the players Padraig didn't recognize, populated most of the deck and benches. As a woman with a small boy on her hand came out the sliding glass door from the cabin, Padraig craned his neck for any sign of Gillian but didn't see her through the crowd.

Some of the chatter lessened as Padraig and Del approached the fire pit. It wasn't his imagination. A few of the boys nodded, but luckily the awkward silence was filled by music blasted from a cabin window. Someone had propped an old radio in the sill, getting the party started.

A cold beer can nudged Padraig's hand. He looked down to see Austin offering him up a beer from the cooler, dripping water, chips of ice still set in the rim. Padraig nodded. "Cheers."

Another sweep of the lawn area in front of the river and no sign of Gillian. And her car wasn't here. Unless she had ridden in with some of the other lads, which aggravated Padraig to think about, but it wasn't like they were exclusive, or that anything had been determined between them at all. He could go inside, take a wander around as if he was having a peek at the cabin to see if she was there, but decided against it. He wasn't needy.

Instead, he followed Del down to the water, popping open the lid on the can as he did. For a small club, their sponsors were generous. He doubted the club would survive without them. Where money wasn't a worry with the clubs back home, unless you were renegotiating your contract for a bigger payout, here, the lack of funding seemed as much a priority as the game. A pity it was a concern at all.

But it didn't seem to get any of them down. The camaraderie of the team was solid, even better than the professional teams he'd played with in Ireland, he had to admit. Remove the cash incentive and it only left passion. And good will. Rugby was a competitive sport back home, like the American's football or basketball, players getting ready for selection since their youth. Here, the sport was still young, and with it came endless possibility.

The river ran a lazy swirl around two of the lads standing midstream, Jimmy with one of those corny hats that held cans on either side of his head, a straw contraption leading down to his mouth. And the other prop, Dave.

Both boys weren't worth a feck for lifting.

Pulling off his shirt, Padraig then tossed it on a beach chair set up at the edge of the water. He stepped timidly down the bank onto one slimy moss-covered rock and then another, half submerged into the water. Cold. He waited a moment, getting used to the river's temp up to his ankles, then stepped gingerly into the riverbed. Sand and muck oozed between his toes as he joined the others center stream.

"Hold this for me, Del, wouldya?" He handed his can of beer to Del, then dipped his arms into the water, rinsing up each limb and splashing over his shoulder onto his back. And then with a backward plunge, he submerged himself completely, rubbing his hands with vigor over his face. As his head breached the surface, a large object splashed right next to his head. He turned to see a rugby ball drifting quickly down the river, chased by Dave.

He looked back to the crowd of lads in the chairs, but only a few laughed. Del slapped him on the back. "Maybe they feel a bit threatened, too, mate."

The ball sailed over his head and Del leaped to catch it in an awkward sideways swan dive. He popped up and shook himself off like a dog, then threw it back to Jimmy, who caught it with ease, then lobbed it forward like an American football. Only then did Del offer Padraig's beer back to him, now full with river water.

"No worries, mate, it's still drinkable. No alcohol abuse here."

Padraig smirked, grabbed the beer, and proceeded to dump it into the river.

"Oy!" yelled Del.

Dave chimed in as well. "Not into the river. What ya trying to do, pollute our bee-you-tee-ful water ways?"

Padraig threw back over his shoulder. "What? You don't pee in it?"

Jimmy had a sheepish grin on his face like that was exactly what he was doing.

When Padraig turned back toward Del, he had stepped farther downstream and had raised the ball above his head as if he was going to throw a lineout. In an instant, Jimmy and Dave raised Padraig out of the water, one on each leg. Del tossed the ball directly at him. In reaction, he tightened his leg muscles, which threw both the boys off balance, and he teetered forward as the ball passed over his head. Face first, he fell into the river on a belly flop.

He came up gasping. "What the feck are ye playin' at?" He swung around and directed his rage at Jimmy and Dave, both wearing huge grins on their faces.

"It's because you don't trust 'em, Irish," Del said from behind him.

Dave nodded and crossed his arms over his chest. Jimmy did the same in echo.

"Let's try it again," Del said.

"Fuck this." Padraig waded toward the bank, but Del's voice stopped him in his tracks.

"O'Neale, that's not a request." His voice had turned serious, deep and unquestionable. Any trace of the lighthearted Del was gone and a different man stood in his place, the rugby ball cradled by his arm at his side. "Do it again."

Padraig squared off with Del, his hands on his hips, water dripping from his soaking shorts down his legs to join the force of the river as it swam around him. Who was going to give? As a veteran player, Padraig knew you always followed your captain. That was what they were there for. But this was fucking ridiculous. As if Del could read his mind, he said in the same stern voice, "It will hurt a lot less to fall in the water than practicing the same move on the pitch."

Pain. And less than a week of meds left. "Fuck it. Rory get us some beers for this shite."

Rory loped off back to the cooler. Del's face broke into a broad grin, his white teeth showing stark against his darker skin. And with that, Del was back, and Padraig was glad of it.

"Heads up!" Rory shouted. Out of the sky, beer bombs rained down into the water.

Two landed by Padraig, an echoing plop on each side of him. He dove his hands into the river, wrestling with the slippery cans but came out victorious. He readied to toss one to the other lads, but saw they had cans of their own. At least Del and Jimmy, Dave was still rooting his second out of a tangle of tree roots and foliage at the bank. When he finally rose with the second in his hand, Del cracked his open with a loud *kish* and raised it in the air. "The first one goes down fast, mates."

They followed their captain, chugging the first beer until empty. Jimmy let out a booming belch behind him, while Padraig patted his sternum bone to release the air, trying to let it out quietly in a big puff from his cheeks.

A chorus of cans opening followed, and then Del got them busy. "If you can lift him with a beer in your hand, you'll be able to lift him in any condition."

Interesting theory. Leave it to a Kiwi to suggest. But the other boys were already on board, and Del had lined up downstream from them, waiting to toss the ball at their makeshift lineout.

The first attempt was a total cock-up, Jimmy and Dave more interested in saving their beers than getting Padraig in the air. He barely was up before he was down again into the freezing water.

"Again," Del said, the ball already poised above his head.

The second try, Padraig was raised higher but he locked his knees, his bum jutting out behind him. The balance lost, he took Jimmy down, landing on top of him with a massive splash. Surprisingly, Jimmy didn't say a word. Just raised his beer in salute and finished it off, tossing the empty onto the shore near where Rory still sat, watching the spectacle.

"Another one, Rory, my boy!" Jimmy commanded.

"Me, too!" Dave yelled.

Rory returned, trailing a small cooler on wheels behind him. Just as the Scot was about to throw out another can to Padraig, the boys lifted him from behind, nice and straight. He caught the beer in one hand before the lads set him back down gently into the sandy riverbed. He tucked the spare into his short's pocket.

He turned his palm out to Jimmy first, then Dave, each slapping him five and congratulating each other on the lift. Del had snuck up behind him and clapped him on the back. "See, mate, relax and trust in the hands of your pack."

He trudged across the river to the other side. "Again," he said. The sun had moved across the sky, and Del had repositioned himself to be directly in front so that Padraig had to squint to see the ball coming. The rays danced off the moving water, causing distraction along with the buzz from the beer that had started in his gut and had moved into his head.

Two more beers down, and the lifts were getting easier, but seeing the ball had become more difficult. Twice, it had hit him smack in the face. Swearing at Del, he took a small rock and sent it flying at the captain, letting the splash tell Del off.

"Irish, you got to trust that your hooker is going to send that ball to you. Don't go grabbing for it, reaching out with those long arms of yours, putting yourself off balance. Those boys will hold you steady if *you* hold steady."

So what was Del saying? He was the problem with the lineout? It was his greatest strength in the game. Always had been. The Kiwi must be drunk to think that Padraig, a paid professional, was what caused their lineouts to be shite. He had played on the international level, a game that the boys in this club would only dream about.

"Now, again. Don't bloody move, Irish. I'll get the ball to you."

So they tried different lifts and counts, most often ending with Padraig in the water, sometimes taking one of the other lads with him. Del just laughed, and they got up and did it again. And then Padraig was laughing with them. His anger had melted away with the buzz, and he was enjoying himself. Splashing with the lads, dunking Del when he got too bossy. They would submerge him, but Del's hand always remained above the water to save his beer.

Chapter 17

Gillian joined the small crowd watching the spectacle in the river, players and friends from both teams shouting each time Padraig went up in the air. It was loud and obnoxious, but Padraig was doing well. Better than that. He seemed to be enjoying himself. And the other boys were enjoying him. The beer possibly helped.

Gillian had never been at the cabin before. She had avoided the plaque, but the place still reeked of Andrew. His scene. His mates. His sport. She felt as if she were fifteen again, entering his room at her mother's request to retrieve dirty laundry and dishes. She rarely had lingered, the smell so offensive, it was suffocating. A combination of body odor, sweat, and cologne overkill, just like the Blues locker room. Andrew's posters were just as offensive—half naked women in risqué positions. Just yuck. Demeaning to all women.

Coach had sent her on a mission to ring the dinner bell so no more walk down memory hell. She shouted, "Food's ready."

Water churned and sprayed as the boys all ran for the bank, jostling each other to be the first out of the water and to the food table. Padraig remained where he was, a half smile on his face. Grabbing her non-burger, a bun with all the fixings except the meat, she set her plate down on an old wooden bench and walked into the water, flinching when her legs met a river that ran deep and cold.

She waded over to him, maneuvering over an uneven bed, tricky rocks, and slimy branches, worn smooth over time from the abrasion of the running water.

"No glasses today?"

"Nope, it's too much of a pain to keep swapping them and my sunglasses, so I have contacts in."

"You look great without them." He continued, "Not that your glasses aren't hot…"

"Ya, ya, I get it." She had even worn flip-flops in lieu of her Converse but had donned her favorite outfit, a white razorback tank and a skull-and-daisy skater skirt over her bikini, which she still wasn't sure she would uncover. Padraig was one thing. The rest of the team and their families? Maybe not.

Stepping into his personal space so that he had to lower his chin to his chest, she lifted the non-burger to his mouth. "Are you hungry?"

He grabbed her wrist to move it out of the way and bent to steal a kiss. Nope, nope, nope. Not ready yet. It was like openly admitting that she was a hypocrite. As he dipped his head, she shoved the non-burger to his lips, squashing the mess against his teeth. He could do little else but open his gob when she shoved half in.

She laughed as he stepped back, poking the loose bits of lettuce, onion, and bun back into his mouth. Then he swiped the back of his wrist across his lips, streaking his hand with sauce.

He washed his arm in the river. "So vegetarians just eat a bun and salad? Toss on some tomato sauce and mayo and call it a burger?"

"It's not half bad. Even Burger King will make you a veggie Whopper with cheese."

"That's wrong in so many ways. If you're going to be a vegetarian for health reasons, why eat that crap?"

Okay, she was a big ol' hypocrite now. She didn't know what to say so she finished the rest of her non-burger while Padraig watched. She could feel the weight of his stare, but couldn't meet his gaze. She was confused by the constant battle between her head and her heart. Logically, she and Padraig were a dead end. For so many reasons. But her heart insisted on trying, insisted there was something more there that should be explored.

Gillian bumped his shoulder with her own in a friendly way.

"Not in front of the lads?"

She defended her action, or lack of action, as was the case. "Sure, Del knows now, but it still seems weird to me." She reached out and rubbed his arm in a friendly but distant gesture, searching his face for understanding. When Padraig didn't move, she dropped her hand from his arm.

"I thought you just started with the team this season?"

"I did, but I knew Coach from before."

"How's that?"

"My brother played for the Blues when I was younger."

An awareness registered in his eyes, but then his face went blank again. "I didn't realize."

"Yeah, I asked Coach not to say anything...ya know, to the boys."

"How come?" He laid his palms against his back and arched.

"Still painful?" she asked, ignoring his question.

Gillian knew he wouldn't pry. Their relationship was still undefined and vague enough that they hadn't crossed over to intimate territory. It was best to keep a bit of distance. Leave things physical.

"Not too bad. Del was right. Easier to fall into the water than onto the ground."

"The last couple of lifts looked pretty good. Really good, actually. I'm impressed."

Padraig spread his legs and put his hands on his hips in a superhero pose. "'Twas nothing for a man of steel, like."

She laughed and then punched him softly in the gut. "Is that you, Irish, joking around?"

He exaggerated the reflex from the punch, bending over, grabbing his belly. "You got some serious action with those arms, Miss Sommersby."

She smiled. "I like seeing you this way."

"I like seeing you in any way." He meant it, and Gillian braced for the embarrassment that usually followed a compliment. Heat crept up her neck but at least she didn't go into a panic and start rambling, which always made it worse.

"How about we go join the others?" She motioned with her head back toward the party on the lawn. As much . as she didn't want to, she needed a breather from the intensity that they created. Plus, her legs were going numb from the cold, and even though Padraig hadn't said, she could see goose bumps rising up amongst the dark hair on his arms.

He laid his hand on the small of her back to lead her to the bank. That was nice, and not too much. Such a simple gesture, yet so profound to her heart. She'd always been so focused on her independence, she'd never let a man try anything like this. Preempting any romantic attempts, she'd thwart their chivalry before they could try. She sighed as Padraig led them both toward the group. So many years wasted having her head up her ass.

They separated as they approached the group. Padraig donned his T-shirt, then headed for the food table. As he scooped potato salad and beans onto his plate, Gillian sat next to Shano's wife and their little boy.

Instead of taking a chair, Padraig stood beside her alone, his plate in one hand, eating with the other. It wasn't a bad day. Someone had turned the music down instead of up, which seemed strange, until one of the young ones started belting out "The Seven Days of Rugby." Their numbers had grown, and now there was a scattering of children running around, a few staying close to their mother's chairs, a couple older ones playing guns with sticks, using the shrubs by the river for camouflage.

Del approached with a couple more beers, handing one to Padraig who dumped his paper plate in the trash to take it. "Cheers."

"Why don't you come sit over with me and the boys? See that blue and white, plastic piece of junk beach chair? It has your name written all over it."

178

When he didn't move, Gillian nudged him in the arm. "Why don't you go?"

"Come on, O'Neale."

Padraig looked to Gillian, but at that moment Tania's little boy chose to climb up into her lap. "I'll be over in a minute."

He nodded and let Del tug him along by the bicep.

Trying not to be obvious, Gillian watched from behind the safety of the toddler.

Rory handed Padraig a full shot glass. "Come on, Irish, I know you know this one." Whether it was the beer or the sunny day or the camaraderie, she didn't know, but when the boys hit the chorus for "Whisky in the Jar," Padraig joined in. And when he did, they honored him, the Irishman, with beers raised high. She was glad for him, that he finally had started to let the walls crumble. But it was at happy times like this that sad memories always crept in. Like she'd never have a moment without Andrew there, hovering, a grayness that eclipsed all the color.

She imagined him, sitting where she was now, beer in his hand and most likely a girl on his arm. He'd been a charmer, all right, and always had a few girls after him. That alone was enough to turn her off jocks. So full of themselves. Insensitive and selfish. Andrew had made the girls sweat it out. Leading them on, using them, and tossing them away. There had been times when she was ashamed to call him her brother.

When two of the lads ran naked into the river, their bits bouncing about, Gillian lifted the boy back to his mom and excused herself. She had nothing against a bit of fun, but she had to pee.

Andrew had always thought her a miss prissy, goodie two-shoes. Wound tighter than an eight day clock, he used to say to her. But that's only because she didn't agree with what he did, how he acted.

She shut the sliding door harder than she expected. Just because she didn't play by someone else's rules didn't mean she was an uptight bitch. And look where following the crowd got Andrew? Six feet under. That was where.

The bathroom door was ajar, so Gillian pushed it open with one finger. Slowly, her heart pounding. What did she expect to find? One of the boys lying in a pool of their own vomit?

Or maybe Andrew. Alive and crabbin' at her again for interrupting his privacy.

But there was only a pile of dirty towels on the floor, the seat up, and soap dripping out of the dispenser onto the sink. She stepped in and closed the door behind her. Taking a deep breath, she circled the room...but felt nothing. No last remnants of Andrew. No ghostly energy lingering here. Of course, it had been five years. And Gillian was sure this was the last place any spirt would want to hang out. She shook her head at her own stupidity. There was no closure here.

A pounding on the door, and Gillian clutched her chest. "Just a minute."

She pulled down her bikini bottoms and peed quickly. There was only one bathroom at the cabin, the boys instructed to pee in the bushes, but there were plenty of girls out there today.

More pounding. "Hurry up!"

Gillian rolled her eyes. Fucking Jenn. Last person she wanted to see. She washed her hands and dried them on toilet paper instead of the towel hanging from the bar. It had seen better days.

When she opened the door, Jenn had her hand up, ready to hammer again. "'Bout time." She shoved past. "Nice skirt."

As Jenn went to shut the door, Gillian blocked it with her hand. "Hold up."

Jenn cocked her fist onto her hip. Wearing only a bikini top and shorts so tight she had camel toes, she looked sluttier than usual. Plus, she was obviously intoxicated. She couldn't hold her pose and slopped sideways, stumbling and then righting herself. Her mascara had melted and ringed the bottom of her lids. "Do you mind?"

"I do. I mind when you slam my favorite skirt."

Her lids half mast with drink, Jenn smirked.

"What is your problem with me, Jenn? I've only been professional to you since I've started with the Blues, and yet you feel the need to treat me with disdain."

"Wha—?"

Gillian wasn't going to get anywhere with her like this. "Never mind."

She let go of the door and left, but not two steps away Jenn spoke at her back. "He's just using you for sex, you know. He's much too hot for you."

And like the coward she was, Jenn slammed the door and clicked the lock.

What an evil cow. Gillian smiled. But obviously feeling threatened. Barbie receptionist was worried. Good.

Chapter 18

His arm had fallen asleep where her head lay, the buzzing in his fingertips unbearable, but he didn't want to wake her. She slept so peacefully, spooned up against his side.

He pulled the hair away from where it had fallen over her face. How could that not bother her? Scratchy…or something. She hadn't moved, so the possibility of getting loose to take his pill was not likely. The meds were in his bag. At least, he remembered putting them there, but after yesterday's party, things were a bit foggy. Panic seized him, and he shivered. Gillian stirred but didn't wake.

Torn between the warmth of the woman lying by his side and the need to take the med, Padraig was thrumming inside. He struggled, and the struggle lasted too long. Minutes that were hours in his head.

He pressed his eyes shut tight, then released them. *Here goes.*

He moved his hand along her belly—soft caresses that feathered over her skin. She groaned in her sleep, and he took that confidence and moved to her breasts. He embraced one then the other, and when she stirred, he ran his fingers over her nipples until they hardened.

Her eyes fluttered open, but she stared out into the distance, caught between sleep and waking. He nuzzled her neck, pushing away her long hair to kiss along her chin.

As he had hoped, she turned into him. A soft smile he couldn't resist, and he pressed his lips to hers. How different everything felt over here. In the States versus back home in Ireland. Like he was on holiday, and nothing was quite real. As if he knew he had to return to a life filled with repetition and work and…what? Nothing.

She wrapped her arms around his shoulders and kissed him, long and sensual before she pulled back and whispered, "Good morning."

She was so close, he couldn't focus and had to withdraw farther to take in her rested face, flushed from the kiss, freckled from the sun yesterday, and so beautiful.

He couldn't talk, so he kissed her, caressing his hands down over her naked body, her skin soft as a warm Irish summer, light and lovely, holding so much promise.

And then the burn began. The hunger to be inside her. As much as he pressed against her, it wasn't enough. There was nothing so stimulating, nothing so right, as the tactile feel of skin on skin. As if humans weren't meant to be clothed, and like children in the sprinklers in summer, would choose the freedom and fun of nudity in the hot sun.

He readied himself with a condom. Scooping one arm around her waist, he pulled her under him and gently prodded at her opening, and then slipped into a heaven on earth. So perfect. So complete. Unlike last night when he was buzzed up and giddy on booze, when the lovemaking had been playful, nips and sucks and laughter. This morning it was slow and sensual—emotionally charged as he used his body to try and show what his mind and words could not communicate to her.

It was a slow build to climax, Padraig holding on until Gillian released with a tremble, pulling him against her chest when she came. And then Padraig let himself go, ducking his head into her shoulder so that she couldn't see how his eyes watered. For the guilt he harbored, for the affection for this amazing woman. But for once, it wasn't for the pain. And yet he craved the pills in that little plastic bottle. Right then, he knew he was messed up more than he'd ever let himself believe. And why his rugby career was here instead of over there.

He drew in two deep breaths to settle his racing heart and to clear his eyes so Gillian wouldn't see. Pecking her on the nose, he threw off the covers. He withdrew faster than she must have expected as a small gasp escaped her. "Sorry," he mumbled and threw his legs over the side of the bed. "Need to get some headache tablets." He faked a laugh. "I'm in bits."

She smoothed her hand over his thigh before he was able to get up. "What does that mean?"

"Got a bit of a hangover."

"I'm feeling rough, myself. Will you bring some back for me? And a gigantic glass of water."

"You didn't even drink," he teased her.

She stretched. "Yeah, but must have gotten too much sun. I feel yuck."

"Grand, so."

Padraig lifted off the bed, a bit of a sway when he did. Her soft hand trailed his leg as he rose. He slipped on his rugby shorts from yesterday, now caked with mud and smelling of stale beer and sweat. Nice. He'd been in better positions. He hooked a left out of the bedroom to where he'd dropped his bag the night before by the kitchen counter. He was pumped up, ready for the pill. It was like when he had to piss real bad. The closer he got to the toilet, the more he had to go. The nearer to his bag, the harder his heart thumped against his chest.

In such a hurry, he snagged the zipper on the fabric and cursed under his breath. It was stuck, and the more he struggled, jamming it back and forth to release it, the more fabric the zipper took between the teeth. "Goddamn it!"

He rocked back on his heels and drew in a deep breath. When he did, he noticed his back didn't ache as much this morning. His knee still hurt like hell, but he had learned to live with the strain years ago. Another couple of deep intakes, and he tried again. This time with gentle motions, breathing deeply in and out of his nose like Gillian had taught them in yoga. Calm. Keep it together. A smile burst onto his face when he freed the side zipper and there it was. Right where he had left it, on top of his dirty socks and the old tape he had ripped off after the game.

"How many pills left?"

Gillian stood leaning against the wall with her arms crossed, his Irish rugby T-shirt over her naked form. Her hair was in a messy bun on top of her head, her glasses on.

He must have taken too long to return to the bedroom or she'd heard him going off and had followed him into the kitchen. She moved into the middle of the lounge room looking vulnerable, unhappy. Sadness radiated from her eyes, but no judgment. He couldn't have borne it if she passed a verdict on his addiction.

He looked away from her to the cupboard. "Eleven."

"To the right of the sink."

His fingers around the handle, he rested his forehead briefly on the smooth wood. "Thanks."

She waited and said nothing. With a pop, he wrenched the cupboard door open and grabbed out a drinking glass. He filled it at the sink and popped the pill in his mouth with his back to her. "I never meant to stay."

"What?"

Padraig shook his head, his gaze stuck on the corner of a chipped tile on the floor.

"What do you mean?" Her question had taken on an edge. Anger roughened a voice normally filled with an iridescence of tranquility and grace. A voice that could calm the angriest of beasts. "Will you look at me, please?"

He turned as she had asked, leaning his bum against the front of the sink. "I don't want to be here. Is that clear enough?" Raising his glass, he took another drink. His throat had tightened from the change in her. "I am only here until my agent can find me a better club to play for."

"Does Coach know?"

"Nope."

"So why are you telling me now?"

He rolled his eyes and released a loud sigh. "I don't know."

"So we aren't good enough for you, is that it?"

"I'm not saying that."

"Yes, you are."

"Gill, come on. For fuck's sake. I need a club that will challenge me."

"Maybe it's not all about you. Maybe you are meant to be here to challenge them."

"They hate me."

"They're intimidated. That's all. But God, Padraig, if you gave them the time, they could learn so much from you." She took a step closer. Still too far away for him to wrap her up in his arms and try to make her understand, but it was better than a step back.

"Why would I do that?"

Her mouth dropped open. "And you call yourself a rugby player?"

He hissed through his teeth. "I do. It's my profession. *My job*," he emphasized.

"Is that all rugby is to you?"

"Right now it is."

She slapped her hand hard on the island that separated the kitchen from the living room. "I don't believe that for a second."

Padraig shrugged. "Believe what you want." As much as he wanted her on his side, his temper had flared and the meds hadn't kicked in yet. Top that with the worst hangover he'd had in ages, and foul was a light word for his mood.

"You know the boys are volunteers at the club, don't you?"

"I do." Swirling his glass, he concentrated on the water that made elliptical movements around the glass.

"They go out there every week as underdogs. The Blues can't compete at the same level as the bigger cities. We are a rural club. We don't have a large pool of talent to pull from, and those who start with the Blues and are any good are recruited by the larger clubs like Chicago. Even the high school kids are usually enticed away to the college programs." She pointed a finger at him. "Which you probably didn't even know or care are up-and-coming in the States." Gillian was on a roll, and Padraig wasn't about to stop her. His anger had subsided, replaced by wonderment of the woman before him. "You know some of the team travels as far away as Boyne City and Harbor Springs to play with the Blues? That's over seventy-five miles away. Just so they get a chance to participate."

Padraig turned his back on her and placed his empty glass at the side of the sink. When he was younger, all he'd wanted to do was play. Like the Blues' players, he had simply just wanted to be a part of a team, playing the sport he loved. When he'd been recognized for his ability, his drive had changed to what he could achieve in the game. But even then, it had still been about the passion. After years and multiple agents, the politics and bullshit of the club sport had drained him.

In a softer voice, she continued. "You could really help the Blues get to the top of their division."

He whirled on her. "Are you done with your preaching yet?"

She looked as if he had stabbed her in the stomach. Then rage surfaced. It had arrived on her face and in her stance way before any words were spoken. A side of Gillian he had not seen, and yet he knew he had provoked her. Why? As if he was sabotaging on purpose the only thing he cared about here.

"Those boys on the team are some of the most courageous and unselfish men I have ever met. Their strength is in the pride they have in their play. They love, bleed, and breathe to keep the club strong and going."

"Why do *you* do it?" He needed to know. She'd been evasive about it long enough.

188

Her eyes watered, and Padraig wondered if she was going to cry. *That* he couldn't deal with. Her anger kept him poised on defense. If she shed one tear, that would be the last of him and he would break, promising her anything to get her to stop. "Because I enjoy what I do. Because it makes my life fuller. Because I believe in them. But mostly because... Ah, fuck you, you don't deserve to know."

"For Andrew?"

Her eyes widened with anger. Her teeth clenched and she took a few slow steps toward him. "Don't you dare change this back on me. This isn't about me. This is about you and your stupid pills."

"What do you know about me?" he yelled. "Absolutely nothing. So don't go judging anything in my life."

She was right on so many levels. Padraig was a shit and had been to the lads. He had stood on a pedestal, believing he was above the Blues and their club. He had put in only a half-arsed effort since he'd arrived.

He was older and on his last professional legs of rugby, but he wanted to get to the World Cup. The drive had been poison in his veins. And only the call to represent Ireland would have relinquished his body of the taint that had cloaked him for years.

Gillian continued when silence hung over them for minutes, the room claustrophobic with tension. "You're right. I don't know you at all." She began to pace back and forth in front of him. "For all I know, you are using me for sex."

"I don't need this shit." He set into motion. She was wearing his only clean jersey, so he grabbed out the wrinkled and dirty Blues jersey from the game yesterday and pulled it roughly over his head. He didn't bother with socks, nor untying his runners that he had slipped off the night before. He crammed each foot in, struggling with the back of the second one. It wouldn't slip on, so he grabbed his bag from the floor and wore it out like a flip-flop.

"So that's it. You're just going to leave."

"Yep."

"Maybe I'm using *you* for sex!" She was yelling now, fuming as she still paced back and forth. "You're just like the rest of them."

Who was the rest of them? He wanted to slam the door. He should have, but he also wanted to be that good man she thought she saw. He controlled his anger enough to let the door click quietly behind him. But the adrenaline kept him going, pounding through her physio room and out the front door. He didn't even think which way to turn, only that he did, and he kept moving.

When he reached the traffic lights and the red hand blinked at him to stay, only then did he take a look around to get his bearings. From the drive, he knew there was quite a distance between her apartment and his house, but he hadn't a clue how to get there. More than anything, this infuriated him. His helplessness here. No car. Shared accommodation. Relying on others for lifts. It was as though he was back in high school instead of one of the best Irish International rugby players. It wasn't that he didn't have the funds to buy a car, but he wasn't planning on staying. How he missed his Toyota SUV from back home. Black and all decked out, even tinted windows. One of the few vanity purchases he had allowed himself. Hell, he was from north side Cork City. His family never allowed him to forget where he was from.

Why the hell had he ended up here? As much as he tried, Padraig could not see any benefit in the future. Like how his ma always said there was a reason for everything. *What is for you won't pass you by.* He had always been taught to take life in stride, to know that one day when he looked back on things, it would all make sense. But right now, his heart aching, his gut about ready to spill the contents on the pavement, he could see absolutely no fucking reason for him to be here.

He kept walking toward the water. From there he could find his way back. He had a few miles in front of him.

Padraig considered calling Del for a lift, but then squashed the idea. He didn't feel like talking to anyone about anything right now, including Gillian. And the worst part was, he didn't have the foggiest notion what his address was. Having glanced at it only briefly on the paperwork, he had relied on lifts from either Del or Gillian, and occasionally, one of the other lads after practice. Like it wasn't important enough to remember because he had one foot out the door. He'd have to describe to the cab driver how to get there and hope he knew more than Padraig did. He had never felt so out of control in his life. Back home, it was comfortable, easy. With the exception of the last six months, things had been going grand.

The traffic swished by, and even the sight of the blue water didn't soothe him. Too much commerce here, too much noise and interruption to the beauty. But it was more than that. His heart, now, was utterly broken. For everything he could have been. For all the regrets he had. He stood there, unmoving as the memories threatened to pound him into the ground.

Padraig blinked out of the reverie. There wasn't one single cab in sight. The streets of Cork and Dublin were chockers full of taxis. Here, he rarely saw a handful at night. Did everyone drink and drive?

At the next gas station, he bought a takeaway coffee and asked for the name and number of a taxi service. After calling to book, he set himself outside on a curb, the farthest away from the door. As expected, people parked as close as possible to the door and left Padraig alone.

The day was already heating up, and it was yet nine in the morning. Exhaust from cars floated over to Padraig as they came and went from the servo. When he closed his eyes, he went into head spins. His stomach lurched, but he held it down. He blinked rapidly and focused on a sailboat on the horizon. When his stomach clenched again, Padraig ran to a weedy area along a fence. Bent over, his hands on his knees, he vomited coffee. His eyes watered and stung. Then he vomited again, heaving until only bile came out in spit.

If the Irish could see him now. In front of a gas station in a foreign land, no family and not one friend to call on, Padraig hit rock bottom. Oh, how the mighty had fallen, and he knew some fans would get sadistic pleasure out of a man brought to his knees. At least there were no cameras and no backlash of media. Sure, very few even knew he was here.

Straightening, he took a couple deep breaths before he made it back to his cement stoop on wobbly legs. Since he had vomited the contents of his stomach, the majority of the pill would have come up as well. He dug for the plastic container again, and with shaking hands, emptied another into his palm. Only ten left.

Chapter 19

Gillian had blown until her lips were sore. When she took a peek at a mirror, a red oval ring had imprinted on her mouth like a mime. Without the white makeup. But the tears were real. Not the painted black drops, but tracks stained both sides of her face.

As much as she hated Padraig right now, she hated the situation more. How the hell did she get messed up with some druggie athlete? She should have kept her distance, helped professionally but remained objective about him and his treatment.

As soon as he shut the door behind him, she'd whipped out her trumpet and blasted some notes of an old marching tune that she knew by heart. With the windows open to the summer air, businesses down the block had then been subjected to an unpleasant, out-of-tune version of "When the Saints Go Marching In." And it was a Sunday morning. Nice. Sure to get some client recommendations that way.

If the Blues weren't good enough for him, then Gillian wasn't. That's what it came down to. And what jock thought band was cool?

Andrew. He had always teased her about playing the trumpet, but he had told her when he was a senior that he had always been secretly jealous. He had chosen sports, and she had gone with the arts. But then he had overdosed, found by their dad in the bathroom at the Blues cabin, the syringe still in his arm. The autopsy had listed steroids, pain meds, and heroin in his bloodstream. Her folks had been completely blind to any of it. They were a middle-class, hard-working, American family. Andrew had been raised in a caring, supportive environment. What had he been thinking?

With her trumpet across her lap, Gillian rested her head back against the couch. For the millionth time, she deliberated on why. But nothing was revealed to her. No matter what she tossed about, she could only come up with stupidity. Ignorance. He hadn't a clue what he'd been doing, what risk he'd been taking. He was just a follower.

She surged to her feet, the trumpet clunking onto the floor.

After pulling her hair into a ponytail and chucking on flip-flops, she grabbed a small wrapped gift from the table and was out the door.

When she turned into her parents' driveway, Gillian realized they were probably at church, not even home. Didn't matter. She'd only come for the car.

She slid the cover off from front to back and thrilled in the reveal of the beautiful, classic car she and Andrew had restored from bare bones. It had been a piece of junk, the frame and floorboards completely rusted through, the body in decent shape but the steering wheel had been missing and the old black vinyl seats had split, pale yellow foam stuffing scattered throughout the car.

They had built her back up to her original glory, even repainting her the color she'd come off the line. Now, the chrome polished, the retro white-walled tires shiny, the horse emblem sitting proud on the hood, it was time to give her a spin.

The only upgrades Andrew and she had agreed on were proper over-the-shoulder seatbelts and a new radio with speakers. Gillian turned up the Alpine loud, and only when she was on her way out of town did she roll down the window. The old way, with a silver handle and black knob. The car purred, eating up the road faster than she had imagined.

She passed the turn-off to the cabin and kept going, rural northern Michigan quilted beyond her windscreen. She blasted Andrew's favorite music—AC/DC. He hadn't cared that it was old-school. He had loved it. She pulled along the side of the road and reached over to roll his window down. That was better. Almost as if he were there with her.

She stomped on the gas pedal and spun out, gravel from the side of the road spitting up rocks under the carriage. Probably should have thought that one through, new paint job and all. At the next intersection, she pulled a U-turn and headed back into town. She wasn't ready to see Padraig yet, if ever. But Junipers on a sunny summer morning was what she needed. Plus, she had a little something to drop off to Charlie.

When she arrived, Matt let her in, dressed in a ratty pair of shorts, no shirt, then promptly returned to the couch where he'd been watching a morning show on TV. He looked none too pleased to be interrupted so early on a Sunday. Gillian stepped on a nude Barbie doll as she walked through the living room to the kitchen.

"Barbies for you or Charlie?"

Junette looked over her shoulder when Gillian stepped through. "Charlie. We don't discriminate in this house. He loves them." She poured a cup of coffee from the percolator and set it on the far corner of the counter for her. "Help yourself to milk and sugar."

Charlie was in his highchair, half of his breakfast of toast and jam around his mouth. The other half he was smearing around his tray, making red circle designs around his little squares of toast.

Charlie squealed in delight when Gillian placed the wrapped present on his tray. There was only a small rubber star that glowed when he pressed it, but he'd be thrilled with the unwrapping more than anything. "This is for you, cutie-pie."

Junette raised her eyebrows at Gillian, asking with the same simple gesture what Gillian asked herself every day. *What's going on?* She didn't press but continued to load bottles into a sterilizer tray for the microwave. Food and dishes were stacked on the counter and in the sink. Junipers looked more haggard than usual, her natural glossy blond hair tied in a ratty bun, her nightgown wrinkled, her one blue slipper missing the heel. When Gillian pointed at the ragged footwear with her mug, Junette stated, "The dog."

Laundry sat in a basket in front of the dryer, some clothes still hanging out the front like a multi-colored tongue, as if someone stopped in the middle of extracting the clean clothes and just left them.

And here she thought her life was hard. So caught up in her own self-misery, she hadn't even volunteered to help Matt and Junette. They could probably use a night out for the both of them. She was the best friend from Hell.

"Can I babysit for you guys tomorrow night?" The microwave dinged. "You know, so you and Matt can go grab something to eat together, or see a movie, or something."

Junette had turned so she stood in the middle of the kitchen, her hands on her hips. "Are you serious?" But then Junette raised her arms in the air. "Yes! Do you hear that, Matt?" she yelled loudly to the other room. "We're going on a date tomorrow night. Yee-hah and fuck yeah and all that shit."

No response from Matt but Junette walked over and gave Gillian a hug. "Thank you."

"I should have offered before."

"That's okay, you're offering now."

"Hey, I want you to see something." Gillian grabbed Juniper's hand and led her through the living room to the door.

As they passed behind the couch, Junette directed at Matt, "Watch Charlie." Matt only grunted and turned up the volume.

They hadn't even closed the door when Junette gushed, "You've got her running!"

"Yep."

Junette continued down the steps. "Oh Gill, she looks fantastic."

"You want to go for a ride?"

Junette gave her a look like, are you kidding me? "Hell, yes."

"Do you want to get showered or changed or anything? I'll wait out here. I don't think Matt is in a very good mood."

Junette already had her hand on the door. "He's never in a good mood lately. And I'm going like this. No one's going to see me. He can watch Charlie for a few minutes. He's perfectly capable."

Gillian hopped in the driver's side. "I've already taken her for a spin this morning to make sure she won't die on us." She set the car in reverse and backed out of the driveway. "What do you think about us stopping on the way back to pick up some champagne and orange juice?"

Junette smiled at her, and years fell away from her tired face. "To celebrate? Of course! You sure on the bubbly?"

"I'll just have a little. I'm driving and it's the thought that counts." Gillian grabbed Juniper's hand and gave it a squeeze. "Plus, I have some news to catch you up on."

"Oh, yeah? Give me every little detail."

"I will, but it has to wait for the mimosas." Gillian stalled to increase the suspense. "I met a guy. No, not a guy. I've fallen for a jock. Everything about him. His anger. His smile. His kisses."

Chapter 20

There were pages of physicians listed in the Traverse City phone book. And they all seemed to be divided into the type of medicine they practiced. All he needed was a GP, a General Practitioner who wouldn't ask too many questions and would give him a prescription for the OxyContin, maybe a larger dosage and preferably with multiple refills.

While he perused the possibilities from family medicine to gynecology services, Del lumbered into the kitchen where he grunted a morning greeting and headed straight to the coffee machine.

Del scraped out a chair, set his mug on the table, and sat with an *umph*. Padraig shook his head as Del scooped two large teaspoons of white sugar into his coffee and stirred.

While Del leafed through the haphazardly stacked, day-old Sunday paper, he said, "Didn't see much of you yesterday. What were you up to?"

"Didn't feel the greatest after Saturday, like, so spent the day in bed." After getting the cab back from the gas station, Padraig had slipped into the house quietly and remained shriveled and unsure in his room the rest of the day. Even though his hangover had finally lulled and hunger pains had taken over, he hadn't wanted to deal with Rory or the captain. The questions, the jabs about Gillian.

He went back to studying the phone book.

"In yours or Gillian's?" Del perused the sports section, a smirk on his face.

Padraig placed a finger at his place. "I was home by midday."

"Oh, she kicked you out, eh?"

"She had things to do."

Finally, Del lifted his face to Padraig's. "I'm glad to see you guys together, mate."

"I don't know if you'd call us together…" Especially after yesterday morning. Whether she even talked to him again was uncertain.

"She's a good one, Gillian," Del continued as he picked up his mug and dropped it into the sink. "All the team is half in love with her, so you be cool to her, eh?"

Anger pulled at Padraig's gut, but he held it in and turned his attention to the phone book once again, but without focus. The words only abstract scratches and lines in front of him. He had never meant to hurt her. Del might be his captain, but who was he to give advice on his personal life? Feck, he had never wanted to get involved in any way. But time stretched on without any contract. At the best, vague answers from his agent by email. *Still in negotiations. Hang in there.* And here he was feckin' knee deep in club shite. He had gone from keeping a distance to engaging with the Yankees, their opinions and character becoming important to him.

"What ya looking for, mate?" At first Padraig thought he was talking about Gillian again. Or about the team, or about life in general. Del now leaned in the door frame, his weight resting on his right arm, the muscles bulging. Under Del's laid-back exterior bubbled a passionate man. One who Padraig had no intention of pissing off. That had become clear after the first week in the States. As supportive and friendly as the Kiwi was, there was something simmering beneath the surface. Not anger like Padraig, but grief. That's what it was. Sadness cloaked by his jokes and good nature. Until that moment, he hadn't been able to pin it. The Kiwi was obviously here dealing with his own demons.

In a better way than Padraig. Obviously.

"I need to see a doctor. You don't happen to have one here that you'd recommend?" Padraig tried to keep his voice as casual and nonchalant as possible.

Del squinted at him, then turned away to knock at the door jamb a couple times as if in thought. "Nope, haven't had a reason to go. Gillian takes care of us pretty good, mate. What do you need to see one for?" He pinned him with his eyes.

As Padraig considered, Rory came around the corner from the stairs, ducked under Del's arm, and entered the kitchen, energetic and happy as always. As grating as it could be at times, especially when Padraig wanted to revel in his own angst, he had come to respect the young man with his hopes and determination. He had been just the same ten years ago. Now, his age hovered above him, a constant reminder of the limited time he had to get to the World Cup, his ultimate goal, the dream that never died. That was the thing about sports, the career life was short compared to other paths. He'd known many players who had been confused and uncertain about their future after they finished playing with their Irish club. Everything they had known for so long came to an abrupt end. And many with families to support. There weren't many options for ex-rugby players other than coaching. Like so many, he hadn't bothered going to university, a decision he regretted to this day. Even to get some business qualification under his belt. Anything. All the more reason he had to get out of here and get some money in from an Argentinean club. Beyond his pride and desire, he needed to look at his future.

"What you lads goin' on about?" Rory asked.

"Padraig here needs to see a doctor."

"Oh yeah, what for?"

"My back," Padraig replied, not meeting Rory's gaze.

"Gillian can help you with that." Padraig heard the implication, the jesting behind Rory's voice.

"It's part of my contract with my agent to be checked by a physician," he lied, and one glance at Del, knew the captain didn't believe him.

Rory had started making one of his vegetable and yogurt smoothies, adding in spinach this morning and a raw egg. "I went to the Med Center on 31 to get antibiotics when I had a chest infection. Must have gotten a bug on the plane over. Hadn't been in the country for a few days before I was in bed for a week." Now, he spooned in peanut butter. Padraig's stomach rebelled at the sight. But the Med Center sounded promising.

"You remember the name so I can look up the number?"

"Aye, I remember it because it was so daft." Over the burring of the blender, he raised his voice. "The Walk-In Clinic. Can you imagine? How clever, whoever thought of that one."

"Did you need an appointment?"

Rory raised an eyebrow at him as if he was the daft one. "No. I think that's why they call it The Walk-In Clinic."

Padraig didn't appreciate the sarcasm but laughed to keep Rory talking. "Is it walking distance from here?"

Rory shook his head. "Nope, that's the problem. It's a bit out of town, maybe half an hour in traffic."

Well, feck. How the hell was he going to get there? Taxi again, but that would be expensive and take the whole day. Better than the cost of the emergency room, though.

Del interrupted his thoughts. "I can take ya, mate, if you really need to go." He joked, "I'll just put it on your drink tab."

As good as it was for him to offer, Padraig didn't want him to, as the drive there and back left plenty of time for questions that he didn't want to answer. Del must have sensed his hesitation. "Or you can take my beast if ya want." He directed his next question at Rory. "I can get a ride with you to the gym, eh?"

"Nae bother, Del, I'm gonna leave in about an hour."

Del questioned Padraig. "Have you driven on the right side of the road yet?"

Padraig hadn't. Another aspect that added to his lack of freedom. No wheels and no mobility, which did more than irk him. "No, but it shouldn't be a problem."

Del and Rory exchanged glances before Del fished into his pockets and pulled out his keys, then dropped them to the table. "Now, don't go crashin' her. She's a beauty." They all laughed. No one would be impressed by the brown junker with rust and a dented back bumper. Padraig assumed Del would be more financially secure having played club rugby in New Zealand, but it wasn't his business and he'd never asked. Even Rory had a newer Ford Focus hatchback.

He fingered the keys and nodded at him. "Thanks, Del, I'll treat her like the fine lady she is."

That rewarded him with a smile from the Kiwi, who must have been content with his answer and turned to leave. Del paused and over his shoulder added, "Bro, if you need help with anything, you know you can come to me, eh? Not as your captain, but as your mate."

The sincerity in his voice yanked at Padraig, almost as if Del had a rope tethered between the two of them and had applied a slight pressure like a leash. His deception to this man was all the more apparent to Padraig, and he wondered if Del knew the same. Shame settled on his shoulders with a dusting, but he shook it off.

Having jotted down the address for the clinic, Padraig said to Rory who was washing his dishes at the sink, "I'll see you guys later at the gym."

"Aye, we'll be there. At the free weights, me helping the ol' man try to lift a hundred kilos again."

Padraig smiled back at him and grabbed his bag from the floor. Rory was six years younger than Del, but what the captain lacked in youth, he made up in a serious head on his shoulders. He was wise in the ways of rugby and team play.

Padraig dreaded the drive as he slid behind the wheel. When he started the ignition, a loud blast of classic rock filled the car, which only jarred his nerves more. He punched the radio off. Having ridden shotgun, that much he knew. Awkward having all the controls on the opposite side. Luckily, it was an automatic, unlike most of the manual cars in Ireland. He adjusted the seat and played with the indicator, which turned on the windshield wipers, furiously whipping back and forth. So...indicator on the other side.

Padraig backed into the street and drove forward, veering into the right side of the road when a car approached him from the opposite direction. An older gentleman in a long sedan stared at him as he passed. If he hadn't been so nervous, he would have offered the auld fella the two-finger Irish flip-off that had relieved Padraig's aggression in the past without offending anyone. The Yanks hadn't a clue what the motion meant, but it was the same as lifting a middle finger at them. A simple fuck-you, disguised but effective.

Their road ended at a T-junction where no cars passed. After taking a right onto the road, Padraig's confidence grew, only to drop to the pit of his stomach at the next intersection. When he came to the crossroads, traffic whizzed by in both directions. To take a left, he had to cross the approaching traffic. Impatiently, he zipped his head back and forth to look for an opening. With none happening, and it was apparent there wouldn't be, Padraig gritted his teeth, prayed to Saint Anthony, and accelerated into the stream of vehicles. One car braked with a fierce squeal of tires. Another honked loudly, but Padraig at least made it to the turn lane.

He turned on his right indicator to merge, but got his windshield wipers again, lashing back and forth as before. "Fuck!" Wipers still beating a path across the window, Padraig accelerated and cut off a car as he merged with traffic.

He cursed the US roads, thumping his hand on the steering wheel. Why didn't they have roundabouts? So much more efficient than a light every bloody mile.

By the time he turned into the drive of the clinic, he was completely frazzled. Taking a couple of deep breaths when he parked the car, he tried to calm the agitation. All this bullshit out of his comfort zone wasn't worth it! Vowing to call his agent as soon as he was done at the doctor's, Padraig slammed the door and headed in.

Clean and bright. New, unlike his local GP he had seen since he was a child. An old red brick terrace house turned doctor's surgery with a worn brown carpet, an ancient chair, and couch, both with deep seat indentations and losing their stuffing. He had been scolded when he was younger for picking at the fluff.

Straight ahead was a receptionist window with a pin board next to it with brochures advertising flu shots and a new drug for diabetes. A glance at an addiction flyer with a hotline made him pause, but then a middle-aged woman at the desk spoke up. "Hi. Can I help you?"

Padraig had to lower his head to see her since he stood taller than the top of the cutout sliding glass. "I need to see a doctor."

"Do you have an appointment?"

He pulled his wallet from a back pocket. "I thought you didn't need one. Walk-in clinic, like."

She smiled. "You don't, but you're seen faster if you do."

The loud waiting room attested for that. When Padraig had entered, he had briefly noticed about a dozen men, women, and children waiting.

"I'll wait."

"Have you been here before?"

"To Michigan?"

"To this medical center."

"Oh right, no, I'm just visiting from Ireland." He made sure to stretch out the *r,* almost like a pirate, to give her the full punch of the accent.

Her smile grew wider. "I thought that's what I heard. But I didn't want to say and get it wrong. I love Ireland."

And yet again. "Have you been?"

"Not yet, but my husband and I are saving our pennies to go next year. We both have relatives we want to visit." What American didn't?

"Be sure to see Cork. That's where I'm from."

"We'll make sure we do." A flirt teased her eyes that came out more like a squint as if she had forgotten how after all the years, her mouth a tight pinch of a smile. "Especially if they make the Irish men all big and handsome like you in Cork."

If it got him in to see the doctor faster, he'd go with it. "Yer lovely to say. Thanks for that. About seeing someone…"

"Oh right, sorry, I was all distracted by your accent and charm." She handed him a clipboard with a sheet of paper and pen. "Fill this out and return it to me." Leaning in closer she whispered, "I'll see if I can put you ahead of a few." Then winked at him.

To be sure. Maybe he had it all wrong. Obviously the Yanks loved the Irish, and he could work it for all its worth. What was that saying… *There are only two kinds of people in the world, the Irish and those who wish they were.* Flattery could get a person everywhere.

After he had completed the form and returned it, adding another smile for the woman, he sat and waited, his forearms resting on his thighs. A telly in the corner was set to a morning show, the hosts sitting in a semicircle in front of the camera. He'd watched this particular one once and that was enough. Talk about narcissistic. All they wanted to do was talk about how the current events affected them, how funny they were, what was happening in their lives. That wasn't news. Without RTÉ, he had resorted to watching the BBC or CNN.

Ignoring the perky blonde on the show, he sat up to see if there were any good magazines to read. Nothing but *People* and *Woman's Day*.

He hadn't prayed since he was a child when his mum and dad took him to mass every Sunday. By the time he was a teenager, his rugby training consumed even Sundays, but his folks allowed him to skip mass, knowing even then that Padraig was headed to the Irish team. Or if not knowing, at least supporting in hope.

He bowed his head into his hands, nonchalant like. *Sweet Mary, please, please let something go my way.* He was begging—he knew it. Then he recited the rosary in his head, leaned back, and stretched his legs out in front of him. And waited for the call.

Not ten minutes later, a young nurse popped her head through the door next to the receptionist window. "Padraig

O'Neale?" She surprised him and pronounced his first name correctly. Must be a golf fan.

After greeting him, she motioned for him to stand on the electronic scale that settled at two-ten.

"What's that in kilos?" he asked her.

Flustered, she turned to a chart on the wall, and when she couldn't find it quick enough, pulled out her phone, presumably to Google the answer.

"Don't bother. It's grand." He had said it gruffer than he meant. Not her fault that the rest of the world used metric while the States was one of the last few countries to continue to use the imperial measurement.

Flustered, she motioned for him to follow her down the hall. "Sorry about that. We had to learn both in nursing school, but I don't use it enough."

When she got him settled into an examination room with a chair, bed, and medical stand, he finally took a moment to look at her. The nurse was not bad. Quite cute—in an American way. Straightened hair with highlights, big chest.

He could tell she fancied him by her nervous gestures and stilted speech, her avoidance of eye contact. But he couldn't get his mind off Gillian. He wondered if anyone would ever compare to her. He doubted it. Now, she was the control that he would base all further experiences on. She was the litmus paper on which all other women would test.

They hadn't spoken, not even by text, since yesterday. He had resorted to checking his phone every ten minutes, but nothing. Badly, he wanted to call her, but didn't know what to say and dreaded the awkward conversation that would likely follow. He'd wait and see her at practice tomorrow. Then he'd know just by looking at her.

So he let the nurse go through the motions of taking his blood pressure and temperature under his tongue without saying a word, no smiles or chatting. When she deposited the black tip of the gauge into a small rubbish bin with a lid that she lifted with her foot, she said, "The doctor will be right in."

Right so. Padraig was ready, the planned speech and replies rehearsed in his head a thousand times.

He was contemplating checking the cabinets for possible meds when, with a soft knock, the doctor entered the room. Barely glancing at him, he extended his hand to Padraig. "I'm Doctor Asgard. What can I do for you today?" Padraig and Gillian had watched the movie *Thor* last week. Wasn't Thor from Asgard? The doctor had another clipboard in his hands, which he placed onto a small counter that housed a tiny sink, box of tissues, rubber gloves, and a clear bottle of extra-long swabs. He pressed the bottom of his pen that opened with a loud *click*.

Only when Padraig didn't respond did he look up. He was younger, probably not much older than Padraig, which gave him hope. But he looked a bit of a wanker with his tightly parted hair and pointy shoes, which shrank the optimism as quick. Probably just out of med school to be working at a clinic like this.

Padraig decided to take the offensive. Rugby was the intellectual man's sport. It required thinking by every player, not just set plays that each man followed like a puppet. The game evolved in seconds, and Padraig knew enough to analyze his opponent's strengths and weaknesses, to think ahead to preempt their moves and counter before they did.

"I'm a professional athlete playing here in a local rugby club and need a refill of oxycodone to help with back pain that I have suffered from since my surgery in December of 2014." It came out in a rush of breath. Padraig had tried to keep his words controlled, hold steady eye contact, show his confidence, but it was as if he could restrain the words no longer. He had held them in for too long, and they surged forth in attack at the poor med student-cum-doctor in front of him.

But it got his full attention. The man raised his eyebrows in a surprised gesture.

The doctor said nothing for a minute, looking over the notes from his clipboard Padraig assumed.

"Do you still have the pain?"

Did a leprechaun love the poitín? Of course he did! That's why he was here, wasn't it?

"Lay on the table please, and I'll have a look."

Oh Jaysus, this was getting worse. Why couldn't he just write the prescription and Padraig could leave? There were dozens of families out there that needed to be seen. More than him. He could still hear the little ones crying, and remembered the mothers trying to soothe them on their shoulders. Guilt washed over him.

Padraig did as he asked, folding his arms for a pillow for his head. The doctor shifted the waistband of his shorts down over his bum, then pressed along his spine. "Does this hurt?"

"Yes."

"And this?"

"Everywhere on my lower back."

"Is the pain from a former injury?"

"Yes!"

The man worked the pressure of his fingers outward and down along his pelvic bone. "And this?"

"Like I said, yes." The words came out more belligerent than he wanted but it was too late to retract them now.

He told Padraig he could get up then. "How long have you been on oxycodone?"

"Six months."

Surprise again in his eyes before the doctor quickly recovered. They must teach repose in med school. Show no emotion or reaction. Keep the calm.

"I see you're from Ireland."

Oh, here we go.

"Oxycodone is a serious narcotic and used rarely in the United States." He paused as if waiting for Padraig's attention. "Mostly because of its addictive nature." Padraig had heard this all before. Another pause. "I've never heard of it prescribed for extended use."

The cunt! It wasn't what he had expected, nor wanted. He was totally off his game on so many levels.

"Before I give you a prescription for the pills," he continued, "I'll need to contact your physician in Ireland to confirm."

That's exactly what Padraig didn't want. There was no way he'd get his local doctor involved, especially after all the bad press. The old man had retired shortly after Padraig's disgrace. Padraig had abused Dr. Doherty's kindness and naiveté in sports medicine. It didn't matter anyway. As a player, he was solely responsible for any prohibited substances. Although Padraig had heard of players trying to shift the blame to a physician, even their agents suggesting it, he couldn't have done that to the old man. Even though the strict liability condition with WADA laid all responsibility with the player, Dr. Doherty could have lost his license after what had happened with Padraig.

He no longer belonged to the Munster squad and had use of the team doctor. Not that he would have helped, anyway. Padraig's anger welled as the realization hit him. It wasn't going to happen.

"Could you at least give me a week's worth while you wait for confirmation?" He had to try. Anything. At least that would give him a chance to pull a few strings over there. Give him a false name or number.

"Unfortunately, I can't do that, but I can offer you prescription strength Motrin which will help in the meantime."

Padraig launched himself off the table. "That won't feckin' help!"

He hovered over the doctor by at least four inches, but to Padraig's surprise, or relief, the doctor didn't flinch. Didn't show any reaction to his outburst.

He scribbled on a small pad of paper. "Well, that is what I can do for you now. If you have the name and number of your attending physician back home, I will make a call as soon as possible and see what we can do for you."

The small room shrank around him, a poster of a human skeleton looming at the corner of his vision. Taking a step back away from the doctor, he drew in a long breath, then let it out slowly. This wasn't the end. He

214

could find another physician, go to the emergency room if he had to. Four days. There was still time.

Chapter 21

The week had flown by, but at the same time crawled slower than traffic on a Cork roundabout. Every day Padraig had gone out to different pharmacies and asked for a few oxycodone tablets. To tide him over until the next day, he'd beseeched them. Charming the receptionist at the first doctor's office had given him the idea. He persisted, targeting the small independent pharmacies just before closing. And it had paid off. Finally, a female pharmacist, after discussing for a half hour her and her husband's trip to Ireland back in 2007, gave him four tabs to keep him going until his supposed appointment the next day. But instead of saving them, he'd gorged, and now he still only had one left.

At practice today, drums beat from the speakers in an intense pounding rhythm, similar to an African tribal dance. Now, this was more like it. Warriors readying for battle. Shivers ran up his spine with the adrenaline. Gillian must have changed tactics. Good on her. And once again his thoughts had circled back to the woman who somewhere was massaging out a cramped muscle. As long as it wasn't the groin.

He told Gillian he would try, and he would.

Mitch smacked him on the back as they moved to reset the scrum, jarring him from thoughts of the sexy American lass. "Pretty good tackle for a second-row."

He reeled to follow the young punk as he moved away. Padraig was about to have a dig at him when Mitch turned back, showing off a large cocky grin. He was joking. With him. That was a good thing, especially after their bad start. Padraig now took all the blame, for Mitch was only a young pup, barely out of high school. Had Padraig been so different?

Padraig returned the jest. "You're pretty fast for a short stumpy dude."

"That's right, tall man, I'd take you on across this pitch any day."

"Okay then, after practice tonight. Length of the pitch."

Mitch had turned so he walked backward. "You're on, Irish."

But Padraig knew it was okay. Mitch had smiled and gestured rudely to him. In a good way, and something only men would understand completely. A woman would have been offended. A man would know he was considered on their level, as their equal.

He waited next to Champ for the front row to stop blathering and reset. The other second-row, Austin, was a quiet fellow but eager like the rest, much thinner than Padraig but only a couple inches shorter. During practice, they normally played opposite sides, and during the last match, everyone had been so focused on directions from the referee, or shouts from Del, it hadn't been the time for niceties. But he had offered him a beer at the cabin. For as much binding as they did together, he barely knew the man, fewer than a dozen words had passed between them. As his wingman, or Padraig's his, that should have been different. For the intimacy of the scrum demanded a trust that few, unless they played a forward position, would understand. Today, that would change.

"So you have any kids?"

He jerked his head around to Padraig. "You talking to me?"

Padraig chuckled and looped his arm around the number four's waist. "Yep, you're the one."

Binding his own arm around Padraig, he answered. "Nope, but I just got engaged to be married."

Coach interrupted their banter with the call. "Crouch—"

"Seriously?" They bent at the hips as one unit, their unbound arms stretched out from either side like crooked wings.

"Asked her this past weekend."

"Bind—"

Both jammed their heads between the hooker and their respective prop. The thick chests of the front row muffled Padraig's, "Congratulations."

The scrum stilled, poised with muscles taut and loaded to spring. Raw energy boiled around him. Unleashed human power restrained by the call of one man, the referee, but today Scotch.

"Set!"

With loud grunts, the two sides of the scrum engaged. Padraig groaned with the rest of them, digging into the ground with his feet and pushing hard through his legs as he'd been taught. Not with their arms, for these were only tools used to hold him to the rest of the animal. The legs were the power, and as usual, the pain traveled up his hamstring over his glutes and splayed along his pelvic bone to center in his lower back at the base.

He yelled out, tunneling the pain into his voice and out of his body. The ache only added to his drive during the scrum. It pinpointed a release for him, a single moment all his aggression and anger purged from him body and soul. He roared as his side gained ground, his fingers digging into Champ's waist and, on his other side, the muscles of the flanker were coiled and ready to run.

First Jimmy, then Josh channeled the ball to the back to Champ, the pack pushing over to try to retain their possession.

And then, like that, it was over. Coach's whistle blew as the inside centre on the other team took their runner down on the first phase. Shoving the ball back between his legs to Mitch, Damian didn't let go of the ball in time so the team was penalized for not releasing. All the hard work in the scrum gone with a simple penalty that could have easily been avoided.

He walked with his hands braced onto his sides, heaving deep breaths. The burn of lactic acid tightened his leg muscles, but the ache was familiar and wanted. He let the irritation of the penalty pass, and while the other team's fly-half set up to kick for three points, he searched the sidelines for Gillian once again.

Whenever he had a moment, he had gravitated toward her, getting as close to the sidelines as possible without seeming obvious. Twice, he had made eye contact. He had smiled and lifted his hand in a small wave. The first time he was rewarded with a flutter of her own in response, the second time she had motioned behind him as Rory had been trying to get his attention.

Surpassing the pain in his back was the gnawing sting in his chest from her absence in his life, made only more apparent when he saw her at training. She had been the light in his dreary days, supportive and uplifting, she

219

could bring him out of his depression and self-loathing with a simple smile or hug.

With that gone, all the sourness of life had returned. And he was lonely, he had to admit. There was only so much gym training and watching bad American telly at nights with the boys he could do. Although, he did like the series called *The Walking Dead*. Zombies. He knew the feeling. He was one of them as he plodded through his time in Michigan. He could almost grasp a glimmer of a future here if it held Gillian with it, but now again, he was lost. Not only would Gillian not return his calls, nor would his agent. As if they had both given up on him.

But the irony that the lads had finally accepted him didn't go unnoticed by Padraig. And the more he came to know them, the more respect he had for the bunch. And maybe, just maybe, playing for the Eagles in a cup wouldn't be that bad.

He had worked hard at practice. He threw himself into the play with wild abandon, often stopping to make suggestions to the other players. Most of them, but not all, were receptive to his constructive criticism and he could feel the shift of their perceptions, even sensing respect from some. He did his yoga that Gillian taught him religiously, twice a day, sometimes three, since he didn't have enough balls to ask her for a massage or physio treatment. And she never had offered.

The penalty kick went wide and he reengaged in practice. They set up for the restart, Padraig's team receiving. The kick went long and straight to Dick, who fumbled it on the twenty and a knock-on was called. Simple and stupid mistakes but the lads' hearts just weren't in it that day.

All the boys were itching to be finished for the start of a long weekend in the US, a holiday called Labor Day, where everyone went off to enjoy the last days of summer. Even Del and Rory had plans to drive to Kentucky where Del had a Kiwi mate that worked at one of the racetracks behind the betting counter. They were pumped with the anticipation. All they could talk about the last few days was the money they were going to win and the ladies they were going to meet and invite back for post-race partying.

They had offered for him to go, too, but he had still hoped to fix things up with Gillian. And the thought of putting on a façade hadn't appealed to him at all. Rewind a couple years, and he would have been there in a millisecond.

What was he going to do? Number one, get a prescription for his meds. As soon as practice was over, he was heading in Del's car to the emergency room, the remaining facility he had yet to try. Perhaps emails and calls to Ireland after. That would take a whole half hour. But rugby season in Europe would be starting up again soon, and maybe his agent would get some interest. Maybe a player would get injured and they'd need a replacement.

The long days stretched ahead of him in a type of foggy misery. With nothing definite, he wished the weekend over before it started.

They were almost done, and Gillian was nowhere to be seen. After the last knock-on, Coach called the end of practice early, and a cheer was raised by most of the boys before they headed off the pitch.

Except for Mitch, who loped his way over to Padraig. Mitch's persistence amused him, and he smiled. A feisty young fella, but he had to give him credit where credit was due. "C'mere then." He motioned for Mitch to walk back with him to the goal line. "You're a glutton for punishment, you know that?"

Bunching up his face, Mitch spit at the ground. "Your legs might be longer, big man, but I've got speed running through these veins."

The wind whipped up as they set their feet to sprint. Dust blew in across the grounds, stinging his eyes. In Ireland, he had played in most conditions, their season starting in the autumn and running through winter. But dust wasn't one of them. Ireland was one of the wettest countries in the world, and dust wasn't part of the equation. Ever. He stood to shield his eyes until the gust of wind passed.

"Come on, you pussy, what are you waiting for? You're just tryin' to delay the inevitable. Your defeat and my victory." Mitch was still crouched ready to spring. Most of the lads had already headed into the locker room, ready to get on with their evening. There were a few stragglers, but none interested in what they were doing on the far side of the pitch. No Gillian, who must have already headed out for her big weekend plans. Jealousy consumed him for a fleeting moment, which he tucked away to burn later. What was she going to do? And more importantly, who was she going to be with?

"You want to put a little wager on it?" Padraig delayed again.

Padraig knew Mitch didn't have much money. He worked in a minimum wage job at a sports store so he could have the flexible hours to pursue the rugby, practices, home games that took up most of the day, away games that took up most of the weekend. He didn't know how the team did it, some with families and holding down full-time jobs, only to rush over to practice at night and spend the rugby season away from their kids. Understanding wives for one. And passion, the other. Selflessness. A trait rarely recognized in high-level professional athletes, Padraig included. A fact made more apparent next to the men he played with now. The American rugby players reminded him of Gaelic Football back in Ireland. You'd not meet more passionate men and followers.

"Twenty bucks," Mitch suggested.

Padraig was an old man next to him. "Why don't we make it fifty?"

Mitch hesitated, most likely wondering if he could afford it. It would probably take him hours to earn the amount at his low-paying job. While fifty euros back home barely got Padraig a round of drinks with his mates.

With a bravado that wasn't convincing, Mitch answered, "It's your money to lose." But then the kid smiled, and Padraig clapped him on the back.

Mitch danced his feet back and forth like a boxer in a ring.

"You going to call it?" Padraig asked.

"Ready, set, go!"

A head shorter than Padraig, Mitch took two to every one of Padraig's strides. When Mitch pumped his arms like a train, Padraig had a fleeting thought he should show Mitch how to run before the little shite pulled ahead of him. Padraig wasn't out of breath, or tired, getting into the rhythm after half the pitch had blurred away, but he could hear large gasps and pulls of air coming from next to him. Mitch was on his last wind.

At the twenty-two meter line, Padraig accelerated with a burst of speed to nose in front of the kid, which resulted in louder gasps, flailing of arms and legs as he dug into his last reserves.

And then, as they were about to cross the line, Padraig let up, slowing imperceptibly. Mitch threw out his chest and stumbled over the line.

Padraig walked over to the lad, still heaving where he lay, and patted him on the back. "Good craic, mate. Didn't think you had it in you."

Mitch rolled onto his back and punched a fist into the sky, letting out an obnoxious *whoop*!

Bending at the waist, Padraig tried to gain his breath, pulling at the hem of his shorts like all men did to give their crotch some space. They both stilled, only the sound of their loud panting filling the void. Then Padraig reached out his hand to help Mitch up, who accepted it with a clap against his own.

Arms around each other, they headed off the pitch toward the locker room.

"You got that fifty on you?"

Padraig snorted. "Of course. I don't lay a bet without having the funds on me."

He glanced at Mitch at the same moment the lad raised his brows and grimaced. Obviously, the kid didn't play the same way. Which made Padraig laugh, and then Mitch caught on, and so they were both still chuckling when they swung into the locker room.

Padraig took a minute to wish each player a good weekend as they left, one after another. No reason to hurry. Nothing to go to. God, a long weekend in Ireland would have meant travel to Europe for a quick trip to Paris or Barcelona, or some big nights out at the bars or clubs in Cork.

He had waved Del and Rory off as soon as he'd finished with the race with Mitch. Both had been loitering around his locker, itching to get on the road. They were driving through the night in hopes of getting to Del's mate before the bars closed. Del had offered his car to Padraig for the weekend at least, tossing him the keys before they blasted out the door singing, "Fuck You, I'm Drunk."

The room was empty by the time he dried off after his shower. He could hear Coach's keys clunk as he locked his office door. Footsteps approached, so he threw on some shorts.

Coach addressed him as Padraig yanked a T-shirt over his head. "You were good with the boys out there today."

"They were good with me."

"Aye, they were. They would have been sooner…"

Padraig swung his locker door back and forth, back and forth, a creak of the metal at each pass, until he had the strength to meet Coach's gaze. "I know."

"I meant to ask you how your pain management is going with Gillian?"

"Fine." Which was a lie on so many levels.

"Yeah? Are you still on the oxycodone?"

"Almost done, like." Which was the truth. One pill left.

"Gillian believes you are a good man, and that's enough for me. I wondered for a while, but glad you came around." When Padraig didn't say anything, he continued, "I've got to get going. Wife has plans for us to leave early tomorrow to go down-state and I have to pack the car tonight. I'll set the alarm now. When you leave, make sure the door is secured behind you. Should be all right."

Padraig nodded. "No worries."

Scotch turned to leave.

"Oh, and Coach, thanks for the opportunity here. I know I haven't said."

Surprise dusted Coach's features briefly. "Nae bother."

"Have a good weekend." Wow, he sounded so...American.

Coach waved without looking back. "You, too, Irish."

The door clunked behind him and then silence. Padraig had never been lonely in his life. From growing up in a large Irish family where there was someone always around to be with, to the camaraderie of his teammates since he was young, he had never lived away from Ireland and never known solitude. Even now, he was unsure if that was what he was feeling.

Eager to keep his mind off it, he busied himself packing his gear bag with dirty training clothes from the past week. Something else he could do that weekend. Laundry. The joys. As he stuffed a clean pair of rugby socks into a zip pocket, the pill container fell out the side, landing with a click and rattle.

Fetching it from the floor, Padraig then placed it on the top shelf of his locker. At eye level, he swiveled the bottle until the label was at the front, his name clearly written on the prescription. *Padraig O'Neale. Take for pain as needed.*

Coach had switched off all the lights on his way out except for Padraig's row. Without the usual noise and smells, the place had become peaceful. Only the one halogen light above buzzed, spotlighting Padraig in a glow of decent light. Having spent half of his life in a locker room, he considered it a second home after the pitch. Even more so than his apartment near Cork City centre.

He debated whether to leave the last pill where it sat in his locker. Then considered throwing it in the rubbish bin. He breathed deep, summoning the strength that was there—somewhere.

The ticking of the clock became apparent as he stood there, warring with himself. In the end, he grabbed the bottle, loudly yelling, "Fuck!" then threw it in the bag, zipped it up, and bashed his way to the door, ricocheting off the locker benches with his gear bag.

Turning off the last light, he pushed open the door with anger and frustration boiling in his veins. When he turned the corner to the parking lot, he stopped abruptly. There was Gillian in a sundress, sunglasses, and bare feet, sitting on the hood of a green Ford Mustang.

Chapter 22

Gillian had just been wondering if she should grab her Converse to drive in when the crunch of feet on gravel jolted her upright. It had to be Padraig. He was the only one left. Player after player had come out and cooed over the car, even Coach. Gillian had appreciated the rise of status in their eyes, some even flirting with her a bit. Dick had wanted to take it for a drive, but no way.

"Took your sweet time, didn't you?" she asked as he approached.

Padraig stopped a few feet away from her. "I didn't know you were waiting for me."

"It was a surprise."

"Is this yours?" He dropped his bag from his shoulder and circled the car, brushing his hand along the side.

She smiled and hopped off the hood. "Yep, all mine."

"She's a beauty. What year?"

"1969."

He chuckled. "The best year." Then paused. "You never said…"

"We never got around to it."

Padraig nodded his head, casting his eyes away from her and back to the Mustang. "Yeah, I suppose we didn't."

"Will you come for a drive?"

"In this baby? Feck, yeah."

"Good, because it's important."

His brows raised in surprise. "Really? What do you have planned?"

"You'll have to come with me to see."

Neither moved toward the other. It was the dance of the awkward and distant lovers, not yet reconciled, any joking shelved for the moment as each walked eggshells to determine the heart of the other.

He shoved his hands in his pockets. "Okay, but I've got to get Del's car back to the house."

"Leave it here."

"At least let me move it under a street light. It's a piece of junk, but Del will kill me if it gets stolen."

"No one is going to take it. Trust me. And if someone did, he'd be happy for it. He could upgrade." She laughed, but it was weak. Her courage was seeping out as fast as a bad oil leak.

"Seriously, Del has all this music from New Zealand in his glove box, and if the car goes, so does his precious music. I have to at least take that with me."

"Fair enough. I'm glad to see you're looking out for Del."

He pinched his lips together and nodded.

Now, she'd done it, but he'd have to take it like a man. "I like your shirt." She pulled at his sleeve, a soft tug, a tentative gesture. She couldn't be cruel-to-be-kind for long.

He glanced down. It was his Munster rugby T-shirt with their logo of a blue and gold rugby ball with three crowns. A buck deer juxtaposed across the form of the ball.

"Oh right, thanks."

"You'll fit in perfectly where I'm taking you." She was excited, but wondered how Padraig would take it all. Especially for what she had in mind.

"Now you have me wondering."

"In a good or bad way?"

"Anything with you is in a good way."

It was like a dart to the bull's-eye of her heart, but she playfully punched him on the shoulder. "Aw shucks, you're such a charmer."

He laughed. "Not really." He opened the side door and stooped to retrieve the CDs. Handing a bunch to Gillian to carry, he finished, "At least not anymore. I used to be."

She rubbed his arm, the first skin contact they'd had in a week, and the impression of his warmth on her hand remained long after she had pulled it away. "You'll get it back."

Wisps of her hair blew across her face, but since her hands were full with music, she had no way of tucking it behind her ear as she normally did. Padraig balanced all that he had in one hand and did it for her. Instead of letting go, he cupped her neck and held on. He pulled at her gently, moving at the same time in her direction where he placed a soft kiss on her lips. It was an apology and a request at the same time—she understood.

She stepped closer and stood on her tippy toes to kiss him back, searching his mouth for the same questions she hoped he held for her. *Do you care for me? Do you want me back?*

She broke the kiss abruptly, just as his hardness had reached her belly through his shorts. Not nice to leave him hanging, but she wanted to get on the road. "C'mon, let's go."

She laughed when Padraig jogged to the trunk of the Mustang where he shifted from foot to foot, like a little boy that had to pee, or one so excited he couldn't sit still. When she opened the trunk, he dumped his gear bag and Del's CDs, the plastic making an almighty clatter. She already had a small duffel and yoga mat packed, along with a large cooler and box of necessities.

He shoved his hands in his pockets. "Can I drive?"

How adorable, but... "No way." Gillian laughed when he gave her a puppy-dog look. That had never worked on her, Andrew having tried numerous times to get her to help with his homework. And as sexy as Padraig was, she wasn't going to give in now. Plus, this was her baby, and the first road trip should be all her pleasure. "Maybe if you're good, I'll let you drive on the way back."

"I'll be good." The way he said it implied lots of things, but nothing was more important than breaking his addiction.

She bit her lip in a smile. "I'm sure you will. Now get in."

When he buckled up, she said, "Make yourself comfortable. We have a bit of a drive ahead of us."

When they were out on the road, Padraig asked, "Are you still mad at me, like?"

"What's with all the likes?"

"That's how we talk from Cork.

She grabbed his hand from his lap. "I'm not angry anymore."

He gave her a look as if he didn't believe it, but squeezed her hand in response. "Grand so." He reached below the seat to pull the lever to push the chair back as far as it would go. When it got stuck and he yanked hard, she scolded, "Hey, easy there, she's no young chicken."

When the seat finally clicked into place, he folded his arms over his abdomen and let out a long, "Aaahhh."

"Make yourself at home."

"Thanks, I will."

"See, why can't everyone else see this side of you? It's like there are two Padraigs."

"There is. I'm like Father Ted and Dougal."

"Father Ted?"

"Yeah, fucking brilliant Irish comedy. I'll have my mum send over some DVDs for you to see. It's hilarious."

That was the most he'd ever offered her, but she tried hard not to let the thrill show. Still uncertain of his feelings, she needed to keep it light, but she'd hedge for some answers later. Sometimes, men needed a bit of a boost. "I'd love that."

They were quickly out of the city limits heading north, rays of the sun flashing in and out of the car windows as they wove their way up Highway 31 to Charlevoix. Padraig seemed happy enough to watch the scenery pass by, and for the first time in forever, she felt like singing along to the music. She couldn't resist and put on her old *80s Greatest Hits*.

"Let's start with something upbeat." She forwarded the CD until the Proclaimers came on. "I'm Gonna Be (500 Miles)."

"Ah Jaysus, no."

"You're Irish. I thought you'd like this stuff. You got all into it when we were at the cabin."

"I was drunk, and we're swamped with that shite at home. Anyhoo, The Proclaimers are Scottish."

"I knew that." She didn't. "Okay, how about this one?"

Madonna's "Borderline" burst from the back speakers.

"Next!"

"But she's so class. You steer while I pick." She pulled the CD case from between the seats. "Go on then, grab the wheel."

"Will you slow down at least?"

She didn't. "You should be used to driving on that side of the car."

"Ha-ha."

"What about Bryan Adams?"

"Feck, no."

"Why don't men like Bryan Adams, one of the best songwriters of the 80s?"

"Too lovey-dovey."

"Pfft. I'm sure you have a romantic side."

He ran his hand through his hair, then gave his head a good scratch. "Maybe. You ready to take the wheel?"

The car wobbled as he tried to control it around a long curve. "Gillian, take the damn wheel or this beautiful car will be smashed on the side of the road with us in it."

There was no way they were going to die. Karma didn't work that way. Or the logarithm of life, whatever someone wanted to call it. "We haven't picked yet."

"Give me the case."

"Jeesh, a bit grumpy again today?"

He snatched it out of her hand. "Now drive."

She did, along the coast toward Charlevoix, the landscape spotted here and there with orchards. Padraig asked what type, and she told him either cherries or apples. Traverse City was the Cherry Capital, after all.

After passing through the small coastal town, they had continued northeast toward Petoskey when Padraig spoke up again. "There are some beautiful towns in Michigan."

His comment gave her hope, even though it may have not been warranted, but it meant a lot to her that he found the same beauty in her home that she did.

They'd decided on random play, the only song that Padraig absolutely refused to listen to was Lionel Richie, and he had forwarded to the next song. "You gonna tell me where we're going?"

Leaning over, she squeezed just above his knee. "Don't worry, it'll be grand, like you say."

"Are we spending the night somewhere?"

Uh-oh, maybe this wasn't the great idea she had daydreamed about. Maybe he didn't think what Gillian thought he thought. Oh, fuck it, anyway. "We are."

"Aren't you working this weekend at all?"

What? Okay, they had their wires seriously crossed. "Nope, have the whole weekend off."

He ran his hands roughly over his cheeks, then around his neck and pulled at his shoulder muscles.

Uncertainty and embarrassment warred for top spot in Gillian's heart. "I didn't think you had any other plans this weekend.... I should have asked...." Shit, what had she been thinking? That he had no other life than her? That because he was from Ireland, he wouldn't have made any other plans on such a big weekend? "I'm sorry. I can turn around and take us back if you want. Did you have other plans?" She thumped the steering wheel. "This was stupid of me. You might be meeting up with others. I didn't even think...."

"I didn't have anything planned. In fact, I was dreading the long weekend with nothing to do. And now here I am, with the only person I wanted to see." His words were like toothpaste on a mosquito bite.

She smiled, and without taking her eyes from the road, reached over and twined her fingers with his, squeezing gently before releasing to put her hand back on the steering wheel. But did he mean it? She hated this typical crap in relationships. All the wondering and nerves. Screw any of that. She'd forge ahead. "You'll love it. I know. My brother and I would go with my dad in the summer to fish and canoe when we were younger. We pretended to track moose and bear, but I don't think my dad would have us anywhere near them. We didn't know that, though. Gave my mom a weekend to herself every now and then. I didn't understand that back in the day. All I could see was adventure and precious time with my dad. And my brother, but we drove each other nuts usually."

"Fish and canoe? Moose and bear? Sweet divine, where are you taking me?"

There was desperation in his voice, which Gillian didn't understand. It both saddened her and put her on the defensive. She'd gone to great trouble getting the car ready, packing groceries and supplies, timing to get him over the bridge, show him something other than Traverse City. And he acted like it was a chore. "It's lovely and private, but I don't want to say much more, or it will give it away."

It came out cold, but he didn't seem to notice. "So this place isn't really in a town, eh?"

With every question, doubt crept further into her head and heart. All she could do was carry through and hope for the best.

Finally, she took the large loop onto 75 heading north, the sun almost directly to their left. The weekend was supposed to thrill Padraig, and if she didn't get a move on, she'd miss the next surprise she had planned. So she sped up and started passing traffic.

"What's the rush?"

"The sun is going to set soon."

"As it normally does."

"Don't be cheeky, as you say."

"Me? Cheeky? I'm a good boy, miss."

His lightheartedness revived her hope in the weekend, and she laughed. "You'll see, not much longer."

The highway ended, merging into Mackinaw City limits. Gillian kept an eye on the sunset to her left, but all she hit were red lights and slow traffic. "C'mon, c'mon move it already!"

She could feel his eyes on her, but she was too busy concentrating on navigating Mackinaw City traffic to explain. When they finally stopped to pay the bridge toll, Gillian motioned in front of her. "Mackinaw Bridge, the fifth longest suspension bridge in the world."

"Pretty impressive."

"The bridge connects the lower and upper peninsulas." As they accelerated up the hill, where there had been one tower became two. Cables were suspended between the massive cement stanchions with others hanging vertically, disappearing over the sides. Opposing lanes of traffic squeezed into smaller lanes once they were upon the suspension, metal barricades down the center separating the cars. There was something exhilarating about crossing a large bridge, being up in the air, the view, the anticipation of the other side. She drew a deep breath, as if it was cleaner from this altitude.

"I assume we are going to the upper peninsula?" Padraig asked.

"And here I thought you were only a cute face."

"Ah, there is so much more to me—"

"Shh," she interrupted. "This is what I wanted you to see. Look to your left." They were at the summit of the bridge, the merging of Lake Michigan and Lake Huron beneath through the Straits of Mackinac. They had almost missed it. The setting sun was a huge half pie sitting on the horizon, fat and the color of a mandarin. Wispy clouds brushed the sky with gold, orange, and purple. "Gorgeous, huh?"

Craning his neck around her, he answered "'Tis."

Gillian pressed against the back of her seat to give him the best view possible, but when she looked over to him, he wasn't enjoying the sunset. He had been watching her, but turned away when she caught him staring. A melancholy seemed to have settled on Padraig. That, Gillian could understand, knowing that spectacular beauty often brought with it an unexplainable sadness. It was as if something so wonderful reminded you of your life, so lost and impotent in comparison.

She tried to break him out of it, acting like a tour hostess. The last thing she wanted was for Padraig to live through any more anxiety. "Over to your right, you should be able to see Mackinaw Island. It's kinda a touristy place, but really nice—no cars and a few great Irish pubs."

While driving over the bridge, Gillian kept her eyes on the road, only glancing at the sunset a couple times. The bridge was narrow and it was a long way down. When they exited off the steel and onto the concrete, she finally spoke. "I have to be honest. I was hoping for more of a reaction from you. I thought you'd be thrilled. It's not every day one crosses the Mighty Mac, especially with that sunset."

He reached over and rubbed her neck. "Sorry, I am"—he paused, as if searching for the right word—"honored that you shared this with me."

"Okay, that's a bit strong." She laughed.

"I am. And sorry for seeming like a grumpy arse. I'm happy right here, right now with you."

"How come I sense a but?"

"No but, and I plan on showing you how grateful I am once we get to…where we're going." He ran his hand up the back of her neck into her hair and tugged lightly. "That's if you let me."

"I might do. We're not long now. Another twenty minutes, and we're there." Not that she didn't want the great sex, but she hoped for more this weekend. To get to know the real Padraig and distract him from those stupid pills he carried around. If her calculations were right, he'd be on his last ones.

Gillian took an immediate left off the bridge after a large Welcome to St. Ignace sign on Highway 2.

"Will we be stopping at the shops on the way? Ya know, for food or anything?"

"Nope, I've got food with me and there is a ton where we are going. My mom and dad keep it well stocked. Well, mostly my mom, who likes to plan in case of emergencies."

"Righto." Padraig drew a deep breath. "I don't have a toothbrush."

"Brought an extra. And deodorant you'd have in your gear bag."

"Lovely... You wouldn't happen to have an extra pair of knickers for me, too?"

She turned to him and smiled. "You won't need them."

Padraig was quiet as they drove west, the last bits of color from the day clinging to the horizon. Only a slice of magenta and gold were left, darkness almost upon them. She slowed and took a right turn and then another quick left onto a dirt road.

At a large recreational plaque for Sault St. Marie State Forest Area, Gillian knew they were almost there. It was the sign she and Andrew had always competed to be the first to see when driving up with their dad. They had always tied, no winners, even if one of them barked out "I see it!" first before the other. They were so attuned to that moment that as soon as one started, the other chimed in, and their dad always had called it a draw.

Padraig opened his window full now that they had slowed, letting the smell of warm summer fill the car with pine and earth. He stuck his head halfway out the window, like a dog would, his dark hair ruffling in the breeze.

They were deep into a forested area, the headlights illuminating only the rutted road in front of them, trees hovering close on both sides to form a tunnel. The bright lights of the Mustang bounced with each dip in the road, flashing up in the trees one moment, down at the weeds and bushes lining the road the next. A pair of green eyes reflected briefly before disappearing back into the brush.

She finally turned into the drive, and the car lights shone onto a small log cabin with a red door. With the same excitement she'd had as a child, she announced, "We're here."

Chapter 23

Gillian bounded out of her seat with a set of keys in her hand. She gestured to him from outside the car. "C'mon in."

The car still running, Padraig followed her. He could see little beyond the cabin in front of him, the trees now dark shapes on the fringes. It was colder than Traverse City. From the small circle of sky above them, the stars shone bright, a bit of the curve of the Milky Way came in and passed out of the viewing area.

She wiggled the keys as if the lock was jammed, but then finally pushed it open with a grunt and a shoulder to the door. Using the flashlight app on her phone, Gillian disappeared into the immediate door on the right. As Padraig stepped through, the smell of mildew and old wood accosted him. It was cold inside, a chill he imagined had settled and rested in the place since the last time someone had stayed.

A quiet hum kicked in before Gillian stepped back into the entrance hall. She reached her hand around the corner to flick a switch and led him into a small kitchen. A large table in the middle with a faded red tablecloth and empty fruit bowl consumed most of the space. She pointed at two doors off to the side. "We'll throw our bags into the one on the right."

He followed as she continued through the far door, turning on lights as they went. Another small card table with a low-hanging stained-glass light fixture centered the room with an antique radio on one side, bookshelves on the other.

"Lots of tables," Padraig noted.

As she stooped at an old black fireplace that divided the tiny dining area from the living room, she said, "Yeah, sometimes we have lots of visitors. You know, family and friends for a weekend."

Stepping up behind her, he watched as she turned the flue and set a match to wood and kindling that had been set over top of old newspaper. It didn't take long for the fire to take to the dry wood, and immediately it softened the room with its glow.

Gillian stood, then placed her hands on her hips. "So, what do you think?"

Padraig looked around, making a show to nod his head. "Nice. Cozy." And it was. An ancient rocker sat directly next to the fire on one side, an overstuffed chair with a pillow on the seat on the other. There were two couches, one directly in front of bare windows that ran the width of the cabin. Blackness behind mirrored them where they stood. Another couch was off to the side, across from a small telly on a stand in the corner.

"Ha! Didn't think men used the word cozy."

"Ah sure, I'm Irish." He smiled. "We are the epitome of cozy."

"Let's get settled and then *we* can get cozy." She playfully punched him on the arm.

Now, that was more like it. Perhaps, he could take this opportunity to redeem himself. Try to explain what he'd meant when they had fought. How he had changed his attitude toward the team and the club.

He followed her back out to the car where she opened the boot, pulled out a box, and motioned to the cooler next to it. "Do you mind grabbing that for me? That's our nourishment."

It only took a few minutes for them to unload all the gear. By the time they were finished, the fire had chased the chill out of the cabin, replacing the rooms with the sweet smell of burning wood. As Gillian busied herself unloading the food from the cooler, Padraig stood out of her way, watching, unsure what to do next. "What can I do to help?"

"Put some music on. Radio is in the next room."

Beside a stack of board games and a large box of cards on the shelves, he found an ancient portable CD player. When he finally figured out how to get it to play, classical cello music burst forth in loud volume, which he turned down to background music. It wasn't something he recognized, but at least it wasn't whimsical harp. It was vibrant and intense, two cellos complimenting each other in harmony.

From the other room, Gillian called out, "This is the duet, 2Cellos. My mom's favorite CD. She had mentioned to me the other day that she couldn't find it. These guys are amazing. Have you heard of them?"

"I haven't."

"So young, so talented."

"Oh, yeah?"

Gillian came through from the kitchen and touched his arm lightly. Enraptured, she stood there, her head bowed, listening to the music. Finally, she spoke. "They are two young guys from the Czech Republic. To have such talent is so sexy. I wish I had the amazing gene in my body."

Choking on his words, Padraig barely forced out, "You do."

She rubbed his arm briskly as if she were wiping away his comment, too embarrassed to acknowledge the truth in it. "Not yet. Maybe one day. You have it."

"The amazing gene?"

"Yeah, you're a very talented rugby player."

Padraig grunted. "I used to be."

With one of her adoring smiles, she said, "And you will be again."

To have such faith in him was... He didn't have the words. How did this amazing woman have so much confidence in him? What had he done to deserve her? Again, he asked himself the same question because he had been nothing short of a cruel bastard since he stepped off the plane onto the tarmac at the Traverse City airport. He could only hope that she saw more than the others did, that she could see beneath the surface to the man he had become through hard work and determination. Not even his ma and da had the confidence that Gillian had in him. It was both heart-wrenching and nerve-wracking at the same time. How could he live up to her expectations?

The music changed to a slower dirge, the cellos crying out pain and loss. He didn't mind it, but the song reminded him too much of Mass. Walking down for communion, his head bowed, hands clasped, humility in his step as his parents had instructed. For what? Redemption, he had never even understood.

To break the sadness creeping up on him, he tried to lighten the mood. "You mean no whale or spa music this weekend?"

Gillian stuck her tongue out at him, which made him grin. "Ha-ha, very funny. Music therapy really works. Okay, I'll admit I got it slightly wrong at first for the Blues, but *you* have to admit those drums are awesome." She unpacked the items in the box, laying them on the table. There were a dozen candles, some he recognized from her apartment, another pack of tea candles that she ripped open. A large flashlight, rubbish bags, a four-pack of toilet paper and a zipped case, which Padraig queried.

"That's a satellite phone. My folks make me bring it up with me in case of emergencies."

Padraig dug his phone from his pocket. "You mean there's no reception here?"

"Nope. Not one bar."

She was right. The phone wasn't even searching for a network.

"And look here, a bottle of wine. Well, well, Miss Sommersby, we are letting loose this weekend, eh?

"Yep." She didn't look at him as she made busy around the kitchen. "We have four nights, so you pick it."

He'd save it for tomorrow night when he didn't have any pills left. Take the sting out of his withdrawals hopefully. "Can I get something to drink real quick?"

"Sure, glasses are in the cabinet behind you. There's bottled water in the fridge. Only well water up here. It's good, but I didn't know if you'd like the taste."

When he filled his glass, he slipped into the bedroom off the kitchen where they had set their bags. It was small with only a dressing table and a double bed with a pastel quilt. His feet would surely hang off the end, but as long as Gillian shared the bed, he'd be happy with that. Her bag sitting next to his was a good sign. As long as he didn't blow it.

He found the pill case that had settled at the bottom of the side zip pocket. At first glance, it hadn't been there and Padraig's heart had missed a beat, but just as panic was about to set in, it surfaced in the leg hole of a dirty pair of boxers.

As he fiddled with the cap, he heard Gillian behind him. "Is everything all right?"

He couldn't look at her. "Sure, no problem."

"How many left?"

He zipped the bag and stood, reaching for the glass of water on the dresser. "Only one." His back to her, he rolled the white pill around in his palm, trying to steady his emotions. Many that he didn't recognize—right now a speedball of tension, anger, agitation.

"Are you going to take it?" Her voice was barely a whisper above the buzz in his head.

He turned abruptly, the pill fisted and at his side. "What do you care?"

She nodded, biting the corner of her bottom lip. "I care."

"Why?"

"Let's just say I've lost enough to the damn things."

Gillian, standing there in all her natural beauty and big heart. If he could only get past the anger, three steps and he'd be there, taking her up into his arms. But he didn't ask for this. Her intrusion into his privacy, his life—all fucked up as it was.

She held out one hand, to placate him, to offer him a bridge to solid ground. If only he could accept. But he knew, before he could receive her refuge, he had to give her something first. But, that wasn't love. At least, not in his book. Wasn't it supposed to be unconditional? And here she was placing parameters on their relationship. Making him fold his hand. Trying to change him.

Her one arm was still out, the other wrapped around her middle.

He licked the corner of his mouth, his tongue darting in and out. They stood on opposing sides, waiting for the other to make the first move. Make the decision for them both.

With his free hand, he clenched his hair tight at the scalp and pulled. "Fuck!"

She didn't move, not an inch. Didn't jump in surprise or startle at his release. Just stood there, her eyes not leaving his for a second. What, did she think he'd take the pill and she'd have to wrestle it out of him? He laughed at the image in his head of Gillian, the waif, hanging off his arm like the monkey bars at school, trying to weight his hand away from his mouth.

"If it's so important to you." He tossed the pill, but it fell short onto the floor, a couple clicks as it bounced near her feet.

He expected her to pick it up. Instead, she stepped on it, grinding it under the ball of her foot. When she lifted her shoe, a bit of white dust remained on the floor. She raised her foot and brushed away any caught on her sole.

She caught his gaze for a second, then turned away and disappeared around the corner.

Padraig eyed the white dust on the floor, but he wasn't that desperate, was he? If he licked his finger, he'd still be able to get a bit up before she came back. He slammed his fist onto the dresser. Fuck! He remembered the drunks on Grafton Street in Dublin, picking through cigarette butts on the ground to plump them up, straighten them out, and smoke what was left. At the time, he had thought how disgusting and low that humanity had become, and here he was contemplating practically the same.

It was only a minute before she returned with a small duster and brush in her hand. Her eyes went immediately to the floor as if she too, thought he would have tried to salvage any that remained. She swept it up in two quick strokes, turned on her heel, and was back out the door. With her absence came the soar of the music. This time he recognized a classical version of "With or Without You," the two cellos rocking the U2 song.

From the bedroom, he could see her pottering around. She opened a drawer and pulled out a knife, and from the lower cupboard, a cutting board. She kept popping in and out of his line of site as she moved around the kitchen. When she next came into view again, she had a large loaf of bread that she began slicing.

Wasn't she going to say anything else?

All of a sudden, Padraig regressed back to a school boy, when he had gotten into trouble at home and had lingered at the top of the stairs, waiting for his mum to yell up to him that he could come back down and join the family. It was as if he waited for the same from Gillian. To accept him again, no matter what transgression had transpired.

He tentatively stepped to the door and leaned against the doorframe where she had previously stood. As she turned to the table, her head lifted as she caught him standing there.

She smiled. "Aren't you going to help?" Without waiting for an answer, she continued, "The fire needs more wood, the wine needs to be opened, and if you are at all inclined, I could use some help getting our dinner ready." She grabbed a couple of jars out of the box they had brought from the car. "Which isn't a dinner at all…more like lots of appetizers." Holding a jar to him, she motioned for him to open it. "You know, a light and easy something."

Padraig stepped forward out of the safety of the bedroom and grabbed the black olives, which he opened with an easy twist and pop. When he handed it back to her, he took another step closer until he could lean on the back of the chair on the opposite side of the table from her.

"So is that it?" he asked.

She looked at him over her shoulder, the knife raised above the bread. "What do you mean? Like are there other jars to be opened?" She laughed as if she was trying to coax him to do the same.

He tried to smile, but it was awkward with the lump in his throat and the tears threatening at the back of his eyes. "You know what I mean."

She stopped, her hand still on the piece of sliced bread she had moved from the cutting board to the plate. In a moment, she was around the table, her arms closed around his waist, head against his chest. His arms wrapped naturally around her. Into his heart, she spoke. "I'll help you."

With nothing else to say, he murmured, "Thank you."

"But I need you to try. I don't think I have the strength to watch you suffer."

Padraig tried to make light of it. "Ach, sure, there'll be no suffering unless I have to hear the moaning whale songs again."

Chuckling, she stepped out of his embrace and punched him gently in the chest. "No moaning whales."

"Thank Saint Anthony."

She rolled her eyes. "I've got plenty to keep us busy. Your body will be so overwhelmed with pleasure, it won't even know any pain."

That sounded promising. "Ya do?"

She ticked them off on her fingers. "Yoga, massage…" She winked, then continued, "Meditation, and I have a new acupressure technique I want to try on you."

"And?" Padraig prompted. As he stepped forward, she stepped back until they were circling the table.

"Nature walks and fresh air, great soul food."

He reached for her but she evaded his grab. "Aren't we missing something, Gill?

"Hmm…" She tapped her finger to her pursed lips. "I don't think so."

Having stalked her out of the kitchen and through the small dining area, they were back into the living room, the dying fire casting shadows on Gillian's legs.

All of a sudden, she was shy. "Perhaps…"

"Admit it."

"What? Sex?"

"Now that's what I'm talking about."

She rolled her eyes, which made him feel two feet tall and question how awesome he thought he was. She had a way in that.

"Did you know that the pleasure from sex, and especially an orgasm, will override any pain you may suffer from? At least while the endorphins last." She laughed. "There is something called the gate control theory. There are two tracks going to the brain, one for feeling to travel on, one for pain. Feeling travels faster on its track to the brain than pain does. That's why moms will rub a sore spot on a child. The feeling of the rubbing will reach the child's brain faster than the pain that is there."

"Lovely." Her smarts turned him on, as well as her ability as a physical therapist, but he couldn't focus on her words for his attention had shifted to her lips and her hands, fluttering about as she became animated in her passion. Her chest rose and fell when she drew deep breaths between strings of words, blurted out as she did when she was overwhelmed with her own excitement.

"Did you hear what I said, Padraig?"

"All of it?"

Gillian shook her head at him. "Doesn't matter, anyway... I'll take care of you."

And that's when Padraig knew his heart was gone. Lost to the woman who stood before him. She bent to feed the fire with wood from a basket beside the hearth. The smell of wood smoke so much stronger and fulfilling than the coal and turf they burned at home in Cork. A slow, melancholy solo cello played, desperation in the notes as the song called out for a response from some unknown lover. The music instilled in him that same sense of yearning.

Gillian's hair had fallen over to one side of her head as she blew on the embers to light the kindling. He could resist no longer and walked up behind her. He grabbed both sides of her hips and rubbed his erection against her backside.

On an airy gasp, she straightened, and pressed her bum against him. He slid his one hand from her hip to her breast then pulled her deeper into his chest and groin, kissing the bare side of her neck. Her hands rested over his, following his fingers to cup and embrace her body. When he led their joined hands over her nipple, a groan hummed in her throat.

As he kissed his way up her neck to her ear, she directed his other hand down to her vulva where she pressed his palm. He dragged his fingers back and forth, the thin material of her dress shifting, causing friction against her sensitive area.

She turned in his arms and shoved him gently in the sternum, forcing him to take a step back. As much as he wanted to pull her back against him, he waited. He braced at a soft ticking at the window. Gillian must have noticed since she smiled. "Just some low branches outside the window. Look at me, Padraig."

He did. Her eyes on his, she lifted her sundress over her head and let it drop to the floor. She paused as if to let him enjoy the view for a moment. She wore soft pink knickers and matching bra with lace at the top. So beautiful his throat tightened.

As if she had orchestrated her striptease with the music, the symphony swelled when she unclasped her bra and let it slip off her arms onto the floor. Her gaze never leaving his, she stepped out of the panties, toeing them to the side. Sweet, sweet agony. But he still waited.

She stepped forward and rose to kiss him gently on the lips. There was nothing he could do but wonder at her calm while a storm raged inside his own body. She pulled his jersey up over his head, then kissed along his collar bones, letting the shirt drop. Could he touch her now? Something told him no, not yet. She ran her fingertips over his chest as if reading Braille, deciphering without words what he held inside, what he couldn't reveal to her any other way.

Hooking her thumbs into his shorts and boxers, she urged both down in one sweep. She helped him to step out, then again ran her fingertips up his legs, back to front, kissing the tip of his cock as she passed. Sweet Jesus, he wasn't that strong. So engrossed in this woman and the play she made with her caresses.

And then silence. The CD had finished, and with the hush, the beating of his heart filled the absence. She stepped into him and sucked first one nipple then the other, her arms around his waist, her fingers trailing up and down his spine.

No more. He grabbed the back of her head and kissed her with urgency, their tongues and lips in a brutal dance for domination. When she broke them apart, he gasped out loud.

She took only a moment to stretch a throw blanket on the floor in front of the fire, then tossed the couch pillows randomly on top. Her hand reached for his and tugged gently.

In the back of his mind, the ticking of the branches at the window registered over the crackle of the fire. Gillian acted a choreographer to his movements, gently directing him over the top of her, where he rested between her thighs. Both of their movements slow and tender, she set the pace, a rhythm he strained against to increase.

His muscles tightened with the need, and when she finally whispered "now" into his ear, a greedy bastard, he filled her, and she arched in response, her breasts beautiful as they spread to her sides. Her face flushed, lips parted. He wanted her deeper so hooked his arm under the small of her back and rolled her on top of him. When she seated his length, he groaned, "Oh, God."

With the fire behind them, her face was in shadows. And he desperately wanted to see what her expression said. Ecstasy? Love? Passion? For he needed to capture this moment to retain for the rest of his life. One that he could recall at whim.

Hold on.

But he couldn't, and he called out her name in his release.

Chapter 24

Here, he wasn't so brave or strong. Not here. Everything so foreign and unforgiving. Unlike Ireland, the US had an undercurrent of panic and rush that didn't permeate the beat of life in Ireland. He couldn't put his finger on it until now. That sensation that he should be doing something, anything other than what he was. Now, he understood. Because that same panic had his gut and balls gripped and twisted into a vise.

Since dawn, he had stood at the glass sliding doors, staring out the back of the cabin. Beyond the back deck was a small clearing around the house, then thick forest. Gillian had said there was a small lake about a quarter of a mile along a path.

As she had promised, she'd filled his night and the early hours of the morning with pleasure, intense orgasms but also tender and soft moments that had kept him busy, his mind on nothing else but Gillian and him. She alternated feeding him, massaging his body, and long sessions on the floor.

He hadn't even thought about the pain in his back or the pills that offered relief. She had been his crutch.

Now, unsteady on his feet, he needed to move to get his balance back. He threw off the blanket, drew the sliding door quietly open, and stepped onto the deck. Cold air engulfed him, his breath misting in front of his face. He could imagine his balls shriveling in protest. He braced against the sudden change, his muscles tightening, goose bumps running the length of his arms. Hopping along on the balls of his feet, he danced to the railing.

Bring it on.

He grasped the ledge that ran the length around the deck, waiting for his body to acclimatize to the biting cold. Gillian had said they were quite far north.

A cacophony of birdsong filled the air, screeches and titters, echoes of the same in reply. It smelled of pine and wet earth. He recognized the evergreens sharing space with other types of non-coniferous trees, maples and birches, a type with a peach-colored trunk, the bark in white peels curling off the tree. A mist hovered above the ground, but no higher than the lowest boughs of some of the trees, maybe up to his knees if he was off the deck.

If he didn't move. If he didn't do fucking something, he was going to go mad with the need.

He did press-ups against the railing, but when that didn't help, he began their game warm-up routine, then finally his stretches. When he dipped to touch his toes, his boys were indeed shriveled to prunes. Poor feckers.

His agitation hadn't lessened, his need consuming every thought, every skip of the imaginary rope as he bounced around the deck like a madman. He grabbed his hair with both fists, a silent scream bursting through his teeth. He wouldn't wake Gillian, who had worked so hard to keep his mind off his need, his addiction. There, he said it. But it didn't feel any better recognizing what it was in truth.

Launching himself over the railing, he landed with an awkward thud in the dewy grass. From a crouch, he shot off toward the trailhead like a runner out of the blocks. Even when the trail grew tighter, branches catching his arms and scratching at his legs, he kept his speed. Any low branch that crossed the path, he flew at, grabbing the rough bark and letting the momentum swing his body forth. He stumbled and righted, limbs flailing to find purchase.

The farther he ran into the woods, the more dense they became, the trail trickling down to little less than an animal passage, overgrown by a leafy ground cover. Up ahead, the sky brightened and an oval of light beckoned. He ran harder, leaping great lengths of earth like a hurdler, his head pounding, a stitch in his side, lungs heaving. His toes stung from stubbing them on the rock and roots on the way.

The sparkle of the water was ahead. The density of the forest lifted, the air refreshing after the heavy scent of moss and decay. As he burst from the line of trees onto the sand, a piece of large driftwood caught his right leg, and by association, his free boys.

The pain was excruciating, thrusting him forward. He tucked and rolled in the sand, letting the slight hill to the water roll him to the edge, as they had done when they were kids on the dunes outside of Crosshaven during the short summers in Ireland.

When he stopped, he curled into the fetal position, waiting for the pain to lapse. He was nauseated from the sting, so much more than in his back. He was going to retch, but then it passed. Padraig unfurled his body until he lay prone, his arms and legs stretched out into a star. The water lapped at the fingertips of his left hand.

His body tingled, blood pumping from the run. The adrenaline turning his senses on high. The soft wet sand, pebbles under his shoulders, the distant cry of a heron, a crescent moon fading in the daylight.

He lay there, spread eagle, for God knew how long. And with every moment filled with inactivity, came again the despair at where he was in his life, what he could have been and who he was now. Nothing, that was what. He remembered the disappointment from his friends and teammates, but especially his ma and da. The looks on their faces after word had gotten out. When he'd met them in the pub. The worst were the endless texts and the media. Fuck the press. And his fans. Jaysus, it didn't take much for loyalties to be lost.

"Are you done?"

He hadn't heard her approach, so lost in his own self-pity. He had to strain his neck to see her over his right shoulder. Only in his jersey, she stood there with a towel wrapped over her arm.

He lifted his head to acknowledge her, then let it fall back onto the sand. "Not really."

"After this weekend, you will be."

"I doubt it."

She dangled the towel over his face, which he snapped out of her grasp and covered his nudity.

"Or maybe just get the hell out in general."

She stood close to his head so that a view of her legs from toe to waist crowded his vision from anything else. And just like that, the fine length of flesh distracted him back from the dark place he had gone.

"C'mon then." She offered a hand up, but he yanked her down to the sand. Her eyes were still glazed from lack of sleep, her face flushed from the same. She had tied her hair up into a messy bun at the top of her head that Padraig released when she rested her upper body on his chest, her legs tucked at an angle behind her.

He ran his fingers through her hair. Beautiful. So much better tousled naturally than when she tied it into a braid.

"That's gonna itch later."

"Huh?"

"All that sand you're getting into my hair."

"I'll wash it for you in the shower."

A slight nod and smile. "That'd be nice."

She began to trace a fingertip around his face, along his eyebrows, then down his nose and around his mouth. He relaxed into the caress and closed his eyes. This woman could do wonders for his nerves. She pressed at one temple, then the other, then worked her way down his nose and mouth, along his jaw line. Almost certainly not random with Gillian, using her acupressure to keep his demons at bay.

"I'm sorry for last weekend."

"I know you are. We wouldn't be here if you weren't."

"I didn't want anyone to know I only plan to be here a short while." God, he could fall asleep right here. "It's not their business, anyway."

"But it is. That's what you still don't get."

"How is my life their business?"

"Because your life intersects their own. Your paths are the same right now. Rugby and the club."

"Perhaps…"

"You can't live your life without impacting others. That's not a choice we have. But you can choose what footprint you leave behind. Do you want to be remembered as a dickhead? That self-absorbed asshole that came over from Ireland?" She had grabbed his hand and was pressing up each finger, starting at the base and working up to the tip.

Jaysus, she wasn't holding back, and the a-word sounded like the devil coming out of her mouth. "How did you become so wise in the ways?"

Her face turned serious. "You don't think I've suffered any loss before? That pain is only reserved for Padraig O'Neale?"

He was a complete tosser, but it wasn't her that made him feel that way. She'd never do something so immature and base. "Andrew?"

"Yes."

"The one who played for the Blues?"

"The very same."

The pieces started to fit. "So you're trying to save me now. Is that it?"

She brushed his hand away and locked eyes with him so there would be no mistaking her next words. "No, I'm trying to save myself."

"By helping me?"

"Something like that, but you have to help me, help you."

"I'm trying, Gill, but you have no idea what I went through over there."

"Then tell me. I'm all ears." She switched to his other hand, repeating the pressure points along his fingers and palm. She worked a circle in his hand, starting from the outside and working her way into the center.

He opened his eyes. "What are you doing?"

"This is a calming technique used on children." She stopped and stared out at the lake as if gathering her thoughts. "OTs use this to calm kids with special needs, ya know with autism or behavioral disorders, if they are worked up or even if they aren't. The pressure has been proven to help them relax. They use it at the schools, training the kids to do it on their own hands when they feel they are going to melt down."

"OTs?"

"Occupational Therapists." Starting at one shoulder, she squeezed along his arm. She counted lightly under her breath until she reached ten at his wrist, then switched to his other shoulder and did the same.

"You're amazing." He stared hard until she brought her gaze back to him. "I am so turned on by your passion for what you do."

She peeked at the towel that had tented at his crotch and laughed. "I can see that." She grasped his hand and held. "I feel the same about you. Your passion for rugby."

"You have no idea."

"I'm still waiting for you to tell me."

And so he did. From the day everything had turned to shit to landing in Michigan almost a month ago. He revealed how his one dream was to make it to the World Cup, that twenty years or more were spent in anticipation of playing for Ireland. He had watched Ireland at every previous Cup, living every moment as if he had been on the pitch with the team. He told her about when the teams lined up for their national anthems, how he craved to be one standing there in the Irish jersey, singing the rugby anthem for both the republic and northern Ireland. He had imagined that day so often that he could feel the wind across his face, the words belting from his lungs. The pride on his mum and dad's faces when he announced it. Celebrating his selection. One of the chosen.

He didn't want to end up middle-aged, watching matches on the telly, having regrets, knowing there could have been a different path for him. He had fucked things up badly but wasn't sure how to make it right.

She listened to his story with no judgment, no advice, no pity or otherwise, only held his hand in hers.

"So that's about it, like. All that time, energy, and work gone—just demolished—in one bad choice." Emotion started building in his throat again and he swallowed hard.

"You still have the Blues. And me."

He turned his head to face her. "I know."

"You do?"

"Now, I do."

"So you're going to try harder? Put your heart into the game here?"

"I have been. Haven't ye noticed?" He smiled to let her know he was kidding.

Gillian made monkey lips at him, which made him laugh.

He pulled at her neck so he could reach her lips. A soft kiss since he didn't know what else to say.

Her lips lingered, but then she pulled away. "How does that saying go? 'As I look back on my life, I realize that every time I thought I was being rejected from something good, I was actually being redirected to something better.'"

Gently pushing her aside, he got up and wrapped the towel around his waist. "Okay, so, let's go eat." He wasn't hungry, not for food anyway, but enough had been said. When they came to the path into the trees back to the cabin, Padraig hoisted her up in his arms. She went willingly, hooking her hands behind his neck.

"This is awful chivalrous of you, Mr. O'Neale."

He smiled down at her. "The least I can do."

Chapter 25

The closer she came to climax, the harder Gillian sucked. It wasn't a choice—it just happened naturally. She'd never done this before, but with a 1969 Mustang for their ride, Padraig must have had it on the brain. He'd suggested it, and she was glad he did. It was one of the most unselfish sexual acts she'd ever participated in, giving on both sides with the benefit of also taking.

When he stopped licking, she pulled away, too, waiting for his next move. It was difficult in a way, this oral sex, when really she only wanted him to be inside her. But then he suckled again, soft, gentle, lovely, and she pecked his length in return, small licks on the top like an ice cream cone.

It must have been his undoing as his attention to her clit became more aggressive, faster, harder. When she came, she groaned with his dick in her mouth, sucking as hard as she could until he yelled to her, "I'm going to come." He yanked out and she milked his length until every drop was out.

"Holy shit, that was..."

Still exhausted from their performance, Gillian could barely move to shift around into his arms. "Awesome?"

He chuckled. "I was going to say fucking fantastic."

"That, too." She snuggled her butt into his groin to prompt spooning, and he complied, throwing his arm around her shoulder and linking his fingers with hers, aligning his legs to the bend of her own.

Within moments, Padraig's soft snoring blew wisps of her hair across her cheek. It tickled, and she wanted to scratch, but didn't want to disengage from their embrace and wake him. She couldn't sleep, but waited until his breathing deepened, then gently slipped from their spoon.

Naked, she grabbed the quilt that was folded and lay over the top of the old white rocking chair in the corner of the room. She wrapped it around herself and quietly left, leaving the door open so she made no sound. Flinching at the click of the sliding door, she slipped out and closed it, leaving a tiny gap to get back in.

September and she could already see her breath in the air. She sat on the first step and tugged the quilt tighter around her. She lay down on her back, her feet still on the second step, her knees bent. It caused her feet to get cold, but the view was worth it. The stars were so much brighter here than in Traverse City, and she soaked the night up.

Having taken an astronomy class her first year in college, she used to be able to identify most of the constellations in the sky, but now she'd forgotten all but a few main ones like Orion and Cassiopeia. Neither was in the little slice of sky open above the trees. But it was still beautiful, and wondrous.

When they were little, they had always begged their dad to let them stay up late enough to see the stars. And this far north, that was as late as eleven at the height of summer. By the time Andrew was in his teens, he was no longer interested, and year after year, he'd grown in his own direction until he no longer wanted to come to the cabin with her and Dad. He'd stayed home to hang out with his friends instead.

Since Gillian couldn't follow the way he went—sports, girls, gaming, and partying later on, Gillian had veered her path in the opposite direction. Like *Ha! I didn't want to hang out with you anymore, anyway.* And they had never reconnected as adults, and that was the hardest part for Gillian, her deepest regret. How she would have liked to know him as the man he had become. Not just an older brother that she adored, that she had worshiped in her own way.

When she allowed herself to think of Andrew, the emotion became too much and tears slipped from her eyes. The starry night blurred to white dots.

She inhaled deeply and shifted her focus to the man sleeping inside. Imagining him, all dark edges but soft lines, eased her breathing. Gillian had thought the more she got to know him, the more his air of mystery would fade and the intensity she felt every time she saw him would lessen. But it hadn't. He was the last person she would have imagined herself with but couldn't bear to think of the days after he left to return to Ireland.

An owl hooted, a long drawn out call for a mate. Or maybe a warning to the other critters that there was a bear nearby. Could be. They had plenty around here. But she was far too drained, emotionally and physically, to be afraid. Of course, any grunting noises, and she was out of there.

She hadn't heard Padraig approach, so when he sat down next to her on the top step, she jerked up to sitting, her hand stilling a heart that wanted to make a break out of the gates.

He wore his tracksuit pants and a T-shirt with bare feet and rumpled hair. "Are you okay?"

She brushed her face with the corner of the quilt. "Ah yeah, just couldn't sleep. I didn't mean to wake you."

"You didn't. I haven't been sleeping well the last few nights, anyway."

Their seclusion here in the woods, the surrounding darkness as black as ink, gave Gillian the courage to ask, "We're probably not at the right time for each other, are we?"

"Honestly, I'm not sure, but you've done more for me in the time I've been here than anyone has in my life."

"All that means is I'm a super-sap."

He chuckled. "You're one of the most wonderful people I've ever met."

"Oh shit, this sounds like the beginning of the talk."

"What talk is that?"

"Don't. You know what I mean."

"You told me once you don't like head games and I'm telling you honestly. You are better than any other woman I've met, and there have been loads."

"That makes me feel a heap better. So it's not just sex?"

"Fantastic sex."

"Yes, fantastic sex, but you're, you're…a testosterone turd."

"Wait a tick, that sounds naff."

"It does, doesn't it? Sorry, it's what I used to call my brother and his friends."

"I don't get that about Americans. You guys categorize everything, put everyone in little boxes with labels, compartmentalize. We don't really do that in Ireland. And Jaysus, we're adults. Too old for that shite."

"You're so right."

"And you're just you, Gill, sexy as fuck, funny, smart. All the Blues think you're class. You could have picked any of 'em. Why me? It's not like I was much of a gentleman a few weeks ago."

"It was the accent."

"Thanks for being honest."

She laughed, but it died at her next thought. "When are you leaving?"

"Honestly, I don't know. I haven't heard anything from my agent, and I haven't a clue what else to do."

"You could stay here."

He turned, and even though the darkness cloaked his eyes, she had penetrated where she'd wanted the thought to go.

"I could."

She had nothing further to say so she laid her head on his shoulder. "Are you cold? I'd offer to share, but I'm naked as a jaybird underneath."

He wrapped his right arm around her and drew her close, both of them shuffling together in an awkward moment. "Nah, this is just a summer day in Ireland."

"Do you miss it?"

"Not right now."

"What about tomorrow?"

"Will you be here?"

She smiled, scuffing her foot across the worn step, pushing flecks of old paint over the edge. "I will."

"Then I won't miss it."

His words warmed her through, and she bit her lip in happiness. She didn't know what to say in return, so asked, "How are you feeling?"

He nodded, taking a small stone from the step and chucking it into the woods. "Anxious. Tense. I want the meds."

"You will for a while, I hear. You might crave it for days, even months from now."

"Will you be here?"

She wanted to laugh, but couldn't. "I will."

He kissed her on the head. "Hey, you're not such a bad trumpet player."

She laughed then. "Thanks."

Chapter 26

When Gillian had dropped him off at the house late Monday night, he'd clung to the door handle, fighting the urge to ask if he could stay at her place. As if she sensed his distress, she'd laid a hand on his thigh and said, "It'll be okay."

That he doubted, but he'd removed himself from her car, anyway. Now he was on his own, and mornings were the worst. As promised, she'd kept his mind off his withdrawal the entire weekend. When he'd become agitated, she'd soothed him. When he didn't want to eat, she'd made him. When he had been a complete shit, she'd ignored him, or redirected him like a parent would a child. In the moment, he couldn't see what she did. Only after the drama had passed did he understand that she'd helped him through the dark patch.

Even when he'd roared at her to take him to a doctor, she'd simply slipped out the door without looking back, yelling over her shoulder for him to chop some wood. Hours later, she had returned from her nature hike and he had, in all his tension, cut and stacked fifty cords of firewood.

This morning all he wanted to do was crawl back into the safe arms that he knew. Gillian. His haven in the shitstorm of his life. His Guinness to a parched Irish throat. His paracetamol to a hangover. His...everything.

But it was time to try this on his own. And give back what he had taken. It had been a couple days since he'd seen her, and his addiction to her was stronger than the oxycodone. He couldn't wait to see her tonight.

He rolled out of bed with little pain. Only a pop and some ligament creaks, but he could deal with that. First stop a music store, some shopping to do, and then cook his arse off. Padraig had never done anything like this before. Feck, he hoped she didn't hate it.

The day flew by as Padraig rushed around town in Del's clunker. He couldn't remember when he had cooked anything more than bangers and mash at home, often eating on the road or with the boys. But Gillian was worth the effort.

As he crowded through the front door overloaded with bags, Del came down the stairs and grabbed some from him. "You ready for tonight?"

"I'd say so. What time is it?" Padraig led them both into the kitchen and set his shopping on the table.

Del set the rest on the counter. "Just after three."

"Seriously? Feck."

"You want some help?"

Padraig overturned bags, everything clunking onto the table. He caught a rolling can before it could tumble to the floor. "Nah, thanks. You and Rory have done enough. I can get this."

"Okay, bro, make sure you keep the blinds closed to the sliding door, eh? Like we discussed."

Padraig unloaded the bags on the counter and grabbed the lentils. "Definitely. I'll tap on the window when we are ready."

"About an hour and a half still?"

"Yeah, I'd say so, but if it goes badly, I might need rescuing sooner so have everyone ready about seven."

Del clapped Padraig on the back as he set a pot on the stove. "It won't go badly. Not unless you burn everything."

"Nice thought, thanks. Hand me that cutting board, will ya?"

"I thought you didn't want my help?"

"That's it, and then bugger off."

Del laughed. "Look at you all nervous. It's cute."

Padraig banged a mallet against the peeled garlic clove. "Fuck off, would you?"

Laughing, Del slipped out of the kitchen, and Padraig got to work chopping onion. He considered the menu classy and cultural, and most importantly vegetarian, but now loomed too complicated. Argh! Okay, deep breath. He was starting all wrong. First, the soup, then the main, then the dessert.

He ran his finger down the soup recipe and started again.

When he looked at the clock next, it was after five. Feck, that was intense. After he slid the crumble into the oven, he scrambled to load the dishwasher while wiping down the counters. Another ten minutes gone. He set the table with dishes that matched and finally placed the opened bottle of red wine and candles on the table. Would he light them now? Another glance at the clock. Yep, he'd be pushing it to be out of the shower and to the door when she arrived.

He searched all the drawers for matches or a lighter. Nothing. He even checked the overhead cupboards, thinking the lads might keep things differently. Maybe stuck in some spare bowls or something. But no such luck. The loud clicking of the kitchen clock had him about to explode. And less than a week without the meds! He took a seat at a kitchen chair, closed his eyes, and slowed his breathing. In through the nose and out through the mouth, just like Gillian had taught them in yoga. The worst time in the world to be jonesing for a fix, but the urges had always come on with stress.

After a few more breaths, an idea came to him. Yes! They had a gas stove here unlike Ireland. He grabbed a piece of paper towel and twisted it into a taper. He lit the end on the stove burner and walked the flaming torch over to the candles. The paper burned faster than he thought, and he'd barely lit both candles when the flames were licking at his fingers. He took one step and tossed it into the sink, and then sprayed the shit out of the mess with the hand nozzle.

He waved a hand in front of his face. The air stunk from the burning, so he cracked a window and ran up the stairs. Padraig had barely stepped out of the shower and dressed when the doorbell rang.

Breathless, his hair still dripping, he yanked open the door.

Gillian stood there in a strapless red and white polka dot dress tied at the waist with a red sash, a bottle of wine in her hand, the green Mustang on the street behind her.

What a sight. And there was something quite different about her, but in his rush and nerves, he didn't make the connection until he had shut the door behind her.

"Wow, your hair is straight."

Gillian raised her hand to her hair and grabbed a strand to twist, but then stopped short and dropped her hand to her side. "Yeah, for the special occasion. It takes me forever to do, so usually I can't be bothered."

"It looks great." He grabbed her hand. "You look great."

She clutched the pendant around her neck, the one he recognized had hung from the car. "Thanks."

"Well, come on then. I hope you're hungry, like." He pulled her into the kitchen and seated her at the table before he took the chance to look at her again. She was gorgeous. Del was right. He was nervous as hell. He placed the Irish soda bread in the middle of the table, a bowl of soup first in front of her, and then in his spot across from her. "If it's too much, I'm sure Rory and Del will be happy for the leftovers." He placed his napkin on his lap. As he was about to dig into his soup, Gillian interrupted.

"Padraig, look at me."

He let his spoon sink into the soup and raised his head. At that moment, he realized water was still dripping from his wet hair down the back of his shirt, so he used his napkin to wipe his neck.

"This is amazing." Gillian gestured at the table. "Everything you've done. It must have taken you forever."

Padraig shrugged, his face heating with her praise. "It was no bother."

"It was." She grabbed his hand from across the table and squeezed. "Thank you."

He summoned a deep breath and a smile. "You're welcome."

"Before we start eating, will I pour us a glass of wine?"

"Oh, shit, sure. I mean, yes, let me do it." He was botching this up big time. Smooth and sophisticated international rugby star had obviously left on a plane back to Ireland already. Thank God, he had thought to uncork it earlier to breathe so he didn't have to struggle with that now. He poured only a quarter of a glass for Gillian and a half glass for himself. He didn't want to presume for her, but it was the thought that counted. Sure, he'd barely given her more wine than a Catholic communion service, less if you were a sinner and went around for a second blessing.

She raised her glass. "To better days."

Padraig repeated her toast. "To better days. Slainte."

After taking a small sip, she tasted her soup in front of her.

"I know it looks like vomit, but it's my mum's favorite."

Gillian laughed out her nose and then covered her mouth with her napkin. "It's delicious. What's it called?"

"Colcannon soup. Cabbage, potatoes, and leeks. I made sure the whole meal was vegetarian." He pointed to the loaf in front of him. "And this is Irish soda bread. It came out a bit harder than I had hoped. I forgot to slice it, but we can just tear pieces off. It's great for dipping." When Padraig tried to pull the loaf apart, it wouldn't budge. Even digging in his nails, the bread wouldn't separate. He tapped it on the table. Solid as a rock.

Gillian laughed. "Just the soup is fine."

Padraig groaned and threw back his head. A feckin' awful start.

"Leave it there on the table, and it will be our centerpiece." She gave him a cheeky grin, which made him laugh.

"The next course will be much better. I promise. I already checked."

Gillian reached her hand over the table again, so he grabbed on and held. "This is all...so nice. You didn't have to do any of this."

Padraig had to admit the ambience was good. With the blinds closed over the back sliding doors and the candles lit, the room reeked romance. He'd forgotten to turn on some music, but there would be plenty of that later. "I did. I wanted to repay you for everything you've done for me."

"Repayment wasn't necessary or expected."

"I know. Still the same...I wanted to."

"Well...thank you again."

"My pleasure. Now, let's eat."

When they were done with the soup, Padraig cleared the bowls and dished up the main. The presentation wasn't great with the pie splatted onto the plates, but at least it was cooked properly.

As they dug in, Padraig began, "So do you want to talk about Andrew?"

A spoonful of lentil Shepherd's pie in her mouth and she groaned, letting the utensil drop to the plate.

"Not really."

Padraig swallowed, the food too hot burning his throat, but he forged ahead. "This is all part of my helping you now. I'm here to listen if you want to talk."

Gillian pushed the food around on her plate. "There's not much to say. Andrew overdosed. He's dead, and I'm still here."

"You sound angry."

"I am."

"Why?"

She finished chewing before she replied. "Because it's easier to be."

"At just Andrew, or...?"

"I know where you're leading, Irish, and I guess you're right."

"I am?"

"Yeah, I blame his dick friends, too."

"Yeah?"

"If Andrew had only used the brain God had given him, he wouldn't be dead now. But nooo...he had to latch onto that bunch and follow them into Hell." She had started out eating like he'd shown her before, the European way, but at some point in her anger she had dropped the knife and was shoveling in the food with only her fork.

"That's a bit harsh."

She sighed. "I know it is. I'm just angry."

"I can see that. Were they some of his mates from school?"

"Yep. I guess he'd started way back in high school, but we hadn't a clue. It just got progressively worse over the years. His friends weren't even rugby players, just gym rats."

"I go to the gym." Padraig needed to tread carefully. He wanted her to open up but not ruin the evening. The best part was yet to come. "Almost every day."

She went to curl one of her ringlets of hair around her finger like she normally did when she was thinking, but must have realized again that her straight hair didn't allow for the soother. She bit her lip instead. "I know. I'm being dumb."

"Nah, but perhaps placing blame a bit."

"It's funny. In high school, Andrew and I grew apart. Him doing his thing and me doing the opposite, but then when I was helping out the football team at college with their physical therapy, I remember these two guys talking in the locker room about how they'd 'tea-bagged' one of the freshman players. I didn't think much of it until they told some third guy it was placing their balls on the guy's head when he was passed out drunk. And then they took pictures. Absolute class."

Padraig stifled a laugh with his napkin. The oven buzzer went off. Saved by the bell. "Hold that thought." He pulled out the crumble and stabbed a piece of rhubarb like his mum had told him. Done. Hopefully to perfection. "Sorry, go ahead."

Gillian had finished her pie and laid her fork and knife across her plate. "How mortifying for that young freshman, and that brainless act reconfirmed my belief that they were all idiots. Cruel, mindless idiots. And I vowed from that day on to only help children and the elderly. But then the opportunity came along with the Blues…"

When Padraig collected their dinner plates from the table, Gillian reached across and poured herself some more wine. In one gulp, she finished the glass. Well, she was letting it out at least.

He set the rhubarb crumble in front of her. "I hope you like this. The topping is oats." He winked at her. "For health and all."

She must have realized she'd become heated and had withdrawn again. Her voice came out in a whisper. "It looks delicious."

Padraig sat down again and cut into his dessert. "If Andrew was anything like you, I doubt he was stupid. Intelligence and addiction aren't related. Sure, there's a long list of genius addicts, and I'm not just talking about the rock stars like Cobain." He kept his eyes on his food and plowed ahead. "Did you know Freud was a coke addict? And Tchaikovsky was on the drink constantly." His defense wasn't just for Andrew, but himself, too. He couldn't stop. "It's not easy getting that monkey off your back."

At this point, his mouth was dry and his throat tight, the last of the crumble barely making it down his gullet. When he went for a drink of wine, it was then he noticed Gillian's tears. They were barely discernible under her glasses, but the candlelight reflected off the tear tracks, shiny like fish scales. He should have stopped.

She stood abruptly, and his heart stopped with the horror. She was going to leave. "I'm sorry. Forgive me."

But instead, she walked around the table and climbed into his lap. Hugging him, she said, "I know that now. I'm sorry, too."

He held her in silence, rubbing her back as she had often done for him. "I'm so sorry. I didn't mean for things to go this direction. I just wanted you to know I'm here to listen if you need to talk. And then things got a bit personal…"

Still clinging to him, she laughed. "I noticed."

He drew her away and placed a gentle kiss to her mouth. "Hey, I have a surprise for you."

"This whole night has been a big surprise."

He slowly unwrapped her from his body and stood, sliding Gillian off his lap to the floor. "But this one is the best yet. If you'll help me arrange some of this furniture…"

Padraig had already placed one of the kitchen chairs by the sink when he glanced up to find her still standing there, a bit bemused. "C'mon, get the other side of the table there."

She did as told and then stood off to the side while Padraig moved the one chair back in front of the table and the other three in a semicircle facing that one, only a couple meters away. He took her hand and led her to the single chair. "Have a seat. I hope you enjoy." He was so nervous he couldn't look back at her as he grabbed his tin whistle from the cupboard and went to the sliding door where he knocked three times.

Ah, the lads were there, just like they had said they would be. Del and Rory followed Padraig to the three chairs where they sat down with their musical instruments in hand. Padraig with his whistle that he had actually bought, Del with his Pringle can he had turn into a shaker by adding rice, and Rory with his flattened Weetabix cereal box and wooden spoon that he was going to use as a bodhran, a type of Irish drum also used by the Scots.

With a nod from Padraig and a whistle intro, Del started in on the first verse of "Green Fields of France," one of the few songs all the Blues players knew for the Dropkick Murphy version, and luckily, one of the few songs Padraig remembered from his youth. Printed musical notes from online, a couple YouTube videos, and a few hours practice, and the song had come back to him.

Rory's bodhran set a nice slow pace, and at the chorus, he joined his voice with Del's who added his shaker, a nice addition to the refrain. Padraig's whistle kept the melody. And so far the boys were taking it seriously, even with their makeshift instruments.

He didn't dare look at her for nerves, and he didn't want to miss a note. The best part was coming, and feck, he hoped the lads weren't drunk. Or maybe hoped they were. Nothing like a pint to get the creative juices flowing.

As practiced, at the beginning of the second stanza, Padraig heard the sliding door open and Jimmy's voice join the others. And then Shano, Damian, Dave, Mitch, Kevin, Austin, Josh and Champ. Even Dick had agreed, although he was probably doing it for the free beer. Padraig had put a tab behind the bar at the Yacht Club for any of the boys who'd agreed to their little musical. But most of them didn't need too much convincing and had wanted to anyway since Gillian had helped all of them as much as she had Padraig.

As their numbers grew, the song became rowdier, but Padraig went with it, picking up the tempo on his whistle. The boys filed in behind Padraig, Del, and Rory. Their singing was so loud, it had drowned out the instruments. Some boys were getting into it, swinging their arms and busting out the words.

He let the boys finish the last chorus a capella, left his whistle on his chair, and made his way over to Gillian.

She had taken her glasses off and was wiping her tears with a dirty dinner napkin. He pulled her into his arms for a big hug. Her feet came off the ground, and he swung her back and forth.

When the last note finally died away, Padraig asked, "Well, what do you think? Not bad for a bunch of rugby players, eh?"

She kissed him sound on the mouth. "That was fucking fantastic."

Chapter 27

The Blues were down by ten, seventy-seven minutes and forty-six seconds on the clock.

Padraig had played in loads of games where his team came back with less time than what they had. But these boys weren't used to pushing through to the end, and any one play could change the favor in a minute. As much as Del tried to keep their spirits up, it was almost as if they'd already given up. It was pissing rain and cold, having gone from sunny and warm at the beginning of the week to frigid by the end, a northwest wind coming down off the lake.

In terms of dedication, the Blues were as strong a team as Padraig had ever played with, but today, for some reason, the forwards and backs didn't click. Passing was sloppy and runs were short and choppy, no fluidity in their movement across the pitch. If they gained any ground, it was through small plays, gutting it out. They were off their groove, and everyone knew it.

Except for Rory. The kid shined in bad weather. He was Scottish, so that explained much of it, but it was more than that. It was as if he reveled in the hope, as if his entire life that's where he'd been, always looking up.

Del kept yelling at everyone to re-tuck their shirts, pull up their socks. Something was up. Gillian stayed close to Coach's side. On Coach's other stood a mature gentleman. There was something about the way he kept asking Coach questions, kept pointing at the pitch that didn't sit right with Padraig. But somehow he was familiar. He stood with legs spread, arms crossed over his chest like an arrogant bastard. Maybe Coach had brought in a consultant. It was not uncommon over in Europe to bring in a fresh perspective, but they had the money behind them there.

Gusts of wind blew hard across the pitch, hindering their kicking game. So they had to stick to running the ball, which didn't give them the distance over the pitch they needed for two tries. They were inching along, gaining a measly meter here and there.

Padraig had been in this position so many times, it barely rocked him anymore. When he was younger, he played poorly in close matches until he learned to tame his anxiety...until he understood there was always another game to play.

The Tri-City Barbarians were currently ranked top of their division. The Irish liked to be the underdogs. They played better when they went into a game where they weren't expected to win. It was as if they played up to the talent they competed against.

At a mad scramble in the mud, Padraig overturned possession for the Blues after stripping the ball one-on-one from the runner before he could release to his team. Instead of passing the ball to the inside centre who had run up beside him, Padraig plowed ahead, gaining a few meters. It took five of their men to bring him down. But too fast, and where was his backup then? No one there to release the ball to.

Under the pile of bodies, he waited for each of them to peel off, his face smashed into the wet earth, the ball still held tightly into the nook of his arm. He grunted when one player's knee banged his head on the way up.

Above the buzz in his ears, Kevin yelled, "You should have passed, Irish."

Yeah, he should have. Since he hadn't released the ball, now it went back to Tri-City's scrum.

When the last Tri-City player was off, Padraig pushed up with his arms only to smash back down to the ground in pain. "Fuck!" His back was on fire. He could barely move his legs. They had already started setting the scrum, when someone finally noticed he wasn't getting up. The referee whistled and called the injury timeout.

He had mobility in his arms, but every time he tried to rise, the same searing pain froze his back and hips, a bolt of lightning down his left leg.

Del approached first and squatted next to him. "How ya doin?"

Padraig wiped some dirt away from the corner of his mouth. "Not great."

When Gillian approached and knelt next to him, Del moved away.

"Your back?" She talked quietly under her breath in the soothing way of hers. Her professional voice, he called it, but right now it was the best sound in the world.

He nodded.

With gentle motion, she rolled him onto his back. Padraig growled in pain. As she'd done before, she performed the AI-joint maneuver, bracing his right leg on her shoulder. He pressed down his left knee into her cupped hands.

"Any better?"

"At least it's no longer in my leg. Now more the middle of my back."

"Okay, arch your back up and squeeze it like you mean it."

There he was tightening his butt cheeks in the middle of the field, every single set of eyes on him. Coach, the Blues, the Tri-City players, the fans and friends on the sideline. *For feck sake.*

"It's not working, Gill. You might have to help me off the pitch."

"Have faith."

Faith? He'd enough of that growing up in Catholic Ireland. Now, his only religion was rugby. Or it used to be.

"I want you to get in the cobra position."

Fucking yoga now? He fancied the knickers off her, but wondered about her sanity at times. When he didn't budge, she directed his movements, rolling him onto his belly, then pulling his shoulders back so his chest lifted off the ground.

What he wanted to do was get up. He wanted everyone's eyes off him, out here, struggling with his pain demons, but he was afraid. Afraid everyone would know. Afraid he'd look a loser.

"Now, come up to standing."

"I don't think I can."

"You can."

Padraig rested there, inhaling the smell of wet grass and earth, trying to build the courage to move.

Gillian smacked him on the bum. "I know what's missing. The special magic. The music therapy." She proceeded to hum.

He couldn't help but laugh. "Stop already. I'm up!" And he was moving, into a squat, and then with a final push, on his feet. He walked back and forth to get the muscles moving again. And sure enough, even though his back still was tight, the pain had mostly gone.

Not the most conventional therapist in the world, but God, he loved her. If there hadn't been a hundred pair of eyes on them, he would have gladly grabbed her up and kissed her right there. When she caught his eye, he smiled and nodded, as much a thank you as he could give her right now. He'd save his appreciation for bed later. Now that his back was better.

Like with the other players, she waited for him to signal he was good, and she walked off the pitch.

A whistle blew and everyone moved to set for the scrum. Not the best position to start in, but he trusted Gillian. Before Padraig bound with Austin, Del approached, cupping his hand on Padraig's shoulder. "All right, mate?"

Padraig smiled. "All good, Del, let's finish this."

With that, Del rallied the boys, shouting encouragements. And in that moment, Padraig felt the momentum shift. The energy in a game was tangible, in the air and in the movements of the players. Not only on the pitch, but fans could feel it, too. He'd been told that even viewers at home often knew the moment when the change happened, the transfer of the rugby spirits to their side. It was contagious, and each member of the Blues buzzed with the new vigor.

The scrum was the opponent's but the Blues pushed hard, no one harder than Padraig, and they moved over the ball, winning it back. Mitch fed it off to the center, who again released it to Dick and then on to Rory. And he decided to kick. *Please, let the ball fly.*

It was better than Padraig could imagine, out of the wind, a low ground kick like you'd see in soccer, and out of play at the twenty-two meter line. The lineout was the other team's, but the boys around him strutted now with a different purpose, and along with Del, Padraig rallied them with calls and swats on the backside. "C'mon, boys, get in there!"

A few of the lads eyed him like he'd gone mad, like Captain Ahab in Moby Dick. He probably looked it, his hair wild in the wind, walking with a slight limp as though he had a peg leg. And like the man on that ship, his passion—no his obsession—had been his undoing.

The clock had counted up to thirty-seven minutes. Plenty of time until they reached the horn at forty, plus a bit of spare for injury time. He shouted again to the team. "C'mon, lads, rally up!" The last couple of months had been moping and half-arsed efforts. But he'd make it up to them now. Like he used to do with his squad back in Munster, he joked, he laughed, and pounded his chest like a gorilla. And with the wind in their sails now, the boys latched on. They could feel the victory, too.

The Tri-City hooker threw short, and the other team tucked the ball into a rolling maul, surging forward, inching away at the green. Exactly what the Blues would have done to burn the seconds on the clock.

Padraig latched onto the ball carrier, pushing with everything he had. Dell communicated their need with the look of an eye, which Padraig understood and shoved harder, yelling for the boys to do the same.

When the whistle came, the Blues celebrated. The call? The Tri-City's maul had failed to move forward. No motion ahead and they had the scrum just past the twenty meter line.

Padraig tapped each of the forwards, a finger to their shoulder or back as they set in their huddle. Like he did back home. It was a ritual he performed with his pack in Ireland. It was a sign to them. *Together now, lads.*

Mitch fed the ball into the middle. The groans of the first three rows were finally, again, music to his ears. They moved in one motion, a unit as strong as anyone would find, pushing forward to move over the ball.

When it was clear, Champ passed out to Del, lucky number thirteen, and that's the last Padraig witnessed. His job was to support the runner, be there and ready for a pass if needed. And he did his job, as good or better than for Munster or the Irish squad. With the rain pelting down, he could have stepped back onto the field at Aviva Stadium. The cloudy skies and wind, the hush of the play, because when he was in the zone, those sixty-five thousand fans didn't exist. Only the play.

The whistle sounded and the roars went up. Del had scored a try.

After celebrating with the boys, he looked to the sidelines for Gillian. She, too, was jumping up and down, hugging Coach. Then she did a little dance, like an Irish jig, and Padraig ached to walk off the pitch, drag her behind him, and leave it all behind. Because now he knew, there was so much more to life.

Rory sent the kick off long and high. Not bad for thirty-mile per hour winds. Padraig made a mental note to make the boy breakfast. Even with the wind behind them, it was still a damn good kick. The Tri-City full back took it in goal beyond the try line and kicked instead of running it out, but the wind was at the Blues' back, and the ball hung high, suspended in the air. The Blues rushed forward, once again feeling the potential hanging like the ball, that this game could still be theirs.

It was a collision of bodies, each man's goal the same—get the fucking ball. But Tri-City won, their left wing grabbing it out of the sky. As if they shared the same gut, Padraig could feel the disappointment in each man around him. But in mere seconds, their pack stormed down on the left wing, and the inexperienced young man ran the ball out of touch.

The lineout was theirs. Time on the clock. Thirty-eight minutes, fifty-two seconds.

Shano wiped the ball, then passed the towel to Gillian. For a second, her gaze met Padraig's, and he read the same excitement in her eyes. Like she'd told him, she believed in the club. And so should he.

Del stepped up to Shano and gave him the play, but it was lost in the wind to Padraig. Jimmy leaned forward and whispered into his ear, "The cabin."

What the fuck did that mean?

Shano launched the ball. It gave them only seconds to react, but Padraig was on it. He was the jumper. Like in the river, Jimmy and Dave hoisted him in the air. At first, Padraig struggled against their hold, so foreign from what he knew, what he understood to be right. He was leaning too far to center, but with a pinch at his leg, he straightened, and the ball came true.

As expected, the Tri-City's line contested the throw, but the boys still held him suspended, and with a push and a war cry, Padraig was launched over the top of the opposing team, ball still in hand. He rolled down the bodies, head over heels and landed on his feet.

Whether it was surprise or uncertainty, men stilled in their spots. Time moved in measured frames around him. But he was on his feet and moving. Not fast for his size, but few in front of him, and he could see the line. Bold and beautiful, the sacred and intangible force drew him toward the goal.

Out of the corner of his eye, forms approached from both sides. He searched for streaks of blue, but all was a haze. The decision, whether he understood it on a conscious level or not, had already been made. Blood lust surged, and beyond anything else, he believed he would get over the line.

Just before the try line, an opposing player latched onto his left arm, dragging him down, and then another at his back. But he still pounded forward and nothing else mattered at that moment but the line. And the ball over the line.

A body hit him hard in the gut, and he lost his wind, doubling over. Stretching, he used all of his frame and launched himself, ball in the lead hand, toward the line. Like Superman.

He landed with an *umph* and had barely caught his breath before a hand tugged hard on his jersey, yanking him to his feet.

There had been no sound, and then, in an instant, noise. Shouts and players all around him, tugging and slapping. He'd scored the try.

The Blues swarmed together, their heads down into one gigantic hug. Padraig would have scoffed if he hadn't been so damn happy. A month ago, he would have disentangled and left for the sidelines, but today he was in the center of it, and the mass of bodies moved like a giant amoeba on the pitch, morphing and changing in shape as some players pulled one way, other lads another.

The Blues conversion attempt went wide, but it didn't matter. They had still won. The final whistle blew, and they raised their voice in song, the same one from the cabin.

When Del finally broke the pack to line up for the other team, Padraig strained to find Gillian. She was packing her gear up in a large duffel, bent over, facing away from the pitch.

As a few stragglers ran past, slapping him on the back for the try, Padraig picked up his pace until he was jogging toward her. At the last minute, she noticed him and straightened just as he rushed to her and grabbed her off the ground.

"Hey!" she shouted, and even though she put up a struggle, he silenced her with his mouth. When she finally returned his kiss, she softened, and he set her on the ground, still holding her. They were snogging right in the middle of everyone, and he didn't give a fuck. Only Gillian.

A loud clearing of throat broke them apart, but neither looked away. Padraig held her gaze until she smiled, and he knew then, that it was all good.

Del punched him in the shoulder. "Coach wants to see you. Like right now."

He finally broke his gaze from Gillian but didn't dare let her go. "Now?"

"That's what he said."

She squeezed his hand. "Go on. I'll be right here when you're finished, and we can head over to the cabin."

He gave her one last kiss, then turned to follow Del. He walked with Padraig to midfield, then pointed toward Coach and the smug bastard behind the goal. "Good luck, mate."

"You're not coming?"

"Nope, he said it was private."

Jaysus. Now what?

The man and Coach were deep in discussion, but when Padraig approached, they both stopped and turned.

Coach didn't hesitate and directed an introduction to the man next to him. "As you know, this is Padraig O'Neale, second-row."

Janey Mack. *Holy shit.* Could it be? He pumped the man's hand. "Good to meet you."

Chapter 28

Oh, shit. Had she just parked over someone's grave marker? Gillian shifted the car and reversed back out the way she had come. She had tried to park parallel to the gravesite, but that wasn't working as Andrew's stone was smack jammers in the middle of a ton of other graves. Her parents had decided on this impersonal graveyard for his final resting place instead of her suggestion, which was to have him cremated and his ashes sailed out to the middle of the Bay.

That was more Andrew.

But then, she couldn't have shown him the Mustang. So there was a reason for everything.

"Did I hit anything?"

Padraig turned in his seat, wrenching his head over his shoulder. "Nah. Just a couple of gravestones. But you did smash some flower bouquets."

"Grrrr…" She drove forward again, nosing the beast in front first, as close to his headstone as she could get. The rear of the car jutted out into the drive that circled the cemetery. She'd move it if anyone needed to get by.

She had spiffed up in a light floral dress for the occasion, except her Converse, and had worn her hair down instead of the braid because Padraig said it was beautiful. This was the first time she'd been out to the cemetery since the funeral, and she was glad Padraig had offered to come with her.

She wiped her sweaty palms on her dress again.

He grabbed her hand and squeezed. "Do you want me to come with you or stay here?"

"Give me a minute, will you?"

"Sure." He bowed his back as he searched for something in his pocket, then drew out a long row of beads with a crucifix at the end. "Would you like to borrow my rosary?"

Gillian smiled at his thoughtfulness. "Nah, that's all right. You keep it."

She walked to Andrew's grave and sat cross-legged beside his headstone. The grass was long, and colored leaves littered the space around her, reminding her of Fruity Pebbles cereal. Probably from the maple tree only a handful of feet away. It was Indian summer in Northern Michigan, when the season went out in a fight, warming the days but cooling the nights, playing with their minds, leading them to believe that winter would never come. The leaves had already started falling from the trees, but a tepid wind still blew from Lake Michigan.

His grave was bare—no gifts or flowers or pictures. Her mum didn't believe in any of that except leaving him oatmeal raisin cookies on his birthday every year, and that was in the spring. The animals had scampered away with the sweets ages ago.

"Well, I got her going, Andy." Gillian motioned at the car with a stretch of her arm. "What do you think? Looking pretty good, huh?"

Gillian paused, allowing time for his response, then continued, "Sorry, I haven't been out to visit you in a while...okay, well never, but..."

Her elbow on her knee, she rested her hand in her chin. "I hate you, you know. What stupid asshole takes too many drugs? Okay...that sounds horrible. I love you as much as I hate you. Is that better?"

A car approached from the direction of the gate and slowed to park about a hundred feet away. Glad she didn't have to move the Mustang, Gillian turned back to Andrew. "I was thinking of calling her Irish. The Mustang. She is green after all. And before you tell me it doesn't sound like a girl's name, it definitely suits her. And since you can't really argue, that's what it's gonna be."

Doors slammed, and Gillian turned to see an older couple, the woman with a cane, start to walk slowly along a cement path to a section of the cemetery scattered with small American flags.

Pulling at the grass made her feel better so she did it again, grabbing chunks and ripping them out, then letting the wind carry them from her open palm.

"You're probably going to roll over, but guess who I'm dating?"

The noise of passing cars filled the void of silence.

"Go on. Guess."

Nothing, and Gillian had started to feel stupid. Everyone had told her it was therapeutic to come visit his grave and talk to him, but she just felt ridiculous.

"Well, I'll tell you." She paused for effect. "A big, buff athlete." Another pause. "You don't believe me? Well, it's true. He's a rugby player, so you'd approve. Not that I give a shit if you do or not, but he plays for the Blues. He's from Ireland so that's my saving grace. He's in the car waiting for me. He came here with me." She backpedaled. "For me."

Her legs had cramped, which was unlike her with all her yoga practice, so she unfolded her legs and stood. "Anyway, I've got a man in my life now. Not sure if he is going to stay or go, but it's a start, right?"

An idea popped into her head, and she headed back to the car. Through the window, she asked Padraig, "Will you hand me the Rubik's cube in the glove box?"

He retrieved it without questioning what she was doing. Instead, he asked, "Are you okay?"

Gillian nodded and took the cube from him. Before she could pull her hand away, Padraig grabbed her wrist and kissed her fingers. "Give a shout if you need me."

"I'll only be a minute more."

She and Padraig had both tried to figure out the damn thing, getting all the colors on the right sides. As determined as she was, they could get no more than two sides, the white and the blue. So she had messed it up again since only two finished sides looked wonky. It was beautiful in its chaotic colors, she thought, beautiful in its non-perfection. And a treasure for him once again.

Gillian laid the Rubik's cube at the center of the headstone. She dusted her bum of grass leaves. "Glad you like Irish. She's gorgeous, isn't she? I'm very proud of us."

As Gillian turned to leave, she noticed the old couple watching her. Too far to read their expressions, she waved quickly and hopped into the car. Over the large hood of the V8, Andrew's headstone wasn't visible, only the tree behind it, but she spoke with conviction. "I'll talk to you later, okay?"

Padraig seemed to realize she wasn't speaking to him and didn't say a word. He must have been getting used to all her strangeness—that it didn't faze him she was talking to the dead while he sat right next to her.

She reversed up onto the drive and then set the car in park. Without glancing back, she gunned the engine for Andrew, then gasped when she remembered the old couple.

Padraig laughed. "Nothing like scaring the old folks to an early grave."

"Oops, shit." She cringed and drove away, laughing with him.

Epilogue

Gillian waited to the side while Padraig checked in at the American Airlines counter. Wearing only jeans and the Blues club hoodie, he could have passed for any traveler. The rugby season for this year had just finished a few weeks ago and he was already leaving. And she still didn't know if he'd be back. She'd hinted, oh, she'd fished for information from him on what his next plan was, but he had given her very little, undecided he had said, didn't know himself.

Boarding pass in hand, he sauntered over to her. She hid her nerves and sadness behind a brave smile.

Last night, they had cuddled while watching *Million Dollar Baby*. She had insisted they watch it before he left, but when the movie revealed the meaning behind his words on their first date, she had cried.

He'd barely said a word throughout the movie. She had lain with her legs across his lap, and he had touched her in sweet, minute caresses, starting with her toes, up her thighs, subtle gestures over her hips, but she still had squirmed.

For once, it hadn't ended in sex, and she was glad. She couldn't have handled the emotional intensity.

Gillian called to him. "Do you want to get a coffee before I leave?"

Throwing his arm around her shoulder, he turned her toward the cozy waiting area. "I'll get them." The airport was decorated like a north woods lodge—stone fireplace flanked by comfy chairs and small end tables with lamps, done in a Frank Lloyd Wright style. She'd lived in Traverse City almost her entire life, but had never really noticed. Her emotions were running so high her senses must have kicked in to keep up. Everything seemed magnified and dulled at the same time.

He retrieved their coffees and made his way back to Gillian who had taken a seat in an area in the corner. When he handed her the skinny latte, she spoke up. "You seem awful full of yourself today. Must be really looking forward to getting home."

Padraig placed his coffee on a table and rested his elbows to his knees. He scanned the room. "I am."

"Ya know, I'd love to go some day. I've always wanted to see Ireland."

He turned to smile at her. "I'm sure you'll get there." Padraig wasn't helping her crazy one bit. Perhaps karma for dragging him to the middle of nowhere and beating the living addiction out of him.

"Do you have someone picking you up at the other end?"

"Me ma. And she might bring my da along, too."

"Moms are great."

"They are."

They were walking tentative circles around each other with their small clipped words. Not wanting to push or prod, they would break the fragile threads on which they hung. Her gut was in bits, her head and heart the same.

"So what are your plans when you get back home?" she asked.

He shrugged, then blew out a long breath. "Not sure. Will see a few mates. Go out for pints. Get some shopping done. Haven't really thought that far ahead."

Their coffees sat on the table between them, growing cold. Gillian grabbed his hand and linked her fingers with his. "You'll keep in touch, right?"

"Of course. I'll text you from my Irish phone so you'll have my number. You can call anytime."

That was better. But when he bit his bottom lip, it seemed as if he regretted the words that had escaped.

"I might be a bit busy when I first get to Cork."

Oh, shit. He was already backpedaling. Gillian swallowed her disappointment. "Oh, right...well, we can email then."

"I need to sell my car for one."

She pinched her eyebrows in confusion.

"I need to pack up some boxes to get them shipped over here. Take care of my finances. Organize the rental of my apartment..."

She jerked so quickly to standing the chair bumped the coffee table, both cups tipping over. There was little spillage with the lids on, so Padraig righted them both and swiped the table with some napkins. Hands on her hips, she stood in front of him. "Why didn't you tell me?"

Over the airport speaker, a female voice, sounding overly happy and rehearsed, announced priority boarding for his flight to Chicago for first class, business, and passengers who needed special assistance. The announcement finished before he raised his full frame from his chair to stand directly in front of her, invading her personal space.

"Aw, c'mere to me." He pulled her into the wrap of his arms, resting his chin on her head. "Gill, I think I'm in love with you. I'm coming back. For the Eagles. For the Blues…" He paused. "But mostly, for you. I'm even thinking of getting a tattoo with Gill—"

"What?" Gillian tried to push away, but he pulled her back into his arms, firm around her waist and back, then lifted her off her feet until her face was level with his.

"I've been offered a position with the Eagles for the World Cup, and I'm going to take it. And I'll stay here and play for the Blues for a while. Until I grow too old and rickety." Padraig smiled. "You know Shano got a spot, too?"

"Seriously? You guys are going to play for the Eagles?"

He chuckled. "That we are."

He kissed her until she melted. When the kiss finally broke, she asked, "When are you coming back?"

"After Christmas."

"Does anyone else know?"

"Only Scotch and Del."

She pushed off him to land on her feet, but a clumsy fall of arms and legs. "They knew before me? When did this happen?"

"Hey now, miss, they had to know. I wanted to surprise you." He tried to draw her in again, but she stepped away.

"I'll need a place to stay…"

Hands on her hips, she made one distinct nod. "You better start looking."

He laughed, but then set a serious tone to his voice so she couldn't mistake his intentions. "I wanted to give you something… Ya know, so you think of me."

He handed her the Munster T-shirt out of his backpack, the one he'd worn when they went north to her cabin. It was folded, but a pungent odor wafted from the fabric. "I didn't even wash it…so you can smell me when I'm gone."

His pinched mouth and convulsing stomach muscles told her he was trying desperately to hold in his laughter.

"Lovely." She had tried to put on a Cork accent, but it came out sounding like "lowflee." It was an awful attempt, but it broke his straight face.

"I thought all the ladies loved the smell of their man close to them to feel safe and comforted when they miss 'em."

"Uh…no."

He exaggerated confusion with a dropped jaw. "What are ya sayin', like? You ungrateful knacker."

She punched him lightly in the gut. "What's that mean? Doesn't sound good."

"I'll let you find out when you come visit."

She couldn't wait. "When?"

"As soon as ya like."

"Okay, I'll book a flight for tomorrow. Will that give you enough time to get settled?"

He laughed. Behind him the line to the gate had diminished to only a few remaining passengers. "Here, I've got to get going. I'll call you as soon as I land."

Even knowing he was coming back, this was harder than she'd imagined. She already missed him and he was standing right in front of her. "I've got something for you, too." She handed him a bag with a box inside. "But you can't open it until you're on the plane."

Standing on her tiptoes, she gave him one last peck, then drew out his arm as she stepped away, giving it one last tug before she let it drop. "I'll see you in Ireland"— she gave him a big grin to take back with him—"or when you get back."

She left out the door as they announced general boarding for his flight. She couldn't help herself and watched him through the window as he picked up his duffel from the floor and moved toward the loading gate.

She wondered if he would wait until he boarded before opening her gift. She chuckled to herself at the irony. Padraig answered her question when he stepped out of the line and waved for the people behind him to pass. He dropped his bag and pulled out the box.

Inside were her very old, very used high-top black Converse. That he hated.

After he opened the lid, he threw back his head and laughed. She couldn't hear the sound, but she could feel it, as strong as if he was standing right next to her.

She realized then she had never said she loved him back. Nothing said "I care about you" better than a pair of stinky old shoes. She chuckled to herself. Nothing said "I love you" better than making that person laugh. Because, above all else, she wanted him to be happy, to lighten his load just for a minute. He hated the damn things so much, he couldn't help but think of her when he saw them. Good. And she'd wear his jersey to sleep at night. After she washed it.

When he slipped back into the line to board, the sun blinded him from her momentarily until he stepped out of its steely path back into the shade of the building.

She'd get another pair of Converse, perhaps red next time.

New Release Newsletter Sign-Up

For new release announcements and exclusive extras, sign up for Cd Brennan's newsletter at http://madmimi.com/signups/152877/join

Meet the Author

Having traveled and lived all over the world, Cd Brennan now enjoys reliving her glory days by writing about them. Feisty heroines with wanderlust or sexy rugby heroes who breathe passion for more than just the sport.

Aussie/Yankee twined, Cd is now settled in Michigan with a rugby player of her own and two wee sons who are *still* adapting to the snow. A full-time editor and mum, her and her hubby still dream of starting up a buffalo farm. And maybe some chickens and pigs, too. She loves rugby, traveling, and all things from the 80s.

Doesn't watch TV so don't chat to her about that, but she loves to hear from readers about anything else! Perhaps some cooking suggestions? She's desperate in the kitchen! Find her on loads of your favorite places.

www.facebook.com/CdBrennanauthor
www.twitter.com/CdBrennanauthor
www.goodreads.com/CdBrennan
www.pinterest.com/cdbrennan2012
Instagram @cdbrennan_author

Want more from Cd Brennan?

Read on for a sneak peek of the first book in the Love Where You Roam series.

Watershed

She left home to find herself...and found love along the way.

Maggie isn't looking for love on her backpacking trip through Australia. She's got enough man troubles back in Ireland. Australia is her escape, a place of adventure where she can create memories to last a lifetime.

But some memories won't be left behind.
Gray is ready to quit hiring backpackers to help with the work on his remote Queensland cattle station when Maggie turns up. She's just passing through, but the connection they forge during the long nights herding cattle won't be so easily cast aside.

CONTENT WARNING: A strong-willed Irish heroine, a stubborn Australian hero, and oceans of difference to bridge for love.

Watershed Sneak Peek
Chapter 1

Maggie

Maggie swatted the flies away from her face. The late afternoon heat was intense, sweat spots forming on her tank top. Her feet were dusty from pacing the side of the road in her flip-flops, and she'd left her big sun hat on the bus, long gone, and no sign of Josephine. For that matter, a single car hadn't passed for the twenty minutes she'd been waiting.

Her fair skin burned under the hot Australian sun. Although she had layered on the sunscreen, her skin hadn't seen this much exposure in the twenty-six years of her life. She reconsidered sheltering under a small clump of bush off the side of the road. Getting to the shade meant digging her trainers from her backpack, and that meant spilling the guts of her belongings onto the side of the Capricorn Highway to find them. It exhausted her thinking about it.

She raised her hand, shielding her eyes from the light, squinting in the direction she imagined Josephine would come. She was somewhere west of Emerald. What would she do if Josephine didn't turn up? She didn't even have any water left.

Heat simmered over the black bitumen. The terrain was completely different than what she'd known in Ireland, where there was an amorphous quality to the landscape. Green fields flowed into green trees, fitting against the gray buildings and sky. Here, everything was so--defined. There was the sky and the land and the one tree in the middle of a paddock a person couldn't help but notice.

Now everything looked a dull brown, not how Georgina had described it. Maggie did recognize, however, the gum trees she had raved about.

"The bush is a beautiful place, not many see it that way. They aren't looking at it right. The gum trees--that's the eucalyptus, you know--set a wonderful fabric to the land with their leaves full of texture and their white bark contrasting against the red soil." Georgina had become animated, waving her hand in front of her like she was painting a picture. "And when it rains, everything turns green in front of your eyes and the rain powers the rivers along beds that were moments before nothing more than rock and weed."

Maggie agreed on the rock and weed. It was everywhere. Long grasses bordered the road and scattered over the land. There were plenty of short, scrub-like bushes, and the cone-shaped statues of red dirt that speckled the canvas must be termite mounds.

Sweat from her forehead settled in the corner of her eye and stung. *Feckin' great.* She swiveled around to look the other direction and caught a glint of metal off the sun.

Someone was coming! Her stomach lurched. As it approached, she watched the mirage change to an old beatup white truck with a metal tray in the back. It had a black snorkel and a large radio antenna on the bull bar.

Please, Mary, let it be Josephine. What if Georgina hadn't been able to ring her daughter? What if they didn't

310

stop? What if they did and the person in the truck was some nutter like the guy in *Wolf Creek*?

Why had she even watched that movie before she came to Australia? She hadn't been able to sleep for four days after she'd seen the horror flick about a remote bushman who helped lost or stranded tourists by towing them back to his camp in the middle of nowhere, only to drug their drinking water and have his way with them. So. Very. Disturbing.

Maggie half raised her arm to wave the driver down, but the vehicle had started slowing. She walked toward the truck as it came to a stop. A dog in the back lunged at its chain and barked as she cautiously approached the window.

"No worries, she's friendly," she heard.

She leaned into the window. Not a fat balding bushman, thank jaysus, but her breath caught.

Instead, the most handsomely rugged man looked back at her. His mussed hair was light brown with natural highlights any girl in Ireland would envy. A strong jaw defined a weathered face with deep lines webbed around golden-brown eyes, as if he spent much of his time laughing.

Strong, slender fingers played with the hat on the seat next to him. Even the man's thumb joints were perfect. He wore faded jeans and a long-sleeved shirt, cuffed to the elbows. If they traveled well, Maggie reckoned this was Australia's best export. She'd heard stories from the other girls on the bus tour about these country men, built strong and fine. Knew how to fix a truck, muster cattle and make a fancy dinner over a camp stove. Supposedly, real gentleman.

Unfortunately, he wore a scowl that darkened his lovely features. Was he scowling at her? What the hell for? Maybe she looked worse than she felt.

Suddenly, blood rushed to her head and she grabbed the door to keep her balance. She tried to speak but everything went black.

Watershed

Available Now on Amazon, Apple, Google, Kobo & Nook